One of his hands came up to grasp hers, his fingers tightening when she attempted to pull away.

James had the feeling that if he let her, she would try to soothe away his imagined hurts, the way a mother did with a child.

But Tori's touch had just the opposite effect. It threatened to unleash the emotions crashing inside him.

"I don't require stroking, Tori. At least, not that kind."

He watched the storms gather in her eyes, and the sight called to something primitive inside him. He had two decades' experience keeping that core carefully controlled. A man led by his emotions would be ruined by them.

But right now, in this instant, temptation was beckoning, and he couldn't summon up a single reason to avoid it.

Using his grip on her hand, he tugged her closer.

Dear Reader,

The weather's hot, and so are all six of this month's Silhouette Intimate Moments books. We have a real focus on miniseries this time around, starting with the last in Ruth Langan's DEVIL'S COVE quartet, *Retribution*. Mix a hero looking to heal his battered soul, a heroine who gives him a reason to smile again and a whole lot of danger, and you've got a recipe for irresistible reading.

Linda Turner's back—after *way* too long—with the first of her new miniseries, TURNING POINTS. A beautiful photographer who caught the wrong person in her lens has no choice but to ask the cops—make that *one particular cop*—for help, and now both her life and her heart are in danger of being lost. FAMILY SECRETS: THE NEXT GENERATION continues with Marie Ferrarella's *Immovable Objects*, featuring a heroine who walks the line between legal, illegal—and love. *Dangerous Deception* from Kylie Brant continues THE TREMAINE TRADITION of mixing suspense and romance—not to mention sensuality— in doses no reader will want to resist. And don't miss our stand-alone titles, either. Cindy Dees introduces you to *A Gentleman and A Soldier* in a military reunion romance that will have your heart pounding and your fingers turning the pages as fast as they can. Finally, welcome Mary Buckham, whose debut novel, *The Makeover Mission*, takes a plain Jane and turns her into a princess—literally. Problem is, this princess is in danger, and now so is Jane.

Enjoy them all—and come back next month for the best in romantic excitement, only from Silhouette Intimate Moments.

Yours,

Leslie J. Wainger
Executive Editor

Please address questions and book requests to:
Silhouette Reader Service
U.S.: 3010 Walden Ave., P.O. Box 1325, Buffalo, NY 14269
Canadian: P.O. Box 609, Fort Erie, Ont. L2A 5X3

Dangerous Deception

KYLIE BRANT

Silhouette®

INTIMATE MOMENTS™

Published by Silhouette Books

America's Publisher of Contemporary Romance

SILHOUETTE BOOKS

ISBN 0-373-27376-2

DANGEROUS DECEPTION

Printed in U.S.A.

KYLIE BRANT

lives with her husband and children. Besides being a writer, this mother of five works full-time teaching learning-disabled students. Much of her free time is spent in her role as professional spectator at her kids' sporting events.

An avid reader, Kylie enjoys stories of love, mystery and suspense—and she insists on happy endings. She claims she was inspired to write by all the wonderful authors she's read over the years. Now most weekends and all summer she can be found at the computer, spinning her own tales of romance and happily-ever-afters.

She invites readers to check out her online read in the reading room at eHarlequin.com. Readers can write to Kylie at P.O. Box 231, Charles City, IA 50616, or e-mail her at kyliebrant@hotmail.com. Her Web site address is www.kyliebrant.com.

For Jason, our budding lawyer.
Good luck on the bar—we're so proud of you!
Love always,
Mom

ACKNOWLEDGMENTS

Because I have so little expertise of my own,
I rely on experts to get the facts straight in my stories.
Special thanks to Jim Harris, of Harris Technical
Services, and to Michael Varat, KEVA Engineering,
LLC, for your patience with my endless questions about
accident reconstruction. Your assistance was impressive
in its scope and ingenuity! And another thank-you is
owed to Norman Koren, for sharing your wealth of
experience in photography. Your kindness was
appreciated more than you can know! Any mistakes in
accuracy are the sole responsibility of the author.

Prologue

Voices from the grave swirled around him, haunting whispers of murder.

James Tremaine stared sightlessly at the scraps of paper laid across the desk before him and reflected that it was an appropriate enough night for ghosts. The wind shrieked through the sky, shaking the windows of the centuries-old estate with demented fists. The dark clouds shot needlelike shards of rain to stab the parched Louisiana ground, to machine-gun against the house. The single lit lamp in the room had flickered more than a few times in the last hour, but its uncertain illumination wasn't necessary. He didn't need the dim spill of light to read the words typed on the bits of paper on the desk. They'd been emblazoned on his mind.

You've got a target on your back.

This project will be your last.

The threats were easily dismissed. It wasn't unusual for competition to rise to a dangerous level in his line of work. But it was the third one, the most recent, that commanded attention. *Your parents' deaths weren't accidents. Yours won't be either.*

The electricity finally gave up its struggle with the ferocious wind, and the room fell into darkness. James didn't notice. He was too busy fighting an internal battle of his own. He hadn't successfully grown a family business into a global security corporation by being easily manipulated. Not even his siblings, *especially* not his siblings, could realize the degree of treachery that lurked beneath every apparently civil contact in his world. As technology exploded daily with new advances, the race to stay ahead of his rivals was a careening, hair-raising ride.

He'd had far more creative schemes than this thrown his way by a competitor intent on beating him to a potential contract: he'd thwarted sabotage at his headquarters; he'd survived two attempts on his life to remove him from competition permanently; but nothing else had felt quite as personal as the words printed on the last note before him.

With cool logic he considered the possibilities, pushing aside for the moment the emotion churning and boiling inside him. The most likely explanation was business, of course. Dredging up his family's tragedy from two decades earlier would distract him from the deadlines imposed by the government contract currently occupying the majority of their manpower. Failure to deliver the newest encryption/decryption package for the Pentagon would remove his company from consideration for the next job, which promised to be even more challenging. Even more lucrative.

With his index finger he traced the edge of the message in the center. Money was another possible motive, he supposed. His family was no stranger to the lengths others would go in order to reap profit by inflicting pain. What was the sender hoping for? To whet his interest for a payoff? But for what? To call off a potential assassin, or by promising decades old information in return?

The messages could just as easily come from a crackpot operating for reasons known only to himself. God knew, there were enough of them around these parts. He didn't need the police to tell him the futility of trying to trace the notes, and with the Pentagon contracts hanging in the balance, just now he could ill afford the resulting publicity.

Lightning lit up the sky outside his den, throwing the interior of the room into momentary relief. A moment later thunder boomed, close enough to shake the graceful antebellum home. But the storm outside paled in comparison to the storm within.

Because there was a still a part of him, a part he was struggling to suppress, that wondered if it could be true.
Your parents' deaths weren't accidents.

He'd read the police reports. Made the identification. He could remember far too well what the battered, mangled bodies had looked like once extracted from the twisted wreckage of the automobile. A vicious memory of the wild, unchecked grief whipped through him, stunning in its power to inflict fresh pain. The twenty-year-old wound throbbed anew, stirring all the old questions that accompany the bitterness of loss. In the end, it was emotion that made the decision for him. Specters from the past tugged at strings of guilt, love and regret.

But it was stirrings of a far different feeling that had

him opening the center desk drawer, smoothing the tip of his finger down the smooth barrel of the snub-nosed .38 inside.

A thirst for vengeance.

Chapter 1

One Month Later

James Tremaine had not yet grown so jaded that he failed to appreciate an opportunity when one presented itself. Especially when that opportunity was the most attractively packaged eye candy he'd run across in more time than he cared to consider. Shaking the rain from his face, he cocked his head for a better view while he peeled off his gloves and, with uncharacteristic carelessness, shoved them into the pockets of his Prada raincoat.

The form balanced precariously on the ladder inside the doorway was only half-visible, but what was observable was unmistakably feminine. Denim clung to shapely hips and snugged across a curvy bottom before slicking down mile-long legs. His gaze lingered on those legs now, and hormones, too long suppressed, flickered to life. It took conscious effort to drag his eyes upward, to where the woman's torso disappeared into the opening afforded by the missing panel in the suspended ceiling.

"You took your sweet time. I didn't know whether you were ever coming, so I got started without you."

Brows raising at the muffled words, James inquired, "Did you want some help?"

He wasn't certain, but he thought he heard a rather unladylike snort. "All that's left for you to do is to hold the ladder. I'm nearly finished here." He moved to obey, putting himself in even closer range to those long legs.

"I think the receptacle's shot, so you'll have to check that out. Probably needs to be replaced. You got the ladder?" Without waiting for a reply the woman started down it. "And you, my friend, can just put in some overtime fixing it. Serves you right for taking so long getting here."

James steadied the ladder with both arms, framing the slender form descending it. "Overtime can be expensive." Her well-formed rear swayed tantalizingly closer with each step she took. For a moment he forgot the grim errand that had brought him here and allowed his imagination free rein. It was doubtful the woman's face could match those incredible endless legs, but a man was entitled to hope. He was partial to blondes, so as long as this was his fantasy, he'd put his money on her being blond and blue-eyed. A rare smile crossed his lips. No, make it green eyes, and somehow he'd have to recover from the disappointment that was certain to accompany the reality.

He'd recovered from far worse disappointments in his time.

Her voice shook him from his reverie. "You can let go of the ladder. I don't have any intention of walking over you to get off it." When he didn't move away, she twisted around, practically in his arms. "So help me, Howie, you'd better not be enjoying this, or…"

Her words stopped abruptly, eyes widening as she realized her mistake. Eyes that weren't green at all, James noted. Instead they were a warm wash of colors that ranged from gray to brown, with flecks of gold in the irises to further defy description. And she wasn't a blonde, either. Her hair hovered somewhere between blond and brown, a poorly cut tangle that reached to her shoulder blades. Her nose was straight, her mouth wide and her jaw stubborn. Her chin had a decided dip in it, right in the center. It was an intriguing face, rather than a pretty one, and James felt a flicker of interest. It had been a long time since he'd been intrigued by a woman.

He watched her swallow and search for words. "Ah…you're not Howie." And then felt a flicker of amusement at her wince as the inanity slipped from her mouth.

He stepped back to allow her to finish her descent. "No. Sorry. I'm looking for Rob Landry. If you can tell him I'm here?"

There was a flash of pain in those changeable eyes, before they abruptly shuttered. "I…can't do that." She turned away, crossed to the lone desk in the room and sank into the seat behind it.

Impatience flickering, James eyed the door in the far corner of the room emblazoned with the man's name. "You mean he's not in? When will he be back?"

"He won't be." The woman's voice was stronger now, an obvious attempt to layer strength over grief. "He died three weeks ago."

James froze, the words seeming to come from a distance. He was too late. If he'd begun this quest a bit sooner, if he'd tracked Landry a little more quickly, he might have answers to the questions that had reared, spawning suspicion that would burn until he could put it to rest with answers.

Answers that wouldn't be forthcoming with Rob Landry dead.

Disappointment welled up, of a much different sort than he'd expected when he'd seen her perched on the ladder. With long practice, he pushed it aside. "I'm sorry," he said belatedly, recognizing both the woman's anguish and her attempt to mask it. "I understand he worked with a partner. I'd like to speak to him, if I may."

"That would be me. I'm Tori Corbett, his daughter." Emotion had been tucked away. The woman's tone was brisk now, her expression professional. "What can I help you with?"

He was beginning to doubt that she could help him at all, but he reached into the inside pocket of his suit jacket and withdrew a business card. "James Tremaine." He handed her it to her but knew from the look on her face that it was unnecessary. She recognized the name and that of his family's company on the card. He expected no less, since he'd worked for nearly two decades to promote both.

Rejecting the position of the chairs facing her desk, he dragged one around to sit beside her. "Your father did some work for mine a little over twenty years ago. After my parents' deaths, his services were again retained. You would have been just a child then, of course, but maybe he mentioned the investigations to you in the time since."

The shock on her face was its own answer, and the disappointment he felt this time had a bitter taste. "Perhaps he had another partner then? Someone who worked with him when he was running Landry Investigations at that time?''

Her gaze fell to her desktop. "No, Dad always believed in a one-man shop until me. I was the first partner he ever had." Her words sounded as though they'd been difficult for her to say. Certainly they were difficult for James to hear.

"He must have left records. I'd like to look through them, with your permission of course." He was a man accustomed to getting what he wanted, and equally adept at applying finesse to get it. But his fabled charm was difficult to summon. He was too close to discovering the answers he sought. Too damn anxious about what they might reveal.

"Our files are confidential." Tori—what kind of name was that for a woman?—swung her chair around to face him more fully. "If you tell me what you're after, though, I could…" Her sentence abruptly halted. "I'm sorry," she amended. "The files you'd want are what? Twenty years old?" James nodded. "I don't have anything that goes back that far."

He felt his blood cool, his stomach tighten. He withdrew his wallet and extracted several bills. Rising, he leaned forward and dropped them on her desk in front of her. "Why don't you check?" he urged evenly. "I'll wait."

She didn't even glance at the money. And her voice, when it came, had chilled by several degrees. "I don't have to look. My father's building was destroyed by a fire around that time. Shortly after, we moved to Minnesota. He didn't reopen an investigating business until we moved back here, three years later."

This line of questioning was a dead end. James hadn't gotten to his position without knowing when to cut his losses. There would be another way. There always was. It would require regrouping, a new strategy. This wouldn't be the first obstacle he'd encountered in his search for the truth. And it wasn't going prevent him from finding it.

He rose. "Thank you for your time. And my condolences again for the loss of your father." She was staring at him, her varied-colored eyes wide, her mouth half-open in protest. And with a vague sense of regret, one that had nothing to do with the outcome of this meeting, he turned and walked out of her office.

Tori Corbett nosed her car up the long driveway leading to Tremaine Technologies and tried to ignore the nerves dancing along her spine. What she was about to do required bravado and guts, both of which her dad had always said she possessed in spades. But the plan that had seemed so logical three nights ago, hours after James Tremaine had left her office, suddenly seemed a little...well, ballsy. Not that she had anything against the quality normally.

But if she was going to continue to run the business she'd learned from her dad, she was going to have to actively pursue prospective clients. And the balance of her bank accounts were stark reminders that work meant continuing to eat. Though they never showed up on her lean frame, she'd always been fond of regular meals.

It wasn't as if Tremaine didn't need her. Although he'd been short on details when he'd visited, she was pretty good at piecing things together. They'd both benefit if he accepted her pitch.

The persuasive arguments she'd rehearsed had seemed perfectly rational on the drive over from New Orleans. And even most of the way through Tangipahoa Parish.

It wasn't until she'd hit the first set of security gates surrounding these grounds that the first wave of anxiety had hit. It had grown progressively worse each time she'd been stopped by yet another guard and required to go through another clearance.

Okay, she admitted, as she slowly drove toward the sprawling complex of office buildings. So her idea of surprising Tremaine by showing up here had been a bit naive. She hadn't taken into account the level of security surrounding his business. Hadn't considered the fact that the only possible way she'd get through each of the successive security checks was by announcing her identity, having it called in to Tremaine himself.

She had ended up being the one surprised, though, because he had obviously cleared her through each of the stops. And maybe that was what had her stomach churning. She couldn't imagine why he'd agreed to see her, unannounced and refusing to state a purpose for being here. While she'd like to believe that it boded well for the proposition she'd come to offer, she couldn't shake the feeling that this meeting was going to end up far differently than she'd planned.

Her battered compact looked jarringly out of place among the sleek luxury vehicles in the parking lot next to the Tremaine Technologies offices. Grabbing her briefcase, she took a deep breath and got out of the car, not bothering to lock it. The class of the others made it highly doubtful anyone would lower themselves to bother with hers. Jogging up the walk, she worked on calming her nerves with a mental rehearsal for the upcoming meeting.

But thoughts of businesslike persuasion were erased when she stepped into the marbled halls of the headquarters for Tremaine Technologies. It took effort for

Tori to state her name matter-of-factly for the man at the desk inside the door, and even more to keep quiet as he led her to an elevator and accompanied her up-stairs. Obviously, uninvited guests couldn't be trusted to wander around inside on their own. Or maybe, she considered ruefully, glancing at her plain cotton shirt and khakis, her appearance didn't exactly inspire confidence. Even the man's dark-blue uniform looked as if it had cost more than her entire outfit, briefcase included.

The elevator doors opened, and the guard led her into an office area roughly the size of her entire house. The floor was polished mahogany, the ceiling vaulted and the woman behind the desk reigning over the area appeared formidable enough to face down intruders with a single look.

''Ms. Corbett,'' the guard at her side said to announce her, and then backed away, leaving Tori alone with the female staring expressionlessly at her. Of an indeterminate age, the woman wore her brown hair smoothed back from her face like two soft wings, framing a face that was aging with grace and gentility. ''Mr. Tremaine is expecting you. He has quite a busy schedule today, however, so if you could keep your meeting brief?'' The way she said the words sounded more like a command than a suggestion, and Tori nodded mutely as the woman stabbed one long-nailed finger at a button on the intercom resting upon her desk. ''Ms. Corbett has arrived.''

A door on the other end of the room opened and James Tremaine filled it, his appearance too sudden for Tori to steel herself against reaction. As it was, she was ambushed by the exact same response she'd had when she'd turned to find herself practically in his arms three days ago.

Ohmygod, it's James Bond. The fanciful thought re-

curred, only to be firmly pushed away. Okay, there might
be a passing resemblance, she conceded. His blue eyes
were the color of the South Pacific and framed with a
fringe of black lashes that matched his meticulously
combed hair. Tall and lean, his body hinted at strength
even clad as it was in impeccable Armani. But the sheen
of danger lurking just beneath his polished surface must
certainly be a product of her imagination. High-tech
CEOs would hardly be likely to radiate an aura of menace, unless the afternoon golf games at the exclusive
clubs he no doubt belonged to were a lot more savage
than she'd realized.

"Tori." His use of her first name jolted her almost as
much as the undisguised warmth in his voice. He opened
his door wider in an unmistakable invitation. "I hadn't
expected to see you again so soon."

So soon? She threw an uncertain look at his secretary,
but the woman had returned to her computer, as if oblivi-
ous to the scene being played out between them. Turning back to Bond—*Tremaine*—she summoned a vivid
smile and approached him. In her line of work, it paid
to be a quick study. "I decided I couldn't wait to see
you again." There was a flicker of amusement on his
face as she played along with his opening gambit, adopting an openly flirtatious sway to her hips as she walked
into his office, not stopping until she was standing square
in its center.

She paused then to assess. His office was furnished in
an eclectic style that mixed eighteenth century furniture
with the functionality of the present. She had an impression of understated elegance with an edge of ruthless
practicality. A bank of computers covered part of one
wall, with the rest of the area utilized as a work space.
His desk sat facing a huge row of windows overlooking

massive oaks draped with Spanish moss encircling a small pond. There was a sitting area across the room, with wing chairs arranged in front of an ornate fireplace of polished walnut. Elegance, style and purpose. The room reflected all of that. She thought it was an equally accurate description of the man who occupied it.

The walls were covered in art that even her untrained eye recognized as genuine. During the short course of her marriage, she'd been dragged to enough museums and art showings to have acquired a modicum of knowledge. She recognized the small Degas hanging side by side with a painting of the French Quarter done by a local New Orleans artist. The next one, a surrealistic seascape was reminiscent of the Impressionist period. And hanging amidst them all, matted and framed with the same care, were three pictures obviously done by a child's hand, with the name Ana scrawled in the corner of each. The detail was the only unexpected note in the space, but she was given no time to dwell on it.

"To what do I owe the pleasure, Ms. Corbett?" With the door shut behind her, the warmth had vanished from his voice, to be replaced by polite interest. It didn't escape her notice that he didn't invite her to sit.

Reaching into her purse, she extracted an envelope. "I came to return something of yours." When he made no move toward her, she approached him, took his hand and pressed it into his palm. Her gaze fixed on his, she curled his fingers around the packet, and tried to ignore the warmth that transferred at the touch. "I don't keep money I haven't earned."

He glanced down, his expression blank for a moment. "Ah. I'd forgotten." He tucked the envelope in the inside pocket of his suit jacket.

"I can't remember ever being so careless with five

hundred dollars, but I guess you had a lot on your mind.''

''I did, yes,'' he replied.

Sensing that now-or-never time had arrived, Tori drew in a deep breath and barreled on. ''Your visit got me a little curious.'' Okay, it had gotten her a *lot* curious, but it seemed wise to gloss over that fact. ''I couldn't help wondering what could have been so important about a twenty-year-old case that would have had you looking up my dad again.''

He lifted an elegantly clad shoulder, the casual gesture at odds with his aristocratic bearing. ''Nothing to wonder about, really. Just tying up some loose ends.''

He was, she decided studying him, lying through his perfectly even teeth. Running the tip of her tongue over the incisor she'd chipped slightly on Ralphie Lowell's head in sixth grade, she considered how to proceed. Although she was something of an expert in the art of bluff and parry, he didn't seem to be the type of man to appreciate such tactics. In the end she thought a straight forward approach would serve best.

''A man like you doesn't check on 'loose ends' himself unless it's a matter of some importance.'' She found it a bit disconcerting to meet his expressionless regard but kept her own gaze steady. ''You could have called, or had any number of your employees dispatched to make the inquiry. That you came in person tells me the nature of your visit was personal. Two decades ago you would have been what? Eighteen?'' Her words brought a frost to his eyes that dispelled any pretense of civility. He wouldn't appreciate that she'd researched him before coming here, although certainly he should have expected it.

She moved away from him, trailing her fingers over

the back of a chair covered in midnight-blue leather with the texture of melted butter. "I've drawn some conclusions about what my dad might have been working on for your father. You never really said that day in the office."

"I didn't, did I? Most would consider that to mean I wasn't interested in discussing it with you."

His expression, she noted with a detached sort of amusement, had gone from frosty to glacial. She was certain she was supposed to be cowering before it. But she'd always had more courage than sense. "It occurred to me that you didn't get what you'd come for on your visit."

A sudden stillness came over him. "You mean you found the files after all?"

With no little regret, she shook her head. "The fire that destroyed Dad's office wiped out an entire city block. No, I mean you came for answers but you didn't find them." Circling the chair, she dropped into it, tilted her chin toward him. "I'm offering to help you get them."

His smile was somehow more insulting than his earlier dismissiveness. "An intriguing proposition from an equally fascinating woman. However, I'm not in need of the services you're offering."

"I think you are." She doubted he was used to being disputed. A man didn't rise to the level he had in the corporate world without encountering his share of yesmen. "Whatever brought you to my office was something you want to keep private, or you wouldn't have come yourself. I can't get you the files you're seeking, but I think I could reconstruct the information that was in them."

Reaching down for her battered briefcase, she placed

it on her lap and snapped the locks open. "You said your father had hired mine. Given the time period you mentioned, I figured this might have been what Dad was investigating." She handed him the stack of newspaper clippings, the headline of the one on top proclaiming, Tremaine Tot Returned Safely. The others in the pile were no less attention grabbing. Kidnapping Plot Foiled. Teenage Boy Local Hero. It wouldn't do for Tori to admit to the curiosity that had kicked in as she'd started researching the Tremaine family. Growing up in Louisiana there was no way she could have avoided hearing the occasional talk about the tragedies that had dogged the prominent family all those years ago.

But immersing herself in the stories, she'd soon grown fascinated by the details. The passage of time didn't lessen the horror felt at the thought of a three-year-old child being snatched out of her bed in the middle of the night; hadn't dimmed the tragedy of the girl's parents being killed in a car accident less than six months after her safe return.

Tremaine made no move to take the stack of articles, and his voice when it came was more than a little disparaging. "If you were half as careful with your research as you'd like me to believe, you'd have discovered that I'm no fan of tabloidism."

Tori dropped the clippings back in the open briefcase. "And your family's no stranger to it. I got that. But a good investigator uses every tool at her disposal, and newspapers are a great place to start." Looking up again, she caught his gaze on her. "Do you have the name of the person who hired my Dad after your parents' accident?"

He didn't respond. He didn't have to. She saw the answer on his face, in the deliberately blank mask that he'd drawn over his features. She sat back, a bit stunned. "It was you, wasn't it? But you were barely more than a kid yourself at the time."

"I've always felt that need dictates maturity more reliably than does age."

She could wholeheartedly agree with that sentiment. Even at twenty-eight her husband wouldn't have approached anyone's definition of mature. Which was only one of the many reasons he'd become her ex.

Thoughts of Kevin Stephen Corbett III were delegated to a particularly shadowy corner of her mind, where she preferred to keep them. "So you hired my dad to investigate your parents' accident?" She didn't need his answer to be certain she was on the right track. Which was fortunate, because he didn't appear disposed to give her one.

"Ms. Corbett..." It was clear Tremaine had reached the end of his patience.

"Earlier you called me Tori," she reminded him.

He drew in a breath, expelled it slowly. "Tori." She decided her name had sounded better on his lips when it wasn't uttered from a tightly clenched jaw. "The only help I was interested in you cannot provide. You can't produce the files and, unfortunately for us both, your father can't answer my questions." He headed for the door, a not-so-subtle indication that the meeting was over. "Thank you for returning the money. I hadn't expected it."

"Then you must be used to dealing with a different caliber of people."

He turned, his lips curving just slightly. "I think we can both be assured of that."

"So if you're the one who hired my dad after your parents' accident, you'd have your own file on that investigation. He wouldn't have kept anything of interest in his that he hadn't shared with you.'' She ignored his stoic gaze, cocked her head, mind still racing furiously. ''And why now? I mean, what would suddenly make you start looking for information that's more than twenty years old?''

There was a definite un-Bond-like muscle twitching in his cheek. ''I just happen to have some spare time on my hands and thought I'd check into a few things I'd been wondering about.''

Tori shook her head, slouched more comfortably in her chair. ''Now you're not even trying. If you're going to lie, make it believable.''

His eyes narrowed. Again she was given an impression of danger lurking just beneath his polished exterior. ''Are you sitting in my office calling me a liar?'' The lethal tone suggested that she backpedal, fast.

It was a suggestion she chose to ignore. ''A not-very-good liar,'' she corrected. ''I'd think it was lack of practice, but given your experience in the corporate world, you must have plenty of that. So I figure it's just me. You don't know me, so you don't respect me enough to expend the energy necessary for a really good story.'' She waved a hand, indicating she wasn't going to take offense. He appeared less than impressed with her forbearance. ''I've given this some thought and I figure something had to have happened to torch your curiosity about those events.''

''You have an overactive imagination.''

She refused to take offense. ''Uh-uh, just an ability to connect the dots. The FBI never did catch whoever kidnapped your sister when she was a toddler, but she was found safe and sound before your family paid a ransom. So it's doubtful that you're interested in that particular investigation. That leaves the one you hired my Dad for. Since you've waited this long, something must have happened recently to convince you there was more to the story.''

His face was impassive. ''Are you finished?''

''Almost.'' Something about his still air had a chill skittering down her spine. She'd trailed unsavory characters through the back alleys of New Orleans and never experienced this level of unease. Shaking off the reaction, she went on with more confidence than she felt, ''You may not have gotten what you came for when you stopped by my office, but I can get it for you.'' When he started to speak, she held up a hand to stop him. ''I understand you've got a brother who has made a name for himself as a detective for the NOPD. He's probably capable of acquiring certain types of information, as well, but it occurred to me that had you wanted to involve him, he would have been the one to show up at Landry Investigations, instead of you.''

She reached into her briefcase again, surprised to see her hands trembling, just a bit. Handing him a file folder, she said, ''You came to me looking for answers of some kind, Mr. Tremaine. Whether you know it or not, you need me if you hope to find them.''

Chapter 2

Chewing on the inside of her cheek was a nervous habit she'd outgrown when she was twelve, so Tori willed herself to stop doing it now. But that flinty-eyed stare Tremaine arrowed at her after glancing at the pictures in the file folder would have mowed down the firmest intentions. "Where did you get these?"

"From a scumbag photojournalist who's a great admirer of his own work." Kiki Corday wouldn't blink at the description, as long as he'd made a buck on the deal. He also never threw away a shot he'd taken as long as there was the remotest possibility he could still cash in this time. He'd certainly cashed in on it. "He assured me they wouldn't have been part of the police file."

"They weren't." Tremaine snapped the folder shut and thrust it toward her again. She felt twinges of sympathy and regret. Sympathy, because looking at old photos of the automobile wreckage that had killed his parents couldn't be pleasant. And regret that she'd been the one to make him do so. "They also don't prove a thing."

"I disagree. They prove that I have sources you don't." She lifted her shoulders, then let them fall. "They prove you need me, or someone like me, if you want information. Check out the other contents in the folder." With a visible show of reluctance, he did so. It took conscious effort for her to push aside a sneaky blade of guilt. James Tremaine was on a quest that was bound to stir up more than a few old wounds. She shouldn't, *wouldn't* feel responsible for his pain. She looked away from him, concentrating on the century-old oaks outside while he flipped through the reports and pictures in the file.

When he spoke, there was a strange note to his tone. "You have a copy of the sheriff's accident report in here. How'd you get your hands on that?"

Her brows skimmed upward. "It's what I do, ace. That's why my license says Investigator. I investigate stuff."

"I've always made it a point to avoid working with smart-asses," he said mildly, continuing to flip through the file. "Bad for the blood pressure, and who needs the aggravation."

It took a great deal of effort on Tori's part to avoid a delighted grin. Not over the smart-ass comment, although truth be told it wouldn't be the first time the description had been applied to her. But his comment could be interpreted, in a roundabout, insulting sort of way, that he might be considering working with her, couldn't it?

Adopting a more conciliatory attitude, she said, "If you hire me you'll have every bit of information that I come across. But I won't always be able to divulge my sources.'' That brought his gaze snapping up to hers, and she didn't flinch from it. ''The sheriff's report was easy enough. All motor vehicle accident investigations are a matter of public record. But I'm thinking that the answers you're looking for won't be found by going through old records, will they?''

He stared hard at her, long enough to have her decide that those deep-blue eyes of his could be strangely hypnotic. Not that Tori was prone to instant mesmerization from a mere look, she thought uncomfortably, but she was a trained observer. She couldn't help but notice things like that.

Nodding toward the file he still held, she said, ''My purpose in coming here was to show you what I can do. I put those contents together in a day and a half. But if you're looking for information other than what was included in my dad's original report to you, I'm going to have to tap completely different sources. And some of them have to remain confidential. It's a condition for their talking to me at all.''

Tremaine flipped the file closed, tapped the edge against his open palm. ''No offense, but I know countless individuals I can hire to look into this for me. Why would I need you?''

She'd been ready for this question, and her answer came smoothly. ''I already know why you need a private investigator, which means one less person you have to share the information with. The fewer people who know, the easier it will be to keep quiet. And it was my father you wanted to talk to. I learned the business from him. I know who a lot of his contacts are…were,'' she corrected herself, ignoring the pang that accompanied the reminder. ''With him gone, I work alone, except for

some services that I contract out. You could go with a
bigger company, one with more manpower, but that just
means more people are going to know about your private
affairs.''

The last was a gamble. By the flicker in his eyes, she
could assume it had paid off. James Tremaine was, by
nature, a very private man. And his quest was an intensely personal one.

''You don't look old enough to have acquired all that
much experience.''

''I've had my license three years, but I'd worked for
my dad on and off for years before that. My mother died
when I was six. I was raised in and around his business.''
She stopped then, one of her dad's favorite sayings drifting through her mind. *Put your cards on the table and
let the client decide if he wants to talk or walk.*

Dragging a matching chair to face hers, he sat, more
elegantly than she had. Somehow she managed to suppress a sneer when she noted the care he took with the
crease in his trousers.

''Decision-making time, Mr. Tremaine.'' Tori leaned
back into her chair, the relaxed pose belying the nerves
scampering along her spine. ''That folder proves I'm
capable of conducting the investigation you're interested
in. I'm also tenacious and a good listener.'' Because that
last had him raising his eyebrows, she shrugged mod-
estly. ''People tend to talk to me. That's a plus in my
line of work. And it might be to your advantage to use
a woman on this case, did you ever think of that?'' At
his arrested expression she knew she'd scored a direct
hit. ''I'm assuming you'll want this kept quiet.''

''Discretion is imperative.''

She nodded. She offered nothing less to her clients.

"As a female I'm apt to rouse less suspicion in certain circles. I can go places, do things, that men can't."

He was silent long enough to have disappointment welling inside her, a slow steady surge. Until that moment she hadn't let herself think of failure, but it faced her now, stark and uncompromising. It was the first job she'd pitched since her dad had died. The first door, since then, to be shut in her face. His death had become a yardstick by which she measured a lot of firsts these days. And lasts.

Snapping the locks shut on the briefcase, she rose, ready to thank him for his time and determined to keep the emotion from her voice.

"I'll give you a week trial." Her mouth dropped, "A thousand a week plus expenses, within reason. At the end of that time, I'll evaluate what you've come up with. If I'm not satisfied, you'll hand over what information you've accumulated and we'll part ways."

"I…" She swallowed hard and tried to recover her power of speech. "All right. I usually give weekly updates, but under the circumstances…"

"I'll want daily reports."

His interruption had her gritting her teeth, but she managed to nod agreeably. She had, after all, gotten exactly what she'd come here for. "All right."

"I'll have my lawyer draft a contract tomorrow. You can wait until after you've signed it, or start work right away, whichever you're most comfortable with."

Now that his decision had been made, he'd changed slightly, she thought. She studied him as he strode to the desk. He'd reverted to type, she realized suddenly. It was the earlier indecision that had been foreign for him. James Tremaine would be a man very much in control of any situation. And now that he'd hired her, now that she'd become just another employee, he was firmly back in charge.

He approached her again with the money she'd returned to him. "You may as well keep this. Half now, and we'll settle the rest at the end of the week. Are those terms acceptable?"

Slowly, she reached out to take the money. "Sure." Taking the cash from him, she reopened the briefcase and dropped the money inside. "I'm assuming you kept the original file my father put together for you. I'd like a copy of it sent over with the contract." She didn't doubt that he still had it. He wouldn't be a man to leave anything to chance.

"I'll do that."

"So." Tori sat down and drummed her fingertips against the case in her lap. "Why don't you tell me what caused you to want to reexamine this? Why now?" She could wait for the file. She didn't expect to find any surprises in it. Her father apparently hadn't encountered any during his investigation all that time ago. Her curiosity was more focused on what had made Tremaine decide to dredge up painful ancient history. He wouldn't be the type to do anything without a reason.

As an answer, he unlocked the center drawer on his desk and withdrew a small white envelope. Crossing to her, he opened it and shook out three slips of paper atop her briefcase. Turning them over, Tori scanned each one, shock layering over adrenaline.

"When did you get these?"

"They began arriving four weeks ago. They were sent to my home, but I have all my personal mail routed to work. I'm here more, anyway."

"The envelopes?"

"I still have them, but a contact of mine in the postal

department assures me they'll be of little use. They were postmarked in New Orleans, all by different offices.''

Her gaze dropped to the notes again, her flesh prickling. ''Have you thought of going to the police?''

''Please.'' His tone managed to be both derisive and amused. ''If someone really means me harm, they aren't going to waste time warning me first. I'd be easier to take out if I wasn't on my guard.''

At the certainty in his words, her eyes met his. ''Is that the voice of experience I hear?''

He slipped his hands into his trousers pockets, rocked back on his heels slightly. The casual pose didn't fool her. She was beginning to doubt that this man ever truly relaxed.

''I don't consider these serious threats.'' It didn't escape her attention that he hadn't answered her question. ''A private lab I occasionally use informed me there were no fingerprints on the notes other than my own. There were several on the envelopes, of course. But it's doubtful any of them belong to the sender, which means the police will likely come up with nothing. With their involvement, there's a higher probability of a leak to the press.''

His tone became clipped, his expression closed. ''My family dislikes publicity. With my sister's recent wedding, and my brothers' engagement announcements appearing in the papers, there's been a renewed interest in our history. My firm is on the verge of landing another sensitive contract with the Pentagon, and the last thing I need are new rumors about my family serving as news fodder to ratchet up slow ratings.''

That was, she supposed, a reasonable enough explanation. Her brief foray into the Corbett family, the Dallas Corbetts—distinguished from the Houston Corbetts pri-

marily by their bank accounts and penchant for social
climbing—had taught her that wealthy people had an
aversion to publicity. Unless, of course, it involved them
handing over a very large check to a suitable charity.

"Let's talk about your brothers and sister for a minute. What do they think about this?" If she hadn't
known better, she would have believed her question took
him off guard. Which was ridiculous, of course. James
Tremaine wouldn't be a man to entertain self-doubts.

"I'd rather not have to tell them," he said finally.
"My sister and her new husband are just settling into
married life. My brothers are both in the process of planning their weddings. Raking all this up again is bound
to be painful, and in the long run will probably be for
nothing. I'd like to spare them that if I can."

She wondered if they would thank him for that, and
thought probably not. But his protectiveness of his family warmed something inside her. She could respect a
man who looked out for his loved ones, even if his tactics weren't appreciated.

Glancing back down at the notes, she observed,
"These could have just been sent by someone looking
to hose you, you know."

"You're most likely correct. But if that's true, the
sender will find that I'm not, as you put it so eloquently,
easily hosed. I won't give in to blackmail."

She almost grinned. There may be a hint of humor
beneath all that tailoring, after all. And she didn't doubt
his words. He wouldn't be an easy mark, which meant
that the sender had grossly underestimated him. Or else
was holding something back that would yet prove truly
compelling.

As if reading her thoughts, he said, "The only note
that interests me is the one about my parents' accident.

I'm not going to pay for any information that this person has, if it comes to that. That's what you're for. By reconstructing the investigation into their deaths, you should be able to answer any questions about what really happened.''

During his speech, the temperature in the room seemed to have dropped ten degrees. She decided it was due to the chill in his voice. ''And what if I find out there was more to their deaths than was ever reported? What then?''

His smile was as brilliant and lethal as a keen-edged blade. ''Then…justice.''

She stared at him while a shiver snaked over her skin. Something about the way he said the word leeched it of its nobility and instilled it with a sense of deadly purpose. ''I won't do anything illegal.'' For the first time, it seemed prudent to point that out. ''I'll use every avenue at my disposal and take advantage of every possible lead, sometimes utilizing unconventional methods. But I'll do it all within the boundaries of the law of Louisiana.''

''Of course. I'd expect nothing less.'' His tone was normal, making her believe she might have misinterpreted it a moment ago. Except the gooseflesh on her arms was still raised, and her nape was still prickling. ''With any luck you can have this thing wrapped up shortly, and we can both go about our lives. I'll contact you tomorrow.'' He approached her, pausing by her chair.

Slowly she rose, sliding the briefcase to the floor. ''Tomorrow?''

''When I messenger over the contract and file that you requested.''

''Ah. Yes.'' Her tongue suddenly thick, she resisted

the urge to wipe her palms on her khakis. He was standing a little too close, as near as he'd been when she'd turned around on that ladder and found herself almost in his arms. Close enough to have her marveling at the deep blue of his eyes, but retaining enough of her scattered senses to wonder at the secrets behind them.

"To our partnership, Ms. Corbett, as brief as it may be."

Her hand raised of its own volition. "To our partnership." His hand engulfed hers. It suited her to blame the skip in her pulse on static electricity. But try as she might, she couldn't shake the feeling that she'd just made a pact with a very sophisticated, very charming devil.

The plaintive cornet of Bix Beiderbecke wailed from the portable CD Tori had carried into the attic. The blues music provided a perfect backdrop for the task at hand. With resignation layering the ache in her heart, she scanned the contents of the space and wondered where in the world to start.

Rob Landry had been an undisputed pack rat, and she didn't doubt that he'd saved more than he'd ever thrown out. Furniture was heaped and shoved into one corner, and overflowing boxes teetered in precarious towers, threatening imminent collapse. There were stacks of newspapers, neatly bundled and piled haphazardly almost to the ceiling beams. Why they'd been important enough to keep was beyond her, but then her dad had been the type to let junk mail accumulate, too, until she came in and tossed it. The man had been able to figure every angle of a case and work a source like a master, but hadn't been able to part with a single scrap of paper.

The memory made her lips curve and her eyes mist.

The pain twisted just a bit, leaving a wound that she knew from experience would throb for some time. Cancer had stolen both of her parents now. First her mother, and now her beloved dad, who had seemed so indestructible. Right up until that day three months earlier when the pain he'd passed off as indigestion had been diagnosed as something a great deal deadlier.

Releasing the breath that had backed up in her lungs, she headed toward the furniture. She'd already been through the downstairs, putting aside the pieces she wanted to save and those that would be donated to the needy. She'd expected this to be easier somehow. The things that he had stored up here wouldn't hold the keen reminders of him, nor still smell of his aftershave. There wouldn't be memories of him here, as there were in every room below. He'd been a big man, but had filled a room more with his presence than his stature. It would be impossible to exorcise those memories from the house, and impossible to live with them. She'd placed it on the market earlier that week.

Tori worked her way trough the chairs and tables that he'd deemed too good to throw out. It took an hour to decide there was nothing in the collection that she wanted to save, and she restacked the pieces. She'd use the corner to separate those things to be gotten rid of from the things she wanted to keep. Most of what she had decided to hang on to was downstairs, but there wouldn't be room for all of it in her small house. It would have to go into storage until she had a bigger place.

The newspapers could be tossed without going through them, she determined, passing by them in an effort to get at the boxes. But she must have brushed the stack as she went by, and the entire pile began a slow-motion sway. With a sense of futility, she leaped aside, just in time to avoid being nailed by the bundles as they tumbled to the floor.

The impact of their landing sent up a cloud of dust that sent her into a spasm of sneezing. When her eyes and lungs had cleared, she glared at the mess accusingly. Her dad had tended to keep any newspapers with articles that caught his imagination, talking vaguely about writing a book sometime when he retired. She'd never been able to imagine him in so sedentary a pastime, but had thought it a harmless enough intention until now.

Muttering a few choice words, she set to hauling the papers into yet another pile, this one designated for the trash heap. The headline leaped out at her from the top one of the bundle, and a quick flip through them showed a collection detailing the trial of the notorious New Orleans Ripper, who'd been caught and tried a decade earlier after killing a dozen women.

With a grimace, she pushed them aside and started some smaller, steadier piles. He'd had varied interests. Some of the papers were articles on fishing, a passion of his, others on the history of the city. But it was the bottom bundle that caught her eye, with a headline very like the one she'd clipped and placed in the file she'd given to Tremaine.

Tremaine Heiress Returned Safely.

With a sense of déjà vu she had a sudden recollection of James Tremaine's face when he'd seen the similar headline in the file she'd given him. A grim mask had descended over his features, but not before she'd glimpsed the bitter resentment in his eyes. He'd made his feelings toward the press and public prying quite clear, but that didn't stop her from reaching out, tugging at the string that bound the papers together. Flipping through them, she found stories detailing the kidnapping and the car accident a few months later. She scanned the stories, but they elicited no information she hadn't found in her research earlier that week. Something clicked in the rereading, however, something she'd forgotten to ask Tremaine about. There had been a third passenger in the car. A third death.

To refresh her memory, she pulled the papers loose, looking for the articles detailing the accident and the follow-up investigation. The passenger's name was given, but she was identified only as a family friend. Tori made a mental note to look up more about the woman.

She set aside the bundle of papers on the Tremaines and finished stacking the rest to be destroyed. But during the task, her gaze strayed more than once to the papers she'd saved. Her earlier excitement at having landed her first job on her own had been tempered by her troubling reaction to Tremaine. She'd thought her interest in the opposite sex had been laid to rest permanently upon the ignoble end of her marriage. Or, to be truthful, months before the official ending. As her husband's criticism and dissatisfaction with her had grown, her hormones had gone dormant at approximately the same pace. Finding him in his parents' pool house on top of Miss Texas Rose 1998 had nearly shredded what was left of her confidence. She'd had enough sense, however, to leave him and their marriage behind. And enough self-respect to first send his canary-yellow Ferarri convertible crashing through the fence to sink to the bottom of the pool. It was the only memory of her marriage that still had the power to bring a smile to her face.

Given that, it was more than a little disturbing to experience that inexplicable…*awareness* when she was near Tremaine. A woman would have to be in the grave not to react to his looks, and so her response to him was only too natural, a cause for celebration, even. But as comfortable as it would be to believe that's all there was, Tori couldn't prevent feeling a sliver of unease. There was something about the man that heightened all her sensitivities, which really wouldn't do. Getting involved with a client was an ethically sticky situation.

A wry grin twisted her lips. Luckily, that was not likely to be a problem. She and Tremaine couldn't have less in common if they'd been born on different planets. Her brief foray into the monied class during her marriage had taught her only too painfully that the rich were, indeed, different.

Moving to the boxes, she hauled down the top one and opened it. A familiar sight inside it surprised a laugh from her. There, folded neatly, was a sweater her dad had worn for more years than she cared to count. She'd replaced it nearly three years ago with one enough like it to satisfy the man, but he must have rescued this one from the trash and hidden it away. Anything that was a favorite of his was always deemed too good to be thrown out, despite its missing buttons and worn-through elbows. What he'd intended to do with it was anybody's guess.

Nevertheless, she found herself folding it with care and setting it aside. Perhaps there was more of her father in her than she'd guessed, because she knew that she'd never be able to part with it now, either.

Beneath the sweater was a file folder stuffed with papers, which she shook out onto her lap. Her throat went abruptly dry as she recognized medical statements dating from the time her mother had grown sick. With hands that shook just slightly, she stuffed them back into the envelope. She could remember vividly when as a nine-year-old she'd packed away most of her mother's things to prepare for their move back to New Orleans. Her death had been the first and only time she'd ever seen her big, capable father helpless.

The envelope beneath was one she recognized. It was a packet of love letters exchanged between her parents when her mother was in the Mayo Clinic. For years they'd been in the bedside table of her father's room. When had he finally put them away? she wondered. Sometime after that instance when he'd come home unexpectedly and found her reading them. He'd been coldly furious, and she'd been ashamed of her snooping, unable to explain that the few letters she'd read had helped bring her mother within reach again, the words painting an almost real form for her that had previously only been viewed through a child's eyes.

A foreign sound had her catapulting back into the present. Looking around carefully, she eyed the piles of junk suspiciously. Any one of them could be a hiding place for some disgusting four-legged creature. Although Tori was an animal lover, most were best enjoyed outside her home.

Rising to her feet she listened again, and her blood abruptly chilled. The noise that resounded didn't come from the attic. It came from the floor below.

Someone was in the house.

The open door and the music that still poured from the CD player left little doubt as to her whereabouts. Scanning the area, she moved silently to the corner with the furniture. She grabbed a small, particularly ugly lamp, removed the shade and light bulb, and wrapped the cord securely around it. Hefting it with one hand, she was satisfied that it would make a useful club.

She heard footsteps below, but no one called out, as she would expect if a curious neighbor or the Realtor had come looking for her. She'd left the front door unlocked, as it had been afternoon when she'd started her task. But a glance out the tiny window showed that it was early evening now. Dusk and shadows would have fallen over the street. Most of the elderly neighbors would have already finished up their dinner dishes and be seated in front of the TVs with their front doors carefully locked.

The footsteps paused, and the attic door squeaked a bit, as if the intruder had taken it in one hand and stuck a head inside the opening to listen. Tori could feel the blood pulsing through her veins. Her heart was beating a rapid tattoo in her chest, but her mind was cool as she flipped the lamp in her hand so the heavier base would be at the top. She'd feel more comfortable under a cloak of darkness, but the switch was at the base of the steps and out of reach.

The first step squeaked under the weight of the tread on it. Whoever was climbing the stairs now blocked her only exit out of the attic. There was another telltale sound. Another step upward. Options limited, Tori melted back into the shadows afforded by the stacked furniture and waited, weapon in hand.

Chapter 3

"You know some people content themselves with a simple hello." James eyed the lamp clutched in Tori's fist, deciding she looked more than capable of wielding it.

"And most consider it rude to walk into people's homes without announcing themselves," she countered, setting the lamp on a nearby table. "How did you know I was here?"

"I went by your place. A rather unkempt individual by the name of Joe, informed me that you might be at your father's." When she didn't respond, he continued helpfully, "Ribbed undershirt? Uncertain hygiene? Pants riding low enough to show far more than most would care to see of his choice in undergarments?"

She made a face that was half recognition, have irritation. "My neighbor's son. He takes an annoying interest in my comings and goings. Must have heard me talking to his mother earlier today." She dusted her hands on her shorts as she approached, cocking a brow at him. "I have to say, when I heard someone moving around downstairs, I considered it might be the real estate agent or a neighbor. But I never thought of you."

Since she was heading toward the stairs, he turned and preceded her down. "Which one were you going to smack with that lamp, the agent or the neighbor?"

"There was an equally good chance it was a street punk looking for an easy score." The words, as much as the matter-of-fact way she uttered them, caused him to pause for just a moment. "It never hurts to be prepared."

"No, it doesn't." He turned, once he'd reached the open door, and studied her. She snapped off the light switch before following him into the upstairs hallway. He wondered how many women in his acquaintance would have dealt with the possibility of a stranger in her house with such cool calculation. There was no evidence of alarm in her demeanor, just a certain competency that was at odds with the unmistakable femininity of those long legs and lean curves. The observation was undeniably chauvinistic, so he wisely refrained from sharing it.

"I did telephone," he offered, surprising himself by making the explanation. "There was no answer at your house, and apparently you've had the phone here disconnected. I decided it wouldn't hurt to swing by and see if I could catch you. You didn't answer the doorbell, but I heard music from somewhere in the house and followed it."

She brushed by him, sending him a sidelong glance before she led him toward the steps to downstairs. "I didn't expect to hear from you until tomorrow."

"I had business in the city, so I decided to drop off

the contract I had my lawyer draw up.'' He held up the hinged file he carried. ''As well as a complete copy of the old investigative report.''

If truth be told, his business in the city could have waited or could at least been delegated. But he'd found it strangely difficult to focus once she'd left his office that afternoon. They'd decided upon a course of action, and now he was anxious to see it through. Anxious to see what answers, if any, her investigation would supply.

''I thought if you had some time tonight, you could go over the contents of the file and decide where you want to start.'' He followed her into a small downstairs living room and, waiting until she'd seated herself on the sofa, sat in a nearby chair. He looked with interest around the room he'd merely glanced at his first time through. There was a battered recliner in one corner, facing a TV and stereo setup. It didn't take much imagination to figure that the chair had been well used by the man who had lived here. Above it hung a sampler, on which someone had painstakingly embroidered the words Integrity Above All Else.

He gestured to it. ''Your work?''

''My one-and-only attempt. It was my dad's favorite saying. He had what some might consider an outdated code of honor.''

James thought of the family crest that hung above the doorway in his family home. Honor. Duty. Devotion. It was the creed that his father had lived by. He and his brothers had grown up attempting to do the same. ''Not everyone,'' he murmured.

When her gaze turned quizzical, he opened the file he carried, took out the contract inside. Withdrawing a gold pen from his suit jacket, he handed both to her. ''I had my lawyer draw up this contract. The terms are outlined clearly in it, and they're not negotiable. We already discussed this, but you'll want to read the confidentiality clause near the bottom. If you or anyone in your employ violates it in the slightest, I'll direct my attorney to prosecute to the fullest extent of the law. Am I understood?''

''As you say, we discussed that earlier.'' Her voice was cool. She scanned the rest of the document, and he used the time to watch her. It was no hardship. She'd tamed that unruly tangle of hair by hauling it up in a knot and securing it somehow. The simple cotton shirt she wore was marred with dust, no doubt encountered upstairs, as were her shorts, which showed an intriguing length of slender thigh.

Not for the first time he noted that she didn't fit his notion of a private investigator. If he was lucky, she wouldn't fit anyone else's, either. Once she'd left his office, he'd been plagued by doubts about the wisdom of his choice. The feeling was too foreign to be borne comfortably. He could put an army of more experienced investigators on the matter, but she might be able to provide the one thing that no one else could—a direct line to her father's old contacts. It was possible that one of them knew something about the case he'd worked that hadn't been contained in the man's report. That, coupled with his reluctance to spread the word of these threats, had cemented his decision. He could spare a week. And if she failed to come up with anything new— He gave a mental shrug. Then there would be time enough to select another individual.

When she was finished, he took the contract, studying the signature with a sense of amusement. ''Your full name is Victoria?''

He noted her barely concealed wince. ''Use it at your

peril. And be warned that the last guy to call me by it lost his right front bicuspid.''

"I'll be sure to remember that. Do you have a cell?'' When she rattled off a number, he jotted it down on the top of the contract, before setting it aside and handing her the hinged portfolio he'd brought with him. ''You'll find mine on the outside of the top file folder. Don't hesitate to call, regardless of the hour.''

"Are you sure?'' Her tone was light, but the expression in her eyes was speculative. ''I don't want to be responsible for interrupting business. Or whatever.''

"Business will take a back seat to your reports, and 'whatever' will have to wait until we get this—'' he nodded toward the portfolio she'd set on the table beside her ''—taken care of.'' Upon reflection, a personal life of any type hadn't been a priority for much too long. Few women tolerated being set aside once he became embroiled in a particularly challenging contract. He tried, and failed, to recall the last time he'd been involved in a halfway serious relationship. If he was actually spending time wondering if his P.I.'s legs were as silky as they looked, perhaps his sister, Ana, was right, and he *was* becoming too focused. Not that he'd ever admit as much to her.

"As long as you're here, I did think of a question earlier.'' She slid to a more comfortable position in her seat and crossed one long line of leg over the other. ''Who was the third person in the car with your parents?''

It took a moment for him to switch mental gears. "Lucy Rappaport. She was the young wife of our production manager and a good friend of my mother's. They'd been on their way to New Orleans, where my father had business. The women were going to shop and have dinner there.'' The subject brought him back with a crude jolt to the business at hand. ''She and her husband had an eighteen-month-old son.''

The tragedy that day hadn't been limited to his family. Marcus Rappaport still worked for them, having risen high enough in the corporation to be his right-hand man. Although he was considered one of the most eligible men in the parish, he'd never remarried. Some losses, James knew, left a void that couldn't be filled.

''The time frame of this case will make it challenging,'' Tori stated. ''Witnesses move away or die. Memories fade. But technology has grown more advanced, too.'' She gave a shrug. ''Maybe that will prove to be to our advantage.'' She began pulling things from the file he'd brought and arranging them in piles around her on the sofa, in an order that made sense only to her. ''At any rate, I intend to reinterview the people who processed the accident scene, at least those I can get hold of. Is the name of the salvage yard the car was sold to included in this file?''

''The remains of the car were destroyed long ago.'' And he knew that precisely because he'd already attempted to trace it. ''There's nothing left to examine with new technology.'' James felt a surge of impatience, which he tempered. There ought to be ways to find the truth that he hadn't thought of…ought to be avenues to explore that he hadn't considered. Not for the first time he questioned whether he'd made the right choice pursuing this thing.

Then he thought again of the note that had arrived today. *Your parents were murdered. You're next.* And then it was really quite simple to recall just why he'd gone down this path. And just how badly he needed answers, one way or another.

He shifted in his chair, tamped down frustration. There was a sense of powerlessness in putting this into someone else's hands, however close he intended to supervise. He didn't much care for the sensation. "I received another message today."

Her gaze was sharp. "What did it say?"

Lifting a shoulder, he said, "More of the same. But it did mention my parents again. If this was simply about extortion, I would have expected to receive the demand for cash already. Or at least some indication of what information the sender has to trade."

"He could just be whetting your appetite until you're anticipating just that, before striking with the promise of more for a price." Her head was still bent over the file, but her voice was certain.

"Sounds like you have a fair idea of how this guy would think."

"Well, I have met my share of dirt bags. And we don't know the sender is a guy." She did look up now, and caught his gaze on her. "Unsigned notes give a guarantee of anonymity, and they're nonconfrontational. They could just as easily be from a woman. But I tend to agree with you. I doubt the sender is after cash. The tone of the messages are a bit too personal. Have you made any enemies lately?"

He gave a grim laugh. "Honey, if we're going to list all my enemies, we'll be here all night." From the arrested expression on her face, he'd managed to surprise her.

"Let me guess. Your magnetic personality or boyish charm?"

He wondered if he should be offended. "Neither, although I can be quite charming, given the right circumstances. But Tremaine Technologies is considered to have made a pretty rapid rise in the global economy in the last twelve years. We're listed as one of the five premiere encryption/decryption software corporations in the world. All modesty aside, there's only one other in this country even in our league, and that's Security Solutions. The biggest contracts in the past four years have gone to one or the other of us.''

She cocked her head consideringly. ''So if your company was out of the running, they'd all go to this Software Solutions?''

''Probably, at least for a time. But sending anonymous notes hardly fits the profile of Simon Beal, its owner and CEO.''

''Don't be so sure.'' Setting aside the paperwork she was sorting, she crossed to an overflowing desk tucked in one corner of the room and pulled a pen and a legal pad from the top drawer. ''Didn't you tell me yesterday that you're being considered for an important new project?''

''Yes, and so are a handful of other companies. Beal is the only real competition, although Allen Tarkington of Creative Technology considers himself in the running.'' Rising, he slipped his hands into the pockets of his trousers, for once not mindful of the crease.

''So any one of those companies, Beal's especially, would have reason to want you distracted right now.'' She jotted a quick note down on her pad before looking up again. ''I assume that this business is competitive, right? Companies willing to do what it takes to get an edge?''

His smile was as sharp as a blade. ''That edge usually takes the form of corporate espionage. Arson. Sabotage. Even the odd bullet on occasion.''

Tori gaped at him, her eyes wide. "Wow. Guess that's where the phrase *corporate warfare* comes from."

He inclined his head. It was an appropriate enough term. "If one of the other business leaders was trying to eliminate me from the competition, I think they'd engage in something more direct than anonymous notes."

Her expression had gone shrewd. "But a direct attack would have police scrutiny turned on them. Maybe this was deliberately planned to be more subtle, and you haven't reacted the way you were supposed to. The whole publicity angle is exactly why you didn't go to the police, but most people in your shoes would have. From there it would be an easy enough task to get the information leaked to the press. Fan the flames a bit, pay off a reporter or two and you have the Tremaine family history, past and present, in headlines and on TV for days, complete with hype and speculation about this newest development. Given the global prestige of your company, the story is sure to be picked up by the Associated Press, and lo and behold, all those Pentagon types are reading about you and your current problem over their morning coffee."

The accuracy of the picture she painted was startling. "You catch on fast. It would be a roundabout way to approach things, but it's conceivable."

"And even better, at least from the sender's standpoint, it's unexpected. So why don't you, for sake of argument, give me the names of the companies in the running for that contract, along with their locations and CEOs?"

James rattled off the information, only half thinking about it. The scenario she'd just described was possible. Entirely possible. And it would somehow be preferable to believe it than to discover that he'd been wrong all these years about his parents' accident. That he had failed them somehow by not suspecting the truth and bringing those responsible to justice.

He was very much afraid that, if true, his failure to act would haunt him for the rest of his life.

Belatedly he became aware that she was speaking again.

"…just a theory."

"I'm sorry, what?"

"I said, right now, with what we have to go on, this is a theory, one among many. I just don't want to overlook anything."

"Nor do I." He glanced at his watch, surprised to find it was nearly nine. "I've taken enough of your time this evening. I should go."

She rose, in a fluid stream of motion that he couldn't help but appreciate. "You're going to drive all the way home tonight?"

He shook his head. "We have a place on Lake Pontchartrain. I'll stay there and drive to work in the morning." He headed for the door, leaving her to follow him. He felt an odd reluctance to leave. It was a sort of relief, he realized, to be able to talk this through with someone. To finally have a plan of action. He'd spent long hours considering sharing it with his brothers, but his first instinct had warned against it. When this was over, when he had the answers he needed, he'd tell them. He owed them that. But until he had something to report, the uncertainty could only cause them pain. He wasn't willing to inflict that unnecessarily, especially if this was just a ploy by one of his competitors.

As the eldest in the family, responsibility was ingrained in him. He wouldn't shirk it now.

Her voice had him hesitating with his hand on the doorknob.

"This thing between you and Beal...have you been keeping score?"

He looked over his shoulder at her. She had her thumbs hooked in the pockets of her shorts, her head tilted slightly. "Running a business the size of mine is hardly a game."

Her tone grew mocking. "So you haven't kept track of who has landed the hottest contracts. Come up with the most impressive technology."

She saw, he thought, entirely too much. "It's not something that can be reduced to win-loss columns."

Tori smiled knowingly. "You're ahead?"

"By three in this year alone." He shot her a feral grin before turning and going through the door. "And I intend to keep it that way."

There were worse ways to spend the afternoon than lolling on a grassy bank, fishing. Tori had an innate appreciation for life's little bonuses, and she was enjoying this one to the fullest. It wasn't often that she could work a case and indulge her love of fishing at the same time.

She cast her line and kept a watch on the man seated forty yards to her left, closer to the pond's edge. The former Tangipahoa Parish sheriff had been retired for almost six years, and from the size of his girth, his love for food at least matched what she'd heard about his fondness for his favorite pastime. It had taken surprisingly few phone calls to elicit the information she'd needed on the man. And the small group of elderly men playing cards in front of his hometown diner had been more than happy to share favorite local fishing spots and directions to them, once she'd provided some winsome smiles and small talk. Picking up their lunch tab hadn't hurt, either.

She'd spotted him on her third stop, on a secluded shady knoll on the banks of the Atchafalaya. For a while she was content to keep her distance. She didn't want him to feel crowded and leave.

Selecting a bright-green lure, she baited the hook and cast her line, settling into a comfortable position to wait. It wasn't for long. Within just a few minutes there was a tug on her line and she surged to her feet, reeling in slowly.

The yellowed speckled sunfish on the other end was a good size, at least sixteen inches, and she allowed it to thrash on the line just long enough to capture ex-Sheriff Halloway's attention. When she was sure she had it, she made a show of landing her prize, holding it up before her to admire it before deftly releasing it in the fish pail she'd brought along.

Thirty minutes later that fish had been joined by two others, and the man down river disgustedly reeled in his empty line, packed up his tackle box and began making his way to a new spot, one a great deal closer to hers.

"Looks like you found yourself a hot spot here."

"Caught three beauts and haven't even been here an hour," she said casually. "This is my first time fishing in this area. Is it always this good?"

Halloway wiped his brow, then adjusted the brim of the straw hat he wore. "Not for me. Not today, anyways."

"Well, you're welcome to try your luck here."

It was the only invitation he needed. Minutes later he had his equipment situated and was settled in a portable folding chair. He cast his line and it fell soundlessly into the river. "You're not from these parts."

"New Orleans." Tori leaned back in the grass, propped on her elbows and toed off her sandals. "Every day off I get I head to new fishing spots." She shot him a sideways glance, a bit concerned at his flushed expression. The sun was searing overhead, though it wasn't yet noon. For the first time she thought he might have been equally attracted by the shade nearby as he was by her fishing success. "Guess you must spend your free time same as me."

He grunted, reeled in his empty line and rummaged in his tackle box to choose a different lure. "I got nothing but days like these. I been retired now near 'bout seven years."

There was a tug on her line. Tori pretended not to notice, although the fact hadn't escaped Halloway. "I'm figuring you must live around here."

"How you figure that?"

"No lunch with you." She smiled easily and pointed to the small basket she'd packed. "I came ready to make a day of it."

"Born and raised 'round these parts," he admitted. "Gal, you got something bitin' at your line, there."

"So I do." With a nonchalance that seemed to set the man's teeth on edge, she straightened, cocked her wrist back and reeled in her fourth and biggest catch of the day.

"Well, if you aren't having Sam's own luck," the man muttered, narrowed gaze envious. "What're you using there?"

She added the fish to her pail, and held the lure up for him to see. "Something my dad used to make himself. Sunfish go wild for it. What do you use?"

"Straight fly lure. Ain't seeing the kind of luck you're having, though."

Seizing the opportunity, Tori reached into her tackle box. "You're welcome to try one, if you'd like." She held out one of the neon lures and it took only a moment before Halloway pushed himself from his chair and came to get it. "I always put a bit of bacon on mine."

"Always use grubs for sunfish, myself." Nevertheless, he accepted the piece of bacon she offered and gave her a smile before lumbering back to his chair.

"So, what'd you retire from?"

"Used to be sheriff of this parish. Got myself elected unopposed every term but two, and neither of them elections was close. Don't know if that means most folks got more sense, or that I got the job done right, but put twenty years in office."

"People must have been satisfied," she said, with an obvious stroke to his ego. "I suppose things stay pretty quiet around these parts, though. Not like in the cities."

"You'd be surprised. Just a couple years ago, Cooter Beecham shot his wife, Emma, stone cold after being married thirty years. That got the parish buzzing, I can tell you."

"I'll bet." Although Tori could care less about Cooter or his questionable ancestry, which Halloway described at some length, she let the man talk. And when he pulled in a sunfish a good foot long, he got even more expansive. "'Course no one was surprised overmuch," he concluded, his story winding down. "Got himself drunker 'n Bessy Bug most Saturdays. Went home after he'd tied one on and thought he saw a ghost standing in his doorway. Ran to get his shotgun from his truck and squeezed off three shots afore he figured out it was Emma in her nightdress."

She took advantage of his pause for breath to say, "I'll bet that created some excitement around here. Did it bring all the reporters in from the city to interview you?"

He looked a little crestfallen at that. "Well no, just the reporter for the local paper. But," his face brightened as he recast his line, "I was on WDSU once, you know the New Orleans channel? Near 'bout twenty years ago, it was. Everybody wanted to talk about that case, yes sirree. There was a mite more interest in the Tremaine family than in Cooter's."

"I think I remember that. It was a car accident, wasn't it?" Tori nodded, her nonchalant manner at odds with the jitter in her pulse. "I'll bet that did bring the reporters crawling."

"Reporters, photographers and more gawkers than a body could shake a stick at. Gruesome scene, it was," he said, shaking his head. "By the time I arrived there was nothing to be done for any of the passengers. Car ran off the road, over an embankment and landed fifteen feet below. Terrible sight." He looked, Tori thought, just a little green at the retelling. "The Tremaines have done a lot for folks 'round these parts. The tragedy was talked about for years. But an accident's all it was, just like I told 'em, and despite all the digging by journalists and P.I.s, that's all they came up with, too."

Since she'd spent the better part of the night reading the reports in the file, Tori was well aware of the conclusions drawn. "They didn't discover anything wrong with the car?" she asked.

"Not a thing, and I had Harris DuBlass look it over special. At that time there wasn't a finer hand with a car than his, and he said it was clean as a whistle. Not much left of it, of course, smashed up as it was. You'll still hear some folks 'round these parts talk about sabotage or some such thing, but I'm here to tell you, the steering and brakes looked just fine. Accident went in the books as plain, old DE.''

It took a moment for Tori to follow his meaning. ''Driver error.''

''That's right. The road had just been reopened after road crews had worked on it for months. There was interest for a while to straighten out that curve, make the road into four lanes, but folks got upset about cutting down the big ol' trees along one side. In the end they just widened it. Most likely Joseph Tremaine took that curve too fast. Only idea I ever come up with. If it happened in these times, they'd probably all survive, what with the shoulder harnesses and air bags. But back then with just the lap belt.'' The older man shook his head. ''Didn't none of 'em stand a chance of living through it.''

''Didn't that surprise you, though?'' Tori asked. ''I mean, he must have been familiar with the area.''

He let out a crow of delight as another tug on his line brought him to his feet. ''I think I got me a big one here.'' He let the line play out a little before reeling it in slowly, watching the fish on the other end thrash. ''Sure he knew the roads like the back of his hand,'' he continued his earlier thread seamlessly, ''but like I said, that road had been changed some. And there's not a one among us that don't get behind the wheel when our mind isn't totally on driving. That's why they call them accidents.''

''I guess there were no witnesses to help clear up any questions.''

''Nope. Just a couple of Bernie Glasser's cows that musta got out and come downriver, and they weren't talking. Leastways, that's the story Glasser gave. Like nobody knew he brung them down regular every morning to avoid the cost of watering 'em. Used to tromp 'em across Cooter Beecham's property like clockwork, and didn't that make the old guy cuss a blue streak. Had a mouth on him, old Cooter did, and he didn't need to be liquored up to let loose, no sirree. Why I remember a time…''

Tori let the man ramble and her mind drift. Ex-Sheriff Halloway's retelling of the accident was different from his report only in the colorful details. Doubt about the cause of the accident hadn't lingered long in his mind, if at all.

If he was right, his conclusion would mirror her dad's. His report had been included in the file, as well, and she'd pored over it with particular attention. Just reading it, imagining him sitting at his battered desk painstakingly typing his findings, had summoned a lump to her throat that appeared only too easily these days.

For the first time she considered the fact that if she arrived at a different conclusion from his, it would mean he'd been wrong. That he'd overlooked something, or been too careless in his investigation. Neither of the possibilities seemed likely. Rob Landry had been meticulous about his work and his reputation. If there had been something to find twenty years earlier, something to support James's fear that the accident had been deliberate, he would have found it. Reported it. And remained on the case until the wrongdoer was brought to justice.

She let out a sigh, only half aware that Halloway had fallen silent. It was highly probable that there was nothing to the claims in those messages about Tremaine's parents. They'd likely been sent to distract him at a time when he most needed to focus his attention on his work.

But the conclusion didn't make her breathe any easier. She couldn't dismiss the threats in the notes as easily as

James did. Even if the car wreck all those years ago had been an accident, he could still have a target on his back. Either way, this investigation could well prove dangerous to him. And if she was honest, the fear that followed that thought was more than just a professional one.

Chapter 4

James peered at the screen, tapping in commands rapidly. "I'm still not satisfied with the speed of the file-wiping function of the software. For optional utility, the task needs to be accomplished twice as quickly."

Marcus Rappaport, Vice President of Production and James's right hand in the company, shook his head. Bracing his hands on the table beside James, he leaned closer to the computer. "Figured you'd raise a breeze about it. But if you're bent on overwriting the data a dozen times in the wipe, it's going to take more time. We can speed it up by doing a sextuple overwrite, which still is twice as often as conventional methods, but…"

James lifted a brow. "Did you actually mention conventional methods in my presence?"

The man straightened, raising his hands in mock surrender. "What was I thinking? But it's getting pretty close to deadline to do more than fine-tune any aspect of the system. Maybe we should just…"

''Adjust the algorithm, compress the oppositional system and, if that doesn't work, see what our new supersonic chip would do to the speed.''

Rappaport gaped at him. ''Do you know how that would impact the cost?''

James pushed away from the computer table. He assumed the question was rhetorical. There was no one in his company as well versed as he in the profit/loss margin of every contract he undertook. ''I have a general idea, yes. It's a last option, but if it comes to that, I'd rather shave our profit than put a product out there that doesn't perform exactly as I envisioned it.''

Marcus stared at him a moment longer, then began jotting notes on a pad of paper. ''This perfectionist trait of yours may be the death of this company yet.''

James was too used to the man's pessimistic nature to take offense. He smiled and rose, clapping him on the shoulder. ''I'm not a perfectionist, Marcus, just fussy. Give the job to Analiese and tell her none of us think it can be done. You know how she responds to a challenge.''

The man visibly brightened. He'd always had a soft spot for James's little sister. ''I'll do that, although your brother-in-law may not thank you if she starts putting in overtime to accomplish it.''

''I'll let her manage Jones.'' Although his sister's husband was overprotective enough to meet with even her brothers' approval, Ana had a gift for wrapping the toughest man around her little finger. James daily counted himself lucky that the lion's share of responsibility for her could now be shared.

''What's the latest on the arrangements for the Technology Expo?''

''I've turned over the final details to Tucker.'' Tucker

Rappaport, the man's son, interned with their company during summers and college vacations. He had one semester left before earning his M.A. When he was finished, James hoped to hire him for good. It wasn't only friendship and loyalty that had him making a place for the young man at his company. The kid was brilliant, with a mind for cryptography that was staggering in one his age.

"Have him coordinate with Jones. I've put him in charge of securing the physical grounds. Better yet, get a meeting set up for the three of us." Regardless of the questions that the anonymous notes elicited, nothing would distract him from business. Projects could be delegated, but his stamp would be all over them, down to the last detail. When he'd picked up the reins of his father's company, with the ink still fresh on his master's degree from M.I.T., he'd also donned a heavy mantle of responsibility, vowing to stay true to his father's vision for the business. In that way, at least, he hadn't failed him.

But now it was the failure of a far different kind that haunted. If there was any truth to the last couple notes, he'd allowed three people's deaths to go unchallenged. He'd let down his brothers. His sister. Not to mention the man standing next to him.

Truth wasn't often delivered anonymously, he reminded himself, jaw tightening. The messages were the mark of a coward, one who wished to inflict pain while staying in the shadows. No one had ever been allowed to strike at the Tremaines without certain reprisal. The sender would learn that all too soon.

James checked his watch, shifting his thoughts firmly back to business. "What about the Micro Secure? Everything set to showcase it at the expo?"

Rappaport nodded. "Corley and Soulieu have been running it on mobile phones, PDAs and wireless equipment, and haven't hit a glitch yet. I think it's going to generate a lot of interest when we unveil it."

"It should do that." In fact, James was counting on it. The specially engineered tool kit they'd developed provided the strongest security available in constrained environments. The advanced safeguards it incorporated would bring a measure of privacy previously unrealized in the area. It would be debuted at the expo, then introduced to the market six months later. The time lag would give their PR department an opportunity to orchestrate the necessary media promotion to whet demand.

Marcus reached for the phone. "You'll want to check on the Micro Secure yourself. I'll tell Corley and Soulieu to wait for you."

As James nodded, his cell phone began to ring. Striding across the room, he took out his cell, checked the caller ID. Then, pulse quickening, he flipped it open and answered. "Tori. I've been waiting to hear from you." It was, he recognized, truer than he'd like to admit. Even as he'd tended to business throughout the day, thoughts of her, and the job he'd hired her for, refused to be banished from his mind.

"Hi. I talked to your ex-sheriff today, who's convinced the accident was just..." Static interrupted her next few words. It sounded as if she was in her car. "...pictures, and I'm on my way to a guy I know, an accident reconstruction engineer. I'll let you know what I find out."

"No. Wait." Aware that his sharp tone had aroused Marcus's interest, he deliberately softened it. "I don't want you to do that alone. I'll go with you."

Annoyance laced her voice, although it remained civil

enough. "That's really not necessary. I'll call you as soon as I know something."

"It's no problem." He checked his watch. "Where should I meet you?"

There was a pause, as if she were reaching for patience. "I'm heading to a bar called Juicy's on the corner of France and LaSalle. But believe me, it's not your type of place."

"Are you calling me a snob?" he asked with genuine amusement. He could almost hear her mental gears grinding. Or maybe that was her teeth.

"Not at all. There's just no need for you to feel uncomfortable. And why come all this way when I can call you with the outcome?"

Since Marcus had ended his conversation, James hastened to do the same. "Because I want to be with you." His words, as well as the deliberately intimate tone of his voice would have his co-worker drawing his own conclusions about his call. "Does this establishment of yours serve food?"

There was an audible sigh, then the blare of horns. He hoped her frustration hadn't caused her to swerve into traffic. "I believe there's a loophole in the Department of Health guidelines that still allows them to refer to it as food, yes."

"Great. We can eat together while we wait."

"Suit yourself." From the abrupt end of her call it was obvious that his insistence hadn't set well with her.

"I told Corley and Soulieu to expect you. Should I reschedule?"

Belatedly, he looked up, saw Rappaport's quizzical look. With a glance at his watch, he mentally calculated the time it would take him to change and drive to New

Orleans. "Set it for 7:00 a.m. tomorrow. I'll meet with Tucker and Jones immediately after."

Marcus nodded approvingly. "Won't hurt you a bit to get out and socialize a little. Celia's always saying that you work too hard."

Celia had been his father's secretary before she'd become his. She regulated his office schedule with dragon like ferocity, and lent the same zeal to her interest in his social life.

James strode toward the door. "Well, considering that I'm about to make Celia a very happy lady, I'll let you inform her about the changes to my schedule tomorrow." He turned his head just enough to catch the stark terror on the man's face, saw the protest forming on his lips. Marcus's reaction had him grinning, but it didn't account for the warm pool of anticipation pooling in his belly.

No, that was elicited by the upcoming meeting with Tori Corbett.

Tori took out her frustration with Tremaine on the pool hustlers at Juicy's. Although they'd seen her play often enough to know better, most of them had more ego than sense. She was up fifty bucks, and her mood had improved accordingly.

Circling the table, she studied the possible plays.

"She's gonna clear the table again."

"No, she ain't. Ain't possible."

"How easily they forget," Tori muttered under her breath. She bent, lined up her shot and banked the six ball off the opposite side to roll directly into the side pocket. Straightening, she observed, "One would think I didn't have your ten in my pocket by doing that very thing, Skeeter."

Skeeter shrugged his nearly seven-foot frame that was at least half as wide as a pool cue and muttered aggrievedly, "Just ain't right, letting a woman play, anyways. How's a man supposed to concentrate when you're all bent over like that?"

"By using your superior skills of concentration, just like I do." With a sure stroke, she used the cue ball to lightly kiss the three, sending it into the corner pocket. She looked up, threw Skeeter an innocent look. "How else do you explain me being able to keep my attention off your god-like physique and on the game?"

Guffaws broke out among the crowd around the table. Skeeter finally found the description too much to resist and cracked a smile, revealing a gold front tooth. "Shoot, if you could play as good as you talked, you'd be on the circuit."

"And if you played as good as you looked, there'd be statues erected in your name." She bent over, studying the lay of the remaining balls. She'd managed to leave herself with no clear shot, which was going to require some sleight of hand. After a few moments of consideration, she made her choice and shifted into position.

It was the quiet that alerted her first. The effect of a stranger walking into a neighborhood tavern was equivalent to a panther stalking through the wilds. The occupants went silent, sizing up the newcomer, assessing the danger, readying for action.

The identity of this particular stranger was never in doubt.

Without glancing his way, she sent the nine ball spinning toward the opposite pocket, bouncing it off the side, where it teetered precariously at the entrance and then, in slow motion, fell into place.

The crowd around the table thinned considerably. She could only imagine that they'd drifted toward Tremaine. Tori decided she'd let him sweat a bit before she called them off. If it gave him a few bad moments, well, maybe the next time he wouldn't be so pushy about inviting himself along.

"You musta wandered in the wrong place, mister." There was a pause, the unmistakable sound of Skeeter spitting on the floor. "I think you ought to wander back out again."

"Since it appears strenuous for you, perhaps you should give up thinking altogether." Tori winced as James's unmistakably cultured tone caused a low rumble to sound across the room. It was time to bring an end to things before he was sent flying back out in the street, with damage to his pretty jaw and two-thousand-dollar suit.

In an effort to distract them, she said, "Who wants to put another twenty on me clearing the rest of the table? Skeeter?"

There was a quick scuffling on the other side of the room followed by a loud thud. With a quick stab of guilt, Tori jerked around and pushed her way through the men encircling the body on the floor. "Dammit, Skeeter, you didn't have to…" And then stared dumbly, first at the body crumpled on the dirty wooden planks, then at the one standing over it, rubbing his knuckles.

James arched one elegant brow, stepped over Skeeter's prone body. The crowd separated for him like the parting of the Red Sea. "Tori. Didn't mean to interrupt your game."

Somehow she managed to close her mouth. Swallow. "No problem. I was just cleaning up."

His mouth quirked. "Me, too." He strolled to the table she'd vacated, surveyed it critically. She used the time to observe him. Far from the suit she'd expected, he was wearing well-worn denim that was faded to white at the most interesting stress points. With the blue polo shirt he had tucked into the waistband, he failed to resemble the Armani-clad executive she was used to seeing. But neither did he look like a regular at Juicy's with their undershirts or ripped tees. Especially with him wearing what looked like Gucci loafers.

Her gaze traveled upward again, lingered on the very respectably muscled wall of his chest. It was difficult to shift her attention once again to clearing the remaining pool balls from the table. It would have been too much to ask, she thought, with an odd jitter in her stomach, to discover that his shoulders owed their width to his well-cut suits. Using her thumb to balance her cue stick, she sent the cue ball smacking into the one, spinning it across the table and into a pocket. Or to find that his long hours at the company had turned his body soft and all too resistible.

She circled the table, noted that Skeeter was on his feet again, but swaying just a bit. Dispatching the five ball, she sent James a cautious look. With one hip propped against the table, arms folded across his chest, he projected a subtle aura of danger. With a jolt of shock, she realized that the power the suits merely hinted at was all too apparent in the more casual clothes. Skeeter had had the misfortune to discover that the hard way.

It was a relief to have something other than the man on the other side of the table to focus on. She sent the thirteen ball to the far pocket and then dispensed with the eleven. Straightening, she chalked her stick, giving the task more attention than was warranted. Why couldn't Tremaine have been like the majority of guys

his age, and let himself go a little? she thought aggrievedly. With the demands of his job, it would be expected.
Even her ex, jock that he'd been in college, had continued his exercise routine only halfheartedly once they'd
gone back to his home in Texas.

"Eight in the left side pocket," she announced, to no
one in particular. Those who had left the table earlier,
in hopes of a good rousing brawl, were shying away
from it now that the stranger had taken up residence
there.

"You've got an easier shot to the right corner," James
noted, observing the table critically.

"The best way isn't always the easiest," she replied
lightly. Leaning over, she took her time lining up her
shot, then banked the eight ball off one side to go spinning into the pocket she'd called. The game finished, she
straightened, set her cue against the table, and, because
she detested cowards, looked squarely at him.

A smile was playing about his mouth as he looked at
the cleared table, then at her. "Showing off?"

She threw a meaningful glance at Skeeter, who was
at the bar, sulking over a beer. "Weren't you?"

"There are times when diplomacy is overrated."
Rounding the table, he took her elbow in his hand and
led her to one of the booths that lined the walls. Once
she'd seated herself, he slid in opposite her. Scanning
the rooms, he raised a brow. "Menu?"

"On the wall."

Following the direction of her finger, he noted the
choices scrawled with colored chalk on the rough plaster
next to the bar. "Interesting display. How do they
change it?"

"Changes wait until it's time to paint," she said
blandly. In truth, she didn't recall any time in her mem-

ory when there had been a change or a paint job. Much of Juicy's dubious charm was owed to its constancy.

He scanned the short listing on the wall. "What's good?"

"Well, if you exchange *edible* for *good,* I can recommend the cajun crawdad platter." She gave him a bland look. Jeans or not, she couldn't see him cracking crawdads and sucking out their brains. Which was really the only way any self-respecting Louisianan would eat them.

"How's the gumbo?"

"Spicy enough to curl strips off your intestines."

He caught the eye of Stoner, the unambitious waiter, and gave him a short nod.

"You'll have to go up to the bar and order," she started, then trailed off as Stoner ambled toward them in what was, for him, a hurry.

"Two bowls of gumbo and the crawdad platter. What do you have on draft?"

Fumbling with the pad he was attempting to withdraw from his back pocket, Stoner reeled off the names of the beers. James ordered one, then cocked an eyebrow at Tori.

"I'll have another Michelob Lite."

Stoner bobbed his head, laboriously writing the order down on the pad. Since Tori had never seen him actually take an order before, it was a sight worth watching.

"Okay." He looked up, seemed to search for some waiterlike lines. "Ummm. I'll get you some silverware. Maybe napkins?" He sent James a hopeful look.

"Excellent." From the slight incline of James's head, Stoner seemed to realize he was dismissed, and moved away.

"That was worth paying tickets for." Tori's bemused

gaze switched from the departing man to the one across from her. ''Did you perfect that talent on snooty maître d's in the French Quarter?''

''Snooty maître d's rarely question the need for table linens, but they do respond to a certain attitude, yes.'' James folded his arms on the table and leaned toward her. ''Why don't you tell me what you've been up to today? Besides fleecing unwary pool players?''

''Well, that was certainly the most lucrative part of my day so far.'' She gave him a brief account of her conversation with Halloway, ending with, ''He's still convinced the accident was due to driver's error. But I went back to my contact, who provided me with the photos in the file I put together for you. I made him a very happy man and bought every picture he had of the accident scene.''

Those sinfully blue eyes of his narrowed. ''I take it he had quite a few of them?'' At her nod, his mouth went flat. ''When did he take them?''

Understanding the meaning hidden in the question, she hastened to reassure him. ''It was hours afterward. The car was still there, though.'' She gave mental thanks that Kiki Corday hadn't been near enough to have gotten to the scene before the bodies had been taken away. He would have had no compunction about snapping whatever photos he thought he could make a buck from.

Stoner brought their drafts to them, setting them down with more care than usual on the table. Waiting until he'd left, she continued. ''The owner of this fine establishment has a setup in the back. He specializes in accident scene reconstruction. I sent over the photos I bought today and a copy of the accident report. He's comparing them and will give us his impressions.''

James looked skeptical. He's the owner and engineer?''

"Don't let the ambiance fool you. Juicy has dabbled in this field for a long time. He finally went back to college a few years ago and got his engineering degree. All his money gets put into the latest equipment and gadgetry, and as you see, little of it goes to overhead. I could have gotten someone with a lot more glitz and polish, but Juicy's cheap and he's the best around.''

James looked toward the back of the bar. "How long has he been at it?''

Because she recognized the impatience in his tone, she reached over, touched his arm lightly. "A while. But genius can't be hurried.''

Touching him was a mistake. She realized it immediately. His heat transferred to her fingertips in a warm flood of sensation, before pulsing through her veins with quick jolts of awareness. The warmth was both an invitation to linger and a warning against the same. She didn't respond to men like this. Ever.

She jerked her hand away with a suddenness that sent her beer teetering. She steadied the glass, then brought it to her lips, sipped. It was more than a bit disconcerting to have her femininity return unheralded, especially summoned as it was by this man. The Tremaine family fortune made the Corbetts look like pikers. And two excruciating years living in that particular vipers' nest had taught her more than she ever wanted to know about high society. Give her the hidden perils of New Orleans's seamy side anyday. At least there she had a fighting chance of figuring out where the knife was coming from.

"You're jumpy tonight.''

Although his observation was made mildly enough, it

was issued in the same voice he'd used with her over the phone. Low and silky, like the stroke of a heated caress.

Giving him a bland stare, she set down her beer. "Not really. There was really no reason for you to come tonight. I'm just going to be sitting and waiting. It could be hours before he's ready to talk to me."

His eyes glinted. "I've decided, this time around, that I'm going to take a more active role in the investigation. I want these questions laid to rest once and for all."

Inner alarms shrilled at the hidden promise in his words. No P.I. wanted a client looking over her shoulder every minute, but her reluctance to work that closely with him came from a far different source. "Leave the investigation to me. You've got other things that demand your attention."

Straightening, he lifted his glass to his lips. "Such as?"

"Well, there's the little matter that someone is threatening to kill you. Why don't we talk about the measures you've taken to ensure against it?"

Judging from the expression on his face, she'd managed to annoy him. "I told you…"

"I know, I know, you don't think a real killer would warn you before striking." With a wave of her hand, she dismissed that argument. "You've admitted to having enemies, past attempts on your life and a compelling reason for competitors to want you out of the way. You'd have to be stupid not to take precautions." She paused, one deliberate beat. "You're not stupid."

"You can't know how delighted I am by your conclusion."

He had, she decided, a rather irritating habit of responding without truly answering. He said nothing more, and Stoner arrived at that time with a steaming tray of crawdads, which he set between them. Then he presented two plates with something of a flourish, napkins and silverware.

She waited until he'd moved away, having obviously forgotten about the gumbo, before she fixed James with a steely stare. "Tell me you've taken measures to protect yourself."

He heaped a plate with crawdads, set it in front of her. "I'm not without resources or common sense."

"Tell me."

Seeming to recognize the steel in her tone, he halted in the process of piling his own plate. His eyes met hers. For the moment, she forgot to worry about what he might see in them. "I take precautions. I've always had to. Bomb sweeps, Kevlar vests, bodyguards... As the level of threat rises, so do my defenses. Does that answer your question?"

It did. It also shook her more than she thought possible. Once again she was reminded that his outwardly cultured world was filled with as many undercurrents of danger as one would expect to find in the toughest dark alley. She watched him as he snapped the head off the crawdad and brought it to his mouth, and her lips curved reluctantly. A man who knew the proper way to dispense with the disgusting-looking, succulent creatures had something in his favor. She reached for her own plate and went to work, discovering an appetite that had earlier seemed questionable.

"Actually, my firm recently has begun expanding into physical security," he surprised her by saying. Dropping some empty shells, legs still attached, to the plate, he scooped up another. "My brother-in-law has a certain level of expertise in that area, and it seemed a natural step for us to take. He'll head up that division when it's fully operational, specializing in antiterrorism tactics and personal safety.''

Attacking the shellfish on the plate before her, she said, ''Then you'll have a ready staff available to protect you. Sounds like a good plan.''

''Plans are all we can make.'' Dropping an empty shell to the growing mound of them, he wiped his fingers on a napkin. ''All the precautions in the world aren't going to be enough to stop someone intent on harm.'' When her gaze flew to his, he held it steadily. ''I don't take unnecessary risks, but in my business I've gotten used to establishing realistic expectations. If someone wants me dead badly enough, sooner or later he's going to succeed. Unless I get to him first.''

Chapter 5

The expression on Tori's face made James pause in the middle of attacking another crawdad. There was a flash of shock there, followed by what, if he hadn't known better, looked like concern. Both were equally intriguing. But before he could comment, she was shrugging, reaching for another crawdad.

"Yeah, you're right. Hey, I have an idea. Why don't you just have a big bull's-eye painted on the back of all those fancy suits of yours? Make it a mite easier all around."

Slowly, his eyes never leaving hers, he reached for his beer, tipped it to his lips. He drank, then lowered it to say, "I don't intend to make it easy for anyone."

"No, I got that." The caustic tone of her voice was matched by the glint in her eye. "You're just fatalistic, right? What's going to happen is going to happen." She snapped off the shell of the crawdad in her hand with just a little more force than necessary. "Seems a little odd for someone in the security business to be saying there's really no way for people to be completely secure. Just a tip—don't pass that line on to your marketing department. I doubt it'll do much for your sales.''

It was on the tip of his tongue to agree with her. It was precisely because he was in the security business that he realized the limitations of the very products and services he sold. No matter how advanced the technology, there were always ways around them for the very, very talented. That was a reality of his field, which necessitated ever newer products, ever more sophisticated technology.

But he swallowed the words, recognizing that her remarks sprang from a far more personal level. He picked up his napkin, deliberately wiped his fingers, then reached out, caught her hand.

He waited for her gaze to meet his before leaning forward to say, ''I like to believe that I'm not without skills in the area of personal safety.'' Her countenance remained stony. It shouldn't have warmed something inside him, something that had been untouched for far too long. His thumb caressed her knuckles, and her hand jerked a little in his. ''I don't have a death wish—there's too much to live for.'' He paused deliberately before adding, ''I've got season courtside tickets to the Hornets.''

It took a moment, but her lips curved reluctantly, even as she slipped her hand away from his. Because her response pleased him, he allowed her to make her escape, and sat back satisfied.

''Courtside, huh?''

He resumed eating. ''Mmm-hmm.''

''Figures.'' The almost angry concern in her voice had changed to unmistakable envy. And then, grudgingly, she admitted, "So, I guess that would be enough to keep you careful. Those seats are tough to come by, even for people with more money than Midas."

He winked at her. "You just have to know the right people."

Tori reached for another crawdad, eyed him speculatively. "How many of those seats did you say you had?"

Enjoying himself hugely, he cracked the shell, dug out the seafood. "Two. Prime position, right across from the team."

"What do you do with them when you can't make it to a game?"

Crushing the tinge of hope in her tone, he wiped his hands and reached for his beer. "Then my brothers use them. Or sometimes my sister. Occasionally someone from work."

She folded her arms on the table and leaned forward. "Don't make me beg, Tremaine. Maybe you and I could reach an agreement. A…a…trade of some kind."

The suggestion summoned more than a casual flicker of interest. Not that he really thought she meant the offer in the way his mind was automatically interpreting it. But her words did elicit all types of fascinating scenarios. Fascinating, because she was as far from his type as it was possible to be. And he was intrigued in spite of it. Or perhaps because of it. "What did you have in mind?"

With excruciating timing Stoner arrived at the booth, carrying two precariously filled bowls. "Almost forgot the gumbo," he mumbled, setting the bowls down in front of them with a definite lack of grace.

Tori sat back, wisely, as it turned out, and narrowly avoided being scalded by the soup that slopped over the side of the bowl. James waited until the man had moved away before observing, "That guy missed his calling. With his light touch he ought to be a surgeon." His words elicited a smile, but the spell had been broken. The fragile link of intimacy between them was gone.

She spooned in some soup, tasted it cautiously. After swallowing, she drew a deep breath. "Oh, my. Hope you don't have ulcers."

He followed suit, took a taste and immediately found his eyes watering. "I didn't before now. That's…an interesting gumbo recipe."

"Yeah, I think they also use it to strip paint. As a matter of fact, I heard a rumor…" Something in the back corner of the bar seemed to distract her, and she stopped talking, laid down her spoon. "Juicy's come out of his lair. Looks like he's ready for us."

With little regret, James slid out of the booth and withdrew his money clip, leaving a bill on the table. Then with a drum roll of anticipation tightening his gut, he followed in Tori's wake, for once failing to give his full attention to the decided sway of her hips. He had no idea what, if anything, to expect from this meeting. But there was no denying that whatever the outcome, there'd be answers of some sort. And answers were something he was increasingly eager to discover.

"What have you got?" Tori didn't bother with introductions, and James was fairly certain it was by design. It suited him well enough. Closing the door behind him, he slipped the tips of his fingers into his jeans pockets and scanned the room she'd led them to. Surprisingly sophisticated computer equipment and peripherals lined the walls. Above the computers the walls were covered with cork board. Displayed there was a series of close-ups of a wrecked automobile. His gut took a quick, vicious twist. The car was instantly recognizable. It made frequent appearances in his nightmares.

He forced his gaze away from the photos to the man Tori was addressing. Juicy's name was the only colorful thing about him. Tall and gaunt, rather than merely thin, his manner of speech was as spare as his frame. The man wore his long, dark hair caught back into a queue that hit him midshoulder blade. From the pallor of his skin, James guessed he spent most of his free time hunched over one of his machines.

"Took me a while." Juicy walked over to a computer terminal and sat down. "You brought me a lot of data. Didn't have a chance to get through it all."

"I know how you like to be thorough." Tori took up a stance behind the man, and James moved to do the same.

"Thought I recognized most of the work." Juicy swiveled his head around to send her a quick look, which she returned calmly.

"I'm sure you did."

Somehow James was left with the feeling that a great deal more had been exchanged in the terse sentences than mere words. The photographer—what had Tori said his name was? Corday—was obviously known to this character.

With a grunt Juicy turned back to the computer. The man pointed the mouse at various spots on the screen and clicked, unfolding several pictures. "Here are the sheriff's pictures of the vehicle and the road. They reported that the car came around this curve—" he traced it with his finger on the screen "—too fast. Driver lost control, tried to compensate by braking." His finger stabbed at the picture of the skid marks on the road. "Car fishtailed, swinging around so the rear end hit the guardrail. The force of that spun the car 180 degrees, and this time it was the front smashing through the rail. Momentum carried it over the edge of the road, down to the riverbed beneath.''

"We read the report," Tori said impatiently. "The question is, do you agree with it?"

"I can see how they came to that conclusion, yeah."

James released a breath he hadn't known he'd been holding. Was that relief he was feeling? He wasn't sure. There were too many emotions churning and bumping inside him to individually identify any one. Certainly it would put to rest a bit of the guilt that had haunted him since the notes started. Guilt that he hadn't done enough. Tried hard enough.

Guilt that wouldn't be assuaged easily.

"What about the other pictures?" he asked tersely. "The ones that weren't part of the report?"

"Like I said, I haven't gotten through everything yet. But I've seen enough to have a few questions."

"What kind of questions?" Tori crowded closer to Juicy, only to be elbowed away.

"Back off and I'll show you." With a few deft strokes he brought up a different set of pictures to the screen, clicking on one to enlarge it. "Here's the front left bumper of the car. Sheriff thought the damage to it came from smashing through the railing. And maybe it did. Might even have hit something fairly solid on the way down to the riverbed." He flexed his fingers on the keyboard. "But it also could have meant the car hit something else before it went off the road."

James stilled. "The report said the road was clear."

Never taking his eyes from the computer screen, Juicy nodded. "There's nothing in the pictures, anyway, but there was a mess load of machinery over on the west side. Why wouldn't the driver head that way? Better to hit a bulldozer than the guardrail.''

"Driver error, the sheriff said," Tori murmured.

"Mebbe." Juicy clicked rapidly until he came to the photo he was looking for. He dragged one of the corners, enlarging it on the screen. "I blew this one up a couple times. This boulder sat at the edge of the road."

"Still does." James never traveled that stretch of blacktop without a part of him wondering about that night twenty years ago. Recreating the scene over and over in his mind. Wishing for a different outcome.

"The ex-sheriff mentioned something about it, too. The parish engineers were working on that stretch of road, widening it. There was interest in turning it into a four-lane, but public outcry killed it. People didn't want the two-hundred-year-old oaks destroyed."

"Whatever." It was clear Juicy had no use for the history. "Looks like the engineers were just widening it up to within a couple feet of that tree there." He tapped a spot on the screen. "But beside it was this rock that probably had sat there since caveman days." With a shrug of his narrow shoulders, he indicated his lack of appreciation of that fact. "See how the dirt around it is disturbed? It had been moved recently."

"The road crew moved it." Tori's voice was flat. She looked at James. "It's in the engineer's report. It was moved back to sit even with the tree to make way for the work, but they left it there to pacify the public upset with the progress."

"You think the car hit the boulder?"

"You wouldn't think so." Juicy stood as he answered James's question and released some pictures that had been tacked to the cork board. "Can't figure a way for the car to swing that far around and still hit it with enough force to cause that kind of damage.'' His pause was full of meaning. ''If that's where the boulder was sitting that night.''

''Well of course it was.'' A bit of James's earlier impatience sounded in Tori's voice. ''We have the pictures to show the scene.''

But James was rounding the man to peer at the pictures in his hand. Reaching out, he took them from him, flipping through the stack until he came to one that stopped him.

His gaze raised to meet Juicy's, who was bobbing his head. ''Wouldn't have thought anything of it if I hadn't seen that picture. It made me stop and look at things a bit differently.''

The pictures were close-ups of the boulder. The rock's position to the road. The flawless face it presented from that direction. But another shot taken from a different angle, intended, James guessed, to shoot the road from a different position, showed the back of the huge boulder. And the fresh scar marring it.

''Suppose that mark could have been made by the dozer that moved it,'' Juicy mused, going back to flipping through pictures he'd loaded on to his computer. ''Not saying that it couldn't have been.''

No, James mused grimly, he wasn't ''saying'' anything. But he'd already planted a seed of suspicion in their minds. ''Are you suggesting the damage to the left bumper is consistent with it having hit the boulder?''

The man pursed his lips, skated a glance toward Tori. ''Wasn't gonna say it that fancy, but yeah, it's a possibility. I'd need to run some tests to be sure. Only thing is there's no way in hell that it could have happened if the rock was sitting the way it is in this picture. Look at this.'' He scrolled down the screen, clicked on close-ups of the guardrail. "A car going at a pretty good clip hitting that railing isn't going to be stopped. It's gonna snap through it and go on down the embankment." He brought up another picture, shot through a night lens, and marked the path the car would have taken. "The damage done to the car's bumper looks more like it hit something solid." He brought one fist to hit his open hand in a loud whack. "Something with no give to it."

"Could it have hit something else as it went down the embankment?" Tori asked. "Another rock, or a tree, maybe?"

Juicy shrugged. "You didn't give me any pictures that showed something big enough in that area, but that don't mean there wasn't something."

"There wasn't." James's tone was final. He'd walked that scene in the days afterward, when thoughts of foul play had haunted him and overwhelming grief had whipped up fury. It had been easier to feel fury and suspicion than it had been to cope with sorrow. Simpler to want to blame a faceless nameless person, than to blame fate. He and his siblings had been orphaned. Another child left motherless. Until that moment he hadn't remembered how desperately he'd wanted to discover a human face to put on that evil.

He still didn't have a face. He didn't have facts. What he had was a *possibility.*

Realizing that Tori was looking at him quizzically, he tucked away the frustration that threatened to swamp him. "I checked the scene myself. There were no sizable trees, only brush. And the path was rocky, but nothing large enough to cause that kind of damage to the bumper."

"Unless impact from the car sent the rock rolling down the hill into the river below."

With an inclination of his head, he acknowledged the idea and addressed Juicy. "What could you do with this if we gave you more time?"

The man all but rubbed his hands together. "I want to go over the rest of the file you brought. Do some photogrammetic calculations. Examine the tire marks. Got the latest here in digital software and laser equipment. Give me a few days and I can run you a 3D reenactment of the accident itself."

"Do it."

Juicy slid a sideways glance to Tori. "The cost…"

"Will be covered. There's a bonus in it for you if you can get it to me sooner."

For the first time, a wide grin spread across the man's taciturn features. "I'll give it top priority."

"Call me the minute it's finished," Tori said, then turned to follow James out the door. He didn't shorten his strides; he couldn't. He had a sudden need for oxygen, to clear his head and fill his lungs.

A need to shake the insidious visions that were already forming, dark and sinister, in his mind.

He only half noted the occupants of the tavern, who eyed him sullenly but gave him wide berth as he made his way through the place. When he got outside, he headed to his car, not at all surprised that it was still there and seemingly in one piece, despite the neighborhood. Walking all the way around it, he did a quick, thorough scan, then nodded at the young hood sitting on the curb beside it. "Any problems?"

The other man shook his head, reaching out for the half of a hundred-dollar bill James offered. Fitting it together with the half in his hand, he stared at it for a moment, then gave a huge grin. "Anytime, mister. Anytime.'' He turned and headed down the street, a bounce to his step.

''Couldn't find anything more conspicuous?''

At Tori's droll comment, he looked over his shoulder at her. ''My tank's in the shop.''

She gave a rather inelegant snort, and circled the Dodge Viper. ''I always wondered what inadequacy men were making up for with expensive…whoa.'' Tori stopped, narrowed her eyes. ''Is this a V-10?''

''Yeah…505 cubic-inch engine,'' he affirmed. ''And it makes up for my personal inadequacy of being unable to go from zero to sixty in fifteen seconds while on foot.''

Further smart-ass comments apparently stifled, she ran an admiring hand over a front fender. ''What's the torque in this baby? You don't mind popping the hood, do you?''

A jacked-up late eighties sedan rolled slowly by. Its windows were cranked down, with rap music and gangster wannabes spilling from them.

Noting their interest, James said, ''Some other time, maybe. I don't think this is the right place for show and tell.''

At his words, her attention followed his and she nodded. ''Sorry. I know a little about cars, but I've never gotten under the hood of one of these. I used to pit crew for a friend, though. I know my way around an engine.''

And it sounded very much like she was itching to get her hands on this one. Despite the darker thoughts summoned by their conversation with Juicy, his interest was piqued. Most women of his acquaintance could identify the car's ignition and little else. He had a sneaking suspicion that her expertise with car engines far surpassed his own, since his was limited to little more than pointing in its general direction.

He felt a flicker of amusement. No, Tori Corbett wasn't at all like the women he generally spent time with. And it was too damn bad for him that he found that so appealing. "So now I have two things you envy—Hornets tickets and this car. Good to know."

Her expression sobering, she came around the hood to stand next to him. Oddly hesitant, she said, "I didn't exactly envy what you must have been going through in there a while ago."

His lighthearted feeling fled, to be replaced with the edge of anger that had been simmering since he'd seen the pictures. Heard the possibilities.

He reached into his pocket and withdrew his car keys. "Don't worry about me. I just wish he'd come up with something a little more substantial." Something that would have provided some answers, for once, instead of triggering even more questions. Something that would put to rest, once and for all, this nagging sense of failure that refused to die.

An image flashed through his mind, of the freshly scarred boulder, followed by another conjured up from his imagination. How easy would it have been, he wondered, to use one of those big Cats to move that rock one more time…into the middle of the dark night road? How quickly could it have been accomplished? In time to take the oncoming driver unaware? To cause an instantaneous decision…between a head-on crash and an unforgiving embankment?

His muscles tensed, and it took conscious effort to keep his fingers from curling into fists. Control had been his mantra for twenty long years, when he'd had to step, much too young, into his father's shoes. He wasn't a man given to rashness. With sheer force of will he pushed back the images that tormented. But he knew they'd return, unbeckoned, when sleep refused to come. Doubts always picked the midnight hours to creep in, when defenses were lowered and darkness dimmed logic.

Skirting the path his thoughts were heading, he used the automatic ignition to start the car. "Have you spoken to Sanderson's Towing and Recovery yet?"

Tori was still watching him with eyes that saw too much. "No, although I plan to. I doubt they'll be able to tell us any more than is contained in the report, but I want to be thorough."

"The original owner is still there." He'd checked out that much, at least, before he'd hired her. The company had been the one to tow the car after the bodies had been extracted, bagging the belongings and doing the necessary cleanup so the vehicle could be sold for parts. "I want to go with you when you talk to him."

"Maybe you should rethink that." Someone came staggering out of Juicy's, threw them a look, then hurried in the opposite direction. The distraction had her glancing away, even as she continued, her voice lowered. "You have a business to run. I'm sure there are things there that require your attention, and I don't expect the visit to come to much, at any rate."

He arched one eyebrow. "Why do I have the feeling I'm getting the brush-off?"

She raised her chin and crossed her arms over her chest. A warrior readying for battle. Gaze direct, she said, "I'm not trying to brush you off, I just don't see the need for you to put yourself through anything else…like you did tonight."

James went still. It was one thing to have the constant

battle between reason and emotion waging war within him. It was quite another for her to sense it. To comment on it. Emotion equaled vulnerability, and he'd spent his life making sure he and his were never vulnerable. "If I didn't know better, I'd think you were trying to protect me."

She uncrossed her arms and let them hang at her sides, as if she was uncertain what to do next. Then one rose, as if of its own volition, to hover between them before resting, ever so lightly, on his chest. "It can't be easy, listening to people talk about that night. Why go through it when you don't have to?"

One of his hands came up to grasp hers, his fingers tightening when she attempted to pull away. He had the feeling that if he let her, she'd try to soothe away his imagined hurts, the way a mother did with a child. But her touch had just the opposite affect. It threatened to unleash the emotions crashing and churning inside him. "I don't need protecting, and I don't require stroking, Tori. At least not that kind."

He watched the storm gather in her eyes, and the sight called to something primitive inside him. He had two decades' worth of experience keeping that core carefully controlled. A man led by his emotions would be ruined by them. But right now, in this moment, temptation was beckoning and he couldn't summon up a single reason to avoid it.

Using his grip on her hand, he tugged her closer. The pulse was hammering at the base of her throat, and he dipped his head to taste it. Her scent lingered there, right there, where the blood beat madly under the skin, beneath his tongue.

Her reaction called to something inside him, a wild and reckless streak that was carefully harnessed but never completely locked away. Most who knew him would swear it didn't exist. But right now it had him, and he was relishing the freedom.

Pressing her lips open with his, he swallowed the protest she would have made. And she would have made one, he was certain of it. However much he demanded control, she strove for it, at least around him. There was a distance between them that she was usually careful to cultivate. Snaking an arm around her waist, he pulled her closer, denying her a physical distance even as he felt her trying to maintain an emotional one.

The taste of her was foreign, forbidden. It called to everything inside him that he sought to tame. This was a bad idea. The worst. The realization didn't make the sudden wanting lessen. Didn't slow the heavy tide of blood from coursing through his veins. And when her tongue met his for the first time, the intimate glide more sure than tentative, he dove headfirst into sensation.

Her response torched his hunger and ignited a need for more. Pulling her closer, he took the sensual battle a step deeper until they were sealed together, chests, hips, thighs. His mouth ravaged hers and was ravaged in turn. The flavor of her was heady, and he couldn't seem to get his fill. He jammed his fingers through her hair, cupped the back of her head and brought her nearer. A moment more, and the need that had risen so fast, burned so fiercely, would be quenched. Just one more instant to satiate himself with the twist of her lips beneath his, the exotic flavor of her that he couldn't have foreseen. Wouldn't forget.

There was a burst of sound in the street behind them, and she started in his arms. Her reaction keyed his own, and a belated awareness of their surroundings filtered through him. The blare of a car horn, the accompanying shouted suggestion, had logic returning.

Releasing her, he took a step away. And then, for good measure, another. The distance helped to keep him from taking her in his arms again as she stared at him, her eyes more green than brown, huge and deep.

"What the hell was that?"

The question, delivered in that faintly aghast tone, was almost enough to have him smiling. Easing a hip against the front fender of the car, he said, "If you have to ask, I must be out of practice." She shook her head furiously, one hand coming out in protest, almost as though she expected him to reach for her again. Which of course, he wouldn't. He folded his arms across his chest, just to make sure.

"Don't go getting all smooth and charming on me, Tremaine. This—" the gesture she made with her hand was unmistakable "—can't happen."

"I couldn't agree more." And then, unable to resist, he added, "Why?"

She'd half turned away, but his question had her whirling back. "Why? Why? Because..." Words seemed to fail her for the moment. "Because it's a terrible idea, that's why. Mucking up business with personal stuff is the worst way to run an investigation."

"Very true. I usually frown on 'mucking up business,' as a general rule."

She peered at him suspiciously, but he was careful to keep his expression bland. "Well then, that's settled. This shouldn't happen again."

"It won't." The words were tinged with regret and filled him with a vague sense of surprise. Her reminder should have been unnecessary. Of course something so inappropriate couldn't be allowed to occur again. He didn't prey on his employees. He was normally quite adept at keeping his personal and business worlds from colliding.

"Okay." She didn't quite manage to keep the wariness from her voice. Backing away, she nearly tripped over the curb. He didn't trust himself to reach out and steady her. "If you're still intent on tagging along tomorrow…"

"I am."

"…how about if we just agree to meet there? I've got the address in the copy of the file you made for me. Is 10:00 a.m. all right with you?"

He thought of the meetings he'd already rescheduled. "Make it one." It would play hell with his calendar tomorrow, but he could go in early, get caught up. He didn't usually have to force the single-minded focus reserved for business.

But right now, watching Tori turn and walk back into the tavern, he had a feeling that focus was going to be more difficult to summon than usual.

Chapter 6

"You didn't hear a word I said."

The feminine words were uttered evenly enough. It was only experience that had James's sense of caution heightening. Raising his brows, he looked directly at his little sister and lied through his teeth. "Of course I did."

Analiese Tremaine Jones tossed her short blond curls and snorted. "Yeah, and pigs fly. I know you have a million things on your CEO mind, oh elder one, but maybe you could show a little interest in the way I'm going to save you about one point five million." After a pause she added, "And a smidgen of gratitude wouldn't be amiss, either."

Assuming what he hoped was a properly chastened expression, James folded his hands and recited the gist of her conversation. "You've figured a way to up the speed on the file-wiping software. Although it's only on paper right now, you're pretty sure you can accomplish the multiple overwrites at least twice as fast as it is cur-

rently, without using our new chip, which—you're
right—will save us a nice bundle of change.''

Her blue eyes, so like his own, narrowed at his glib
summary. ''And how did I say I was going to accomplish it?''

Neatly dodging that bullet, he gave a careless shrug.
''Through genius, of course. I expected nothing less of
you.'' To divert her from his lack of attention, he added,
''You must have been here all night working on it. I
can't imagine Jones is too happy about that.''

Her smile was innocent. Too innocent. ''Nice try, but
we're still talking about you. It's not like you to be distracted when we've got this much going on. I mean,
that's how a normal person would react.'' She delivered
the dual compliment/insult with the smoothness of family. ''Whereas you…you thrive on pressure and deadlines.''

He reached out, yanked a curl before she could duck.
''Brat. We're forty-eight hours from delivery of the Pen-
tagon contract and within a week of the Technology
Expo. I have just a few things on my mind.''

''Mmm-hmm.'' Analiese twirled around in her chair,
studied him speculatively. He reminded himself that this
woman, despite her deceptively petite angelic looks,
could put a bloodhound to shame if she caught wind of
anything suspicious. ''What about the bid on the newest
Pentagon contract? They announce their selection soon,
don't they?''

''They do, yes, but we'll be ready.'' Nothing, especially not some cryptic notes from an anonymous coward, was going to delay the bid. He made a mental note
to speak to Jones about beefing up the security around
their homes, and especially surrounding Ana. He wasn't
willing to take a risk with her well-being.

She waited, but when he offered nothing more, she made a face. "Secretive to the end, as usual." Giving a theatrical sigh, she switched topics. "What time did you come to work this morning? It was well before dawn, I know that."

"Early." He strolled past her, crouched down to look at her computer screen. Once he'd gotten home from Juicy's, there had been little chance of sleep. The information the man had given them triggered a seemingly endless stream of scenarios playing across his mind. Which just heightened his frustration, because he was no closer than before to finding definitive answers.

But that hadn't been what had had him bolting from his bed before the clock had struck three. Those hadn't been the only visions that had haunted him, keeping sleep at bay. Every time he'd shut his eyes, there'd been a sexy, sultry image of Tori drifting behind his eyelids. A memory of the faintly exotic taste of her. The way her body had fit perfectly against his. Followed, of course, by all the reasons she could never be in his arms again.

Since self-torture really wasn't his thing, it had seemed more productive to get up, dress and go to work. As Ana had pointed out, he certainly had enough going on here to keep him busy.

His fingers went to the keyboard, and he was immediately elbowed for his efforts. "No way, this is my baby." Slapping his hands away, she added, "You put me in charge, right?"

"Of course, but I was just…"

"…going to go back to your own office and leave me alone? Brilliant idea." Ana stood and gave him a small shove. "I'll let you know when I get this off paper and functioning. Should be before I leave this afternoon."

With real reluctance James tore his eyes from the keyboard. One of the most difficult lessons learned in running a company this size had been learning to delegate. And it never got easier. "I'll check in later. I have a…an appointment. I'll be off property for a few hours."

Ana stopped shielding the keyboard with her body and surveyed him. "What kind of appointment?"

Back on familiar ground, he dropped a kiss on the top of her head. "One that's none of your business. I'll catch up with you tomorrow."

She fell back in her seat, folded her arms across her chest and stared at him, her suspicious little brain obviously clicking away. "What's wrong?"

Determining that discretion was definitely the better part of valor, he began moving to the door. "Nothing. Just a lot of irons in the fire."

"Which isn't out of the ordinary for you. So there's trouble or a woman. Which is it?"

"Save that imagination of yours for solving the overwipe problem. You're wasting it on me."

From the dejected look on her face, he'd managed to convince her. "Probably. I don't know what I was thinking…there hasn't been a woman born who could tear you away from work when you were busy. Not that we all wouldn't pay money to see you fall hard and fast, but…"

He closed the door with a quiet *snick,* effectively shutting her out. Unfortunately, he wasn't as successful at shutting out the thoughts conjured by her words.

It wasn't a woman dragging him away from work, he thought, striding back to his office. Ana was right, no female had ever had that kind of control over him. But there was a decades-old mystery to be solved, and

damned if he was going to quit before he had all the
answers.

The fact that Tori Corbett was all wrapped up in that
mystery was just a detail he'd have to learn to ignore.

Tori leaned against the counter of Sanderson's Towing and Recovery and flipped through the papers the
owner had obligingly dug out of the filing cabinet for
her. He'd been obliging, at least, once she'd flashed a
hundred-dollar bill in front of him. She didn't think Tremaine would worry overmuch about the cost of her cure
for the man's reticence. He struck her as a man interested
in results, and money had a nice way of eliciting coop-
eration.

Thoughts of what else had interested James Tremaine
last night had the pages trembling in her hands and her
focus on them blurring. She'd recovered, almost, from
the rocketing response his touch had fired in her. But it
would be a while longer before she was able to forgive
herself for becoming a mass of stuttering hormones in
his arms.

Her sudden scowl had the proprietor backing carefully
away from the counter. Maybe she hadn't done herself
any favors by steering clear of men since her divorce.
Surely if she hadn't been abstinent for so long, she could
have tempered her response a bit better. As it was, she
was very much afraid that had it not been for the interruption, she'd have jumped the man's bones then and
there.

And what an ignominious conquest that would have
been, she silently jeered at herself. Ripping off James
Tremaine's shirt in front on Juicy's, in one of the seed-
iest neighborhoods that side of New Orleans. With her
luck, some enterprising cameraman would have been

around and the pictures could have been adorning this morning's tabloids. If mortification built character, they'd be erecting a freaking statue in her name right now.

Scanning the second paper in the file, she flipped it over to look at the next page. The only consolation she'd had in the long sleepless night that had followed their parting was that she'd been the one to step back. Eventually. And once she had, it hadn't taken long for sheer horror to replace the desire pumping through her veins. Getting involved with a client was inviting all sorts of seamy complications. Getting involved with James Tremaine in particular was about as bright as throwing herself in front of a fast-moving bus.

She'd lived, briefly and unhappily, in his monied sphere once. Or at least as close to it as she ever wanted to be. The people she'd met then, her ex and in-laws especially, had epitomized the term *shallow*. She'd encountered puddles deeper. She wasn't going to willingly dance the upper crust two-step ever again.

As the door opened behind her, her attention was captured by the sight of her dad's scrawled signature on the page. She slowed, read more carefully. It wasn't unexpected. In the file Tremaine had copied for her, there had been mention of this place, as well as the lack of any useful leads it had elicited. Still, there was an odd pang knowing she was following in his path, literally and figuratively.

Because her eyes wanted to mist, she blinked them rapidly before straightening to look at the man who'd joined her at the counter.

"Tori." The slightly intimate note to his voice jump-started her pulse, conjuring up a smoky image of their kiss last night. He must have come straight from the office, as he was fully decked out in corporate warrior mode. She recognized the Savile Row suit and Versace tie, but was forced to admit that in his case, the man definitely made the clothes, and not vice versa.

When she was certain her voice would be steady, she said, "Mr. Sanderson was kind enough to dig around for the records on the car's recovery." She nudged the pages toward James and waited as he thumbed through them, skimming quickly.

He looked up and flicked a glance at the apple-faced, narrow-shouldered man behind the counter. "You the owner?"

The man straightened, hitched up his pants. "That's right."

"You wouldn't have been at the time this car came in. Is your father still around?"

Sanderson pursed his lips. "Pa don't have much to do with the business anymore. He's semiretired."

"Is he around?"

"He's probably out back."

"Good. Get him." His words were repeated politely enough, but imbued with unmistakable command.

Tori watched the owner shuffle out the back door, into what was presumably a shop area. Irritation arrowed through her. Tremaine had managed to accomplish with two words what she knew intuitively would have cost her another fifty bucks. "Neat trick. Do you do magic, too?"

James slanted her a look as he spread the papers out to peruse. "I thought you were going to wait for me."

"Traffic wasn't too bad and I arrived sooner than expected." She inched away, just to give him room. Certainly not because she needed the physical distance between them. Nodding toward the papers, she added,

''There's nothing of interest here. Just a record of the call and costs for towing and storing the car until it went to salvage. A notation made by the mechanic who conducted the physical examination. My dad collected the personal effects for you?''

''There wasn't much.''

Sympathy stirred. The page hadn't detailed the contents of the box her father had picked up. The ladies would have had purses. Perhaps a shoe or two had jolted loose in the crash. She tried to suppress the mental image of James, barely more than a boy, receiving that box, symbolic of the responsibility that circumstances had thrust upon him.

The man that walked through the back door was wiping his hands on a greasy cloth. Although his careful gait and the seams etched into his face bespoke at least eight decades, his gaze was alert enough as he surveyed them. ''I'm Guy Sanderson. M'boy said you wanted to see me?''

''We wanted to ask you a few questions about a vehicle you recovered twenty years ago,'' Tori put in smoothly. She picked up the file folder and held it out so he could see the label on it.

Jamming the cloth into one hand, he reached the other deep into the pocket of his coveralls, drew out a pair of glasses. ''Can't read a damn thing without my bifocals,'' he grumbled. ''' Course at my age, I guess I'm lucky I still have my sight.'' He peered closely at the folder, moving his lips silently. Then he swung his head slowly from one side to the other. ''Don't recall it exactly. Mebbe if I take a look at them papers...''

James pushed them together and handed them to him. But rather than taking them, the old man stared hard at him. ''Seen you before,'' he said. ''Take me a minute

to recollect where…'' He snapped his fingers. "I know.
It was in them society pages my wife always has laying
around. Fancy folk going to useless shindigs.'' He stared
harder at James, and then studied the page lying on top
of the papers.

"Tremaine.'' His gnarled fist thumped on the counter
soundly. "Yep, I 'member now.'' He nodded sagely.
"Nothing wrong with my memory, just takes longer to
get it working at my age. Yer the one what runs that
comp'ny nearby. We towed the wreckage from the accident what killed your folks. Terrible accident, that.''

Tori sent James a quick look. If the older man's verbal
meanderings had awakened bad memories, it didn't
show in his expression. "That's what we wanted to talk
to you about. The papers list every part you managed to
sell off the car.'' The frame, two tires, axle rods, bumpers and windows had been a loss. Everything else imag-
inable had found a new home, down to the ash tray and
cigarette lighter.

Sanderson nodded. "There's nothing left of it now,
though. See?'' With one bony index finger he stabbed
at the faded imprint stamped across the top page. "It
had been stripped down to its frame, and that was sprung
so it was pretty worthless. When there's nothing useful
left we sell it for scrap metal. This one has been gone
for, oh…'' He scratched his jaw, stared into space.
"Seems like two, three years now.''

Glancing at the date affixed below the stamp, Tori
found he was correct. Maybe his memory would prove
useful yet. "What about the front left fender? From the
accident photos it appeared seriously damaged, yet you
still managed to sell them.''

"People look for something in better shape than what

they got.'' The man shrugged. ''It was pretty banged in but still had good to it.''

''Do you remember the fender, specifically?'' James crossed his arms, leaned against the counter. ''Any idea what it had come in contact with?''

A shrug was his only answer. ''Don't pay much attention to that kind of thing. I go over the vehicles once real good when we get them. Clean them up some.'' With a quick glance at James, he seemed to think better than to go into detail. ''Make a note of what we can mebbe use and list it all down. That way when someone asks we can find the information real quick. Got us a computer 'bout ten years ago, and that makes the whole thing a lot easier, I can tell you.''

''You don't remember seeing anything special about that fender?'' Tori probed further. ''The accident report noted that it had slammed into a guardrail and then through it.''

Raising his shoulders, Sanderson responded, ''Don't recall any details about the car. Too long ago, and we handle nearly a hundred wrecked vehicles each year. Although seems like this was the one…'' He started turning the pages, studying each of them intently. ''Yep, I thought so.'' With a start, Tori realized he was pointing at her father's signature. ''I 'member this fella. He's the one what collected the personal effects. Had him a signed release form. From you?'' His gaze shifted to James.

At his nod, the man went on. ''I remember it special 'cuz I ain't never seen one of them gadgets before. Never have since, tell ya the truth.''

''What gadget might that be?''

She'd obviously spent too much time in Tremaine's company, Tori thought, because she was able to discern the sliver of impatience layered beneath the civility in his words.

"You know, that—what do you call it—tracking thing. Lets you follow whoever you plant it on. That was a first for me. Guess with your outfit into that high-tech security stuff, you're used to that sort of thing. If I could afford it," he mused, his gaze going faraway, "I'd get one of them things to plant on my braggin' dog. Tell ya, when it trees a coon it's all I can do to…"

"You're saying you found a tracking device in the car?" James's voice was precise, his expression still. But emotion emanated from him in waves. For some reason Tori was reminded of an explosive waiting to detonate. "How'd you know what it was?"

"I didn't, and that was a problem," Sanderson replied. "And I always did a detailed list of the effects I gathered from the car to return to the family, so's there's no confusion later about what was or wasn't in there. Had no idea what that thing was, so I had to ask."

"Who did you ask?" she questioned.

"The one who come and picked up the belongings. Made him sign for them." He stabbed a gnarled finger at the signature again. "Rob Landry was his name."

The room tilted and the floor seemed to shift beneath her feet. Tori tried to speak, found speech beyond her.

"You're sure?" James asked.

Sanderson nodded emphatically. "Dead sure. 'Member it clear as last week. When I fetched the box for him, I showed him that gadget, told him I'd been puzzling over it. He took a look at it and said right off the bat what it was. Guess he'd seen some before."

"That's impossible," Tori said flatly. She'd recovered her voice and with it came indignation. "You must be mistaken."

That drew a glare from the old man. "Missy, I might be old but my memory's in working order. How the heck would I have come up with the name for it when I'd never seen anything like it before?"

She opened her mouth to answer, but James beat her to it. "We want to thank you." He held out his hand, and after a moment the older man accepted it. "We've wasted enough of your time, but you've been very helpful."

Partially mollified, Sanderson gave a dismissive wave. "Not like I'm punching a clock these days. Y'all have a good trip back now."

Doing a slow burn, Tori waited until they were outside before pulling away from James's grasp on her elbow. "That's a load of bull. The man's obviously going senile." Her irritation made her strides long enough to keep up with James without problem.

"Maybe."

Certain she'd misheard him, she stopped in her tracks. "What? You can't believe that garbage. He even said he didn't know what it was that he'd found in the car."

The sun was brutal overhead, bringing an instant sheen of perspiration to her skin. With deliberate movements James slipped off his suit coat, folded it over his arm. "He also said your father identified it for him. Do you think he'd recognize a tracking device if he saw one?"

"He…" The question threw her off balance. "Yes, of course, but the fact that it wasn't included in Dad's report means that there's another explanation."

He inclined his head, slipped his free hand in his pants pocket. "I'm listening."

For some reason, his stance, his words, made her want to kick him. "Sanderson is probably mixed up. He must have been thinking of another vehicle, or this whole thing could be dementia induced. He's not exactly a spring chicken.''

''True.'' The very reasonableness of his tone set her teeth on edge. ''He seemed pretty sharp to me, though.''

''If there was a tracking device in that car it would have been in Dad's report.'' Her tone was flat. ''It's as simple as that. Who knows what happened? Maybe, and this is a big maybe, Dad thought that's what it was, but under further examination found he was wrong. There'd be no mention of it in the report if he'd mistakenly identified it.''

The glare of the sun gilded his dark hair, streaking its inkiness with gold. ''I think you're forgetting something. There was nothing in the box that even came close to fitting that description. I went through the whole thing. My mother's and Lucy's purses had opened and the contents were strewn across the inside of the car. I had to identify which belonged to my mother before bundling up Lucy's belongings for Marcus.'' He paused, as if ready for her protest, but she couldn't summon one. Not then. ''There was nothing in that entire box that wasn't identifiable. That device, or whatever it was, wasn't included in it.''

''You don't know that,'' she said stubbornly, ''because you have no idea what it was Sanderson was referring to. Heck, who knows, maybe Dad was having fun with him. All I know is that I don't particularly care for what you're suggesting.'' She hadn't been aware that the volume of her voice had raised until he glanced around. Following his gaze, Tori saw they'd attracted the attention of a few people in the parking lot.

He took a step back. Voice clipped, he said, ''There's no use having this discussion out in the sun when we can talk in air-conditioning.'' Without waiting to see whether she agreed, he turned, strode toward his car.

The air conditioner was already turned on when she yanked open the door, dropped into the passenger seat. And even churning out thick, warmish air, it was better than the temperature outside. It did nothing, however, to dispel the temper that was bubbling inside her.

"Let's look at this logically, shall we?'' James released the steering column to move it out of his way and half turned in the seat to face her. "The messages, which may or may not be credible, suggested the accident might have been deliberate.''

"One message,'' she muttered, his reasonable tone making her jaw clench. "The others didn't even mention it.''

Ignoring her, he went on. "The expert that *you* lined up,'' his faint emphasis was unmistakable, "using pictures that *you* discovered also came up with some questions about the way the accident happened. Juicy came up with a pretty far-fetched possibility. But if he was anywhere close to the truth…''

He didn't go on. He didn't have to. A tracking device could have alerted the killer to when the Tremaine car was coming, so the scene could be arranged in time.

The chill that broke out over her skin wasn't completely owed to the air-conditioning kicking in. "This whole thing is getting more far-fetched by the moment. Look, I know my Dad. Integrity was his code. He would never have been involved in something shady, and he'd never double-cross a client. There has to be another explanation.''

"There may be. But under the circumstances…'' James took his wallet from his pocket, opened it and took out some bills. "Perhaps it would be best to part ways now."

His words acted as a sucker punch. Inwardly reeling, she stared dumbly, first at the bills, then at him. He spoke again, but it was hard to listen when the buzzing in her ears seemed to get louder by the moment.

"Ours was a trial relationship, remember? And upon reevaluation, I think it's best to terminate it. If nothing else, there's a possible conflict of interest here."

Fury, hot and ripe, clogged in her throat. And something else. Something that felt suspiciously like hurt. It took effort to nod, reach for a calm tone. "Because you think my dad might have sold you out twenty years ago. And me...I'd just do the same, is that it?"

Because she refused to reach for it, he dropped his hand, still holding the bills. "This isn't about you or me. You're reacting emotionally, but we have to consider the facts."

The knowledge that he was right did little to dissipate her anger. "Damn right I'm reacting emotionally. I tend to do that when someone calls my father a crook. Or worse, an accomplice to murder. But that's just me." She bared her teeth, fingers scrambling for the door handle. "You're right. It'd be better for both of us if we parted ways." She pushed the door open, swung out of the car. "And you can keep your money. I don't want it. I'll see this through on my own, and when I do find proof disputing your ridiculous scenario, I'm going to take great satisfaction in making you eat your words."

The heat scorched her the moment she stepped out of the car, shooting up from the soles of her feet to her brow. But it was nothing compared to the furnace that was stoked inside her. She needed to get away from this man, before she did something she'd regret. Like going for his throat.

She ran to her car nearby. But when she went to open the door James was already there, his palm pressed flat against the window. Gone was the cool reason he'd just treated her to as he'd dismissed her. Gone was any semblance at civility. Menace shimmered from him in waves. "You're off this case, Tori. All the way off. You no longer work for me in any capacity, and that means you won't be doing any investigating in this or related issues. It's over."

Jutting her chin out, she met his narrowed blue gaze. No doubt competitors quaked beneath it. But she wasn't so easily cowed. "Wrong, ace. I may no longer work for you, but I can investigate whatever I damn well please. And I will. The only difference is, I no longer have to keep you posted about my findings. Now get your hand off my door, unless you want to chance losing it."

His piercing regard didn't waver. His mouth was flat and grim. "You don't want to piss me off, Tori. I make a dangerous enemy."

She didn't need his words to know that. The man was dangerous, regardless of the nature of the relationship. It was just too damn bad that her defenses, usually so reliable, had turned to putty about the time he'd walked into her office.

Her smile brittle, she fumbled for sunglasses, jammed them on her nose. "Surprise, surprise. Here's a news flash for you. You make an even more dangerous employer. You strike me as the kind of man who knows when to cut his losses. This is a battle you can't win. I'm looking into my father's part of this investigation, and there's nothing you can do to stop me."

She shoved his hand off her car, and surprisingly he let her. Yanking open the door, she slid into its suffocating heat and turned the key in the ignition. "You have far better things to worry about then me, anyway. Like the person who wants you dead. You might want to concentrate your energies on that instead of wasting them defaming a dead man's reputation."

And with that she slammed the door and drove off.

Chapter 7

He'd handled her badly.

The knowledge ate at James, making the trip back to his company seem longer than it should have. He'd managed more tact when firing people, even while sending them away with a lukewarm reference and a dismissive severance package. Hell, he'd dispatched ex-lovers with more finesse.

And that, really, was what gnawed at his gut now. He'd wounded her with his words. She hadn't been able to disguise the hurt in her eyes. That sight, and knowing he'd been responsible for it, sent a sneaky blade of guilt through him.

Expertly he guided the car through the twisting parish back roads, for once taking no pleasure at the vehicle's smooth handling. The fact was that Tori Corbett drew a response from him that he wasn't always able to control. Which was another reason it made good sense to cut off all contact with her. The one thing he insisted upon in his life, both personal and business, was restraint.

Tori threw a wrench into that, and even worse, she represented far more complications than he wanted to contemplate. Of all the possible situations he'd envisioned when he'd decided to reopen this case, somehow he hadn't considered that the P.I. he'd hired twenty years earlier might not have been honest with him. That he might have discovered information suggesting the accident was anything but, and then covered it up.

The countryside zipped by with a blurring speed reflective of his thoughts. There were too few facts and far too many possibilities. But if Sanderson was right and there had been a tracking device found in the car, that would dovetail neatly with the spin Juicy had put on things yesterday. It would lend more credence to the prospect that the "accident" had been anything but. Landry knowing about the device and keeping it from James would be, at best, incompetent.

And at worst, criminal.

Jumping to conclusions wasn't a sport he usually engaged in. He reached for his sunglasses, flipped them open with one hand and settled them on his nose. Solutions were best arrived at after a careful analysis of all the data. Then options could be weighed and a specific course of action selected. But the one thing this case was short on was data. How the hell did he do an analysis when every day brought more questions than answers?

He'd made the decision to check into the warning messages based only upon the reference to his parents' accident. And although he hadn't yet discovered a smoking gun, enough troubling questions had arisen to warrant a continuation.

Without the help of Tori Corbett.

He pressed more firmly on the accelerator, unmindful for the moment of the posted speed limit. It was the best decision. The *only* decision. He couldn't blame her for defending her father's reputation. Hell, maybe she was even right. He could appreciate her loyalty to family, but he couldn't take the chance that it would blind her to discovering the truth. In her desire to clear her father's name, she might overlook something. Or worse, keep something from him that placed Landry in an even worse light.

This time, regardless of the outcome, he was determined that all doubts would be put to rest, for good. He had to ensure the integrity of the investigation. And the only way to do that would be to start over, with another investigative company.

It would mean bringing another P.I. up to speed but that shouldn't waste more than a day or so. He had plenty of contacts in the field. Finding someone to replace Tori wouldn't be a problem. In fact, it would eliminate more than a few. A man wouldn't present the distraction she had, and certainly wouldn't include a connection to Rob Landry that had so suddenly and completely complicated this case.

No, he could replace Tori easily enough.

But even as he had the thought, an unwanted memory flashed through his mind. Of the moments he'd had her in his arms, the surge of heat, the sudden, urgent punch of desire. He wasn't used to a simple kiss stirring up need quite so quickly. Wasn't used to fighting the temptation to ignore a lifetime of control for the promise he'd tasted in her.

He glanced down, vaguely surprised to see the speedometer had crept up past eighty. It was easy enough to speed in a car like this, but he was usually better at choosing the place and time to do so.

Deliberately he slowed to a more moderate pace, and set the cruise control. When this was over, he'd take some time, shed obligation for a while and indulge...various passions. Maybe take his sailboat down to the Gulf and spend a week battling wits with the tide and the wind. To enjoy the theater with an attractive, intelligent woman, and share Sunday brunch in bed with her the next morning. In short, to get back to a life that recently had become devoid of much besides business.

But before that could happen he had duties to perform. He was too accustomed to the mantle of responsibility to feel its burden overmuch. There were details to attend to at work, and his highly honed competitive edge wasn't going to accept anything less than the awarding of this latest contract he'd bid on. Once he'd hired a new investigator, he would have to rethink his other obligations, delegate where he could and begin planning for the next project.

The art of delegation had been one he'd learned under duress, but it was a necessary skill in his field. He was still reluctant to put the investigation of his parents' accident solely in the hands of another, however. What would have happened if Tori had been the one to go to Sanderson's alone? Would he have ever heard about the tracking device being found in the car?

Jaw tightening, he decided that there was no way to be certain. But surely with a different operative on the case, one with no personal stake in it one way or another...

A sudden thought hit him then, wiped his mind clean. There was no denying that Tori's stake was intensely personal. Intensely emotional. So he couldn't bring himself to believe that she wouldn't do exactly as she'd vowed, and continue investigating on her own.

His blood abruptly iced. She'd been maddeningly correct when she'd asserted he couldn't stop her.

The only difference is, now I don't have to keep you posted about my findings.

She was right, damn her. The realization hammered at him, taunting and persistent. There was really very little he could do to prevent her from poking about wherever she chose. He was neatly, irrevocably, trapped. The fact that he was constrained by his own decisions didn't make the matter easier to swallow. Firing Tori hadn't solved his problem, it had compounded it. Because with no way to keep her from continuing on her own, all he'd managed to do was to ensure he had no access to whatever she discovered.

He cursed, long and fluently, then set his mind to doing what he did best; figuring the angles, planning strategy. Hiring another investigator would guarantee the case was still being looked into, but it wouldn't gain him access to the progress she was making. Her connection to Rob Landry complicated this case all too hell.

And it also represented the closest link he'd find to the dead man himself. With a feeling of resignation mingled with anticipation, he reached for his cell phone.

James's intercom buzzed as he was sorting through the piles of mail Celia had efficiently bundled on his desk. "Mr. Jones to see you, sir."

His mouth quirked. There was very little his secretary didn't handle with equanimity, but it was obvious from the slight inflection in her voice that she still didn't know what to make of Ana's new husband. Big, tough and battle-scarred, the man's past was shrouded in mystery.

What was known was that he'd been running a charter boat business in the tropics when Analiese had hired him for a secret caper that still had the power to make James's blood run cold. He'd managed to keep Ana safe while they dodged a corrupt country's military, and for that, James was willing to looking beyond the man's shadowy past and accept him as his brother-in-law.

It was an undeniable bonus that the man possessed skills gained in that unspoken past that came in handy at Tremaine Technologies, and that his wife had convinced him to sell his boat and utilize them.

"Send him in." Going to work on the pile of mail laid neatly on his desk, he reached for an envelope opener as his office door opened.

Jones entered the room, eyed the blade in his hand. "Going armed now?"

James held it up. "After making Ana work all night, I thought I might need a weapon when I saw you again."

Grunting, the other man dropped into a chair before his desk. "No one makes my wife do anything she doesn't want to, so I figure she couldn't tear herself away from the project. But from now on, I told her she was to call me for a ride. I don't like her on the roads after she's been up all night. She nearly got sideswiped by a truck on her way home this afternoon."

Everything inside James abruptly froze. "Did she get a look at the driver?"

His brother-in-law rubbed his jaw. "Hell, I doubt it. She probably wasn't at her best, running on no sleep. She just didn't see the guy coming until he was right on top of her. She was pretty shaken up when she called. Matter of fact, I was going to head home as soon as I talked to you."

It probably had nothing to do with the threats. James

told himself that, and almost believed it. "Did she think it might be deliberate?"

Jones stared at him, his face going grim. "Any reason to believe it might have been?"

James set the envelope in his hand down on his desk. "Probably not, but I want everyone around here to be extra careful. There have been…threats. Nothing specific," he added, not quite honestly, when he saw the man's expression. "They're aimed at me, but I don't want to take any chances. Can you make sure she travels to and from work with you for a while?"

"Yeah, but she's gonna kick unless I tell her the truth."

Considering that, James nodded. "With everything we've got going on right now, we make a bigger target than usual. You can tell her there have been some anonymous messages. We're just being careful."

Jones's scrutiny was implacable. "The threats are directed at you?"

"It's not the first time." The words were no more than the truth. The only difference this time was the reference to his parents. And he definitely wasn't ready to make that known to his family. "Because Ana works here, she should be extra cautious. You, too."

"I'll tighten the security on the grounds," Jones said. "And you better start taking precautions, too. Use different cars each day. Take different routes."

"I know the drill." He'd walked this path before, in times where the threats were more certain, the intent more deadly. Compared to those situations, these messages were almost too nebulous to take seriously.

Except for the note about his parents. And now that it seemed as though there just might be something to the assertion in that note, perhaps he was going to have to treat all the messages with a bit more credulity.

"Wouldn't hurt to take the limo around for a while," Jones suggested laconically. "With the armored doors and reinforced glass, it's a bit safer. I'll make sure it's inspected each day."

James grimaced, ripped open another envelope. With only a glance at its contents, he placed it in a pile for Celia to deal with. One of the things he hadn't yet learned to delegate was letting someone else have first look at the mail. It seemed easier for him to do it, and then to pass the pieces on to whichever employee necessary.

Belatedly he realized Jones was waiting for a reply. "Let's wait a while longer on that." He preferred driving himself, and would continue to do so for as long as possible. "All our cars are protected by Safe-T, which reduces some of the risks." The Safe-T system, their own creation, sounded an alarm if anyone touched the vehicle.

"Okay." His brother-in-law stood and shot him a rare grin. "But once Ana finds out what's going on, you might have to change your mind about that. And a lot of other things." He sounded as though the prospect of his wife taking on her oldest brother gave him a great deal of pleasure. James didn't doubt his assertion. Though she was the youngest by several years, there wasn't a one of the Tremaine males who didn't tread warily to stay off Analiese's radar. She was as fiercely protective of them as they had always been of her. He refused to consider her frequent assertion that it was no more than they deserved.

He sliced into another piece of mail, slipped the letter out and perused it. "You could do me a favor and try and keep your wife in check.'' The suggestion sounded too much like a plea, even to his own ears. ''Try to deflect her attention away from this news if you can.'' The letter was placed in a pile to be routed to Marcus later.

''Sorry, pal.'' Jones sounded anything but. ''But I'd sooner get between a mama bear and her cub. No matter how I play it, when she hears about these threats, you're going to have to handle her.'' He walked through the door. '''Fraid you're on your own when it comes to dealing with the fallout.''

He was entirely too old to experience this feeling of dismay at the possibility, James thought, sorting rapidly through the rest of the mail. But the response he was about to make went unuttered as his hand froze in the act of reaching for the next piece in the pile.

A plain white envelope labeled with his name, with no return address.

She should have told him to go to hell, Tori fumed, as she followed the guard silently up to James Tremaine's offices. The urge to do just that when he'd called had been overpowering. But he had a habit of overriding everything he didn't want to hear. It would be so much more satisfying to do it in person, she consoled herself. To listen to his ''proposition'' and then tell him, in succinct terms, just where he could stick it.

The elegance of the building's interior was lost on her this time. She was too busy thinking of all the ways she'd like to see Tremaine suffer. Like staking him out on a slug-infested anthill. Or, likely more painful for him, to take a well-honed knife to his closet of European suits. Preferably while he was wearing one of them.

''Ms. Corbett, sir.''

Ignoring the guard, Tori walked into James's office carrying the sheaf of papers she'd brought with her. As she swung the door closed behind her, she fixed the man behind the desk with a disparaging glare.

"Tori. Thank you for coming. I wasn't certain that you would."

If the warm smile and civil tone were meant to soften her, they failed miserably. "Really?" Her voice was mocking. "And here I was under the impression that you're quite used to getting exactly what you want, when you want it."

"You'd be surprised. Where you're concerned, I'm not certain of much. Come and look at this."

Her gaze dropped to his desk top and her stomach abruptly hollowed out. Without hesitation she rounded his desk, peered at the note with its typed message:

"Withdraw your bid or be the next in your family to die."

For the moment, her irritation with him was forgotten. "This came today?" At his nod, she said, "What bid do you think it refers to? The new one coming up with the Pentagon?"

"It has to be. It's the only one on the horizon that matters." He stared at the note for a moment. "I'm beginning to believe that was the purpose of these messages all along. To serve as a distraction from the business at hand."

"Except that it's looking as if the sender might have been right, and maybe your parents' accident was deliberate. Does that mean he made a lucky guess, or did he have actual knowledge of what happened twenty years ago?"

"That's exactly what we're going to find out."

She was transfixed by the transformation of his ex-

pression. The cool, savvy businessmen wore a feral mask
that was as chilling as it was startling. It took a moment
for his words to register, but when they did, she straightened and took a step back. "We? Uh-uh, buddy, you
fired me, remember? My only stake in this mess now is
clearing my dad's name."

He swung the chair to face her, his hands clasped
calmly across his chest. "You're here," he pointed out.
"Perhaps only from an urge to take a swing at me, but
you did come. That tells me you're at least willing to
listen to what I have to say."

The sting of his words wasn't lessened by the fact that
they were true. However satisfying it would have been
to hang up on him earlier, his request had tugged at her
curiosity. Because she couldn't refute his words, she
stalked to a chair, sat and slid to a more comfortable
position. "It's your party, ace."

"It occurred to me that our purposes aren't completely
at odds." He'd slipped into CEO mode, all shrewd logic
and reason. "There's no reason we can't continue to
work together, keeping certain details in mind."

"It occurred to you that you couldn't stand not knowing what I was up to," she disputed. "You could afford
to hire an army of P.I.s, if you weren't particularly concerned about discretion, any number of whom are capable of conducting this investigation. But they couldn't
run the assignment and keep track of what I might be
discovering."

There was the slightest smile on his face. She decided
it didn't soften his expression at all. Especially not while
his eyes remained speculative. "Yes. I think perhaps I
was too hasty when I suggested we terminate our partnership."

"And now, knowing that you think the worst of my

father, and of me, I'm supposed to forgive and forget and join up with you again, just because you're afraid I might discover something your new guy doesn't?'' She pretended to consider the thought for a moment before suggesting, ''Bite me.''

''The invitation doesn't lack appeal. But our arrangement could be mutually advantageous. If it is discovered that my parents' deaths was murder, it will become a police matter. From there, it's inevitable that publicity will ensue. I can make sure your father's name is kept out of the resulting media frenzy.'' His regard was direct, the aim of his words on target. ''I can tell you from experience that reputations are fragile things. And the taint of scandal is difficult to remove, especially for a man already dead.''

The insinuation was impossible to miss. She let out a bitter laugh. ''You son of a bitch. Are you threatening me? You'll put your own spin on things, implicating my father, if I don't agree to help you now? You're unbelievable.''

''I didn't exactly say that.''

''You implied it.'' She couldn't remember when she'd hated a man more. And it was strangely ironic that right now she was burning with far more righteous indignation than she had when she'd walked in on her ex playing mattress tag with the empty-headed beauty queen. There was just something about James Tremaine that inspired the most violent reactions.

''What do our reasons matter, really, as long as we both get what we want? You get the answers you're looking for, and I remain apprised of all your discoveries.''

His voice was reasonable. Too reasonable. ''To be sure I don't hide something, you mean.'' She tried to match his cool by shoving emotion aside and considering his offer. "I want your offer in writing."

"You'll have it."

Tori wasn't thrilled with the idea. She'd been free of him, for a few hours at least. But she hadn't been free of doubts—or of a niggling fear that she didn't even want to admit to. She was still convinced that Sanderson had made a mistake. But she wasn't willing to chance her father's reputation being smeared forever.

"All right." Trepidation knotted in her gut.

"Did you bring the information on insurance companies that I asked for?"

Without a word she got up, dropped the papers she'd brought on his desk. He picked them up, flipped through them quickly. "We've got work to do. Follow me."

He rose from his desk and strode to a door on the opposite side of the room. She remembered him using it one other time, the first time she'd come here, trying to land this assignment. With every fiber of her being, she wished she'd never made the decision to do so.

Trailing after him, she stopped short in the doorway, gaped. What she'd assumed was a file storeroom of some sort was, in fact, a smaller office space. It too was lined with computers and peripheral devices whose functions she could only guess at.

"Isn't this a little redundant?"

He'd already placed the papers she'd given him next to a computer and sat down in front of it. "The existence of this space is, of course, covered under the confidentiality clause you signed. Are we agreed?"

"Of course," she said stiffly. But her mind was racing. She knew just enough about technology to have a glimmer of what he was planning, without being completely sure it was even possible.

"This looks like a hacker's paradise. Please tell me that you're not planning on breaking into databases."

"It's not strictly 'breaking in' if they leave a way to infiltrate it." His smile was wicked and, if she wasn't mistaken, laced with anticipation.

He was gazing at the computer screen, fingers already dancing over the keyboard.

"But is it legal?" There was a tickle on the back of her nape, and she looked around uneasily.

"'Legal' is relative."

"Yeah, but jail isn't. What is it exactly you're looking for, anyway?"

This time he did stop, and looked up at her. "I'm going to shift my focus a bit. What if the accident really was murder? What would the motive be?"

On surer ground now, she got up to pace. "Motives for murder are pretty concrete. Greed—for power or money—jealousy. There are variations on those themes, of course, but that's pretty much what it boils down to."

"So we'll tackle those motives one at a time. Greed for power would point to one of my father's competitors. And we'll get to them later." There was a note that had entered his voice that sent a shiver skating down her arms. "But right now we're checking out money."

She stopped midstride, jerked to look at him. "You're checking to see who benefited from your parents' deaths twenty years ago?"

"It's a long shot," he concurred, switching his attention back to the screen. "But anyone can buy an insurance policy on anybody, and since the settlements aren't public information, the only way to be sure is to look for myself."

"What's the sentence for hacking these days?" she asked. In spite of herself, she went behind him and looked over his shoulder. With a shock she realized he was already in to the files of the first insurance company on the list. She checked her watch. It had taken him all of about three minutes. "Lucky for the world that you decided to turn your skills to good instead of evil."

"Companies like these don't even make it challenging." He sounded more than a little disappointed. "I'm going to print out the files and you can start checking through them for the names and dates we're looking for." The printer began to whir as it began the task.

"Aren't there ways for them to tell someone has been in their files? What if they trace this back to you?"

"This computer is totally secure. And all of my equipment is protected by a dandy little firewall I designed myself. Any attempt to probe this computer and there'll be a nasty little virus sent back along the path the hackers use, trashing a lot of expensive equipment at the other end."

Reaching for the first printed sheet, Tori took the highlighter James handed her and set to work. "Well, at least you trust me this much."

"I'll double-check it later."

She gave a bitter little smile. His focus on the screen before him was absolute, his tone offhand. But she knew exactly what he meant. They may be partners again, but nothing had really changed at all. He still didn't trust her.

And she certainly didn't trust him.

Chapter 8

Tori found it difficult to gauge the passage of time, holed up in the windowless room. She rubbed her eyes, which seemed to be on fire after hours of perusing the printouts. She slid a gaze at James, seated next to her. He'd finished his sneak computer attacks on the list of insurance companies an hour earlier. Some had merged, resulting in name changes, which had required some research to discover. Two had gone out of business altogether. But he'd successfully infiltrated the rest, with an ease that bordered on the criminal. She tried not to think about the jail sentence that would be leveled at an accomplice to the crime. Not to mention the threat to her license if his acts were ever discovered.

Integrity, above all else.

Her dad's voice sounded in her head, as clear as if he were standing next to her. And in that moment she knew she'd risk anything, everything, to prove to Tremaine that he hadn't sold him out all those years ago. She wasn't going to let the man beside her destroy her father's memory.

With renewed purpose she returned to the printouts. She'd run through them first and highlighted all the settlement dates that would be in the right time period. Now she was looking for names, but despite her brief respite, the words still insisted on blurring on the pages. She'd actually turned a page and started on the next before belated comprehension registered. Flipping back a sheet, she ran her finger down the list until she came to the one she was seeking.

Frowning, she asked, "Who's Dale Cartwright?"

James looked up. She noticed, with a touch of irritation, that other than heavier-than-normal eyelids, which somehow on him just managed to look sexy, he didn't show any effects of pulling an all-nighter. While she'd spent half the night running a hand through her hair, which was probably even now standing on end, his looked perfectly groomed. Tori was fairly certain her clothes looked as though they'd been worn for a week. He'd shed his suit jacket and rolled up his sleeves, but somehow managed to still look fresh. She decided in that moment that she could hate a man like that.

"He was my father's partner."

"What?" Surprise quickly turned to annoyance. "You never told me your father had a partner when he died."

"He didn't. Although they'd started the business together, my father had bought Dale out three or four years earlier. Why?"

As an answer, she shoved the paper at him, pointed halfway down the list. "His settlement upon your father's death was almost as large as that of your family's."

James studied the paper for a moment. "I remember that my father had one on him, as well. It's not uncommon for business partners to take out policies on each other. That way they can afford to buy out the estate's interest in the company after the death. They had a contract drawn up giving each other that right."

Tori made an attempt to smooth back her hair. "Is he still alive?"

Nodding, James added the man's name to the list he'd kept of those receiving settlements. "When they parted ways, he started a company of his own, on a much smaller scale. He focused on providing security officers to businesses and gated communities, and didn't do much with technology. He's been retired for about five years or more."

When she didn't say anything, merely looked at him, his voice grew testy. "He's my godfather, Tori, and a close family friend. I don't know how we would have coped after the accident if he hadn't been there for us."

Their relationship was an intensely personal one. She understood that. She also understood that it couldn't be allowed to blind them to the possibilities. With as much diplomacy as she could muster, she said, "Let's see what we've got so far."

After a moment he slid the list he'd made over to her. The largest settlement by far had gone to the surviving children. "Who was the trustee of your estate?"

"My grandmother. She moved in with us after the accident and still rules the house with a genteel iron fist." Obvious affection laced his tone. "It couldn't have been easy raising a second family, but with the help of the willow tree in the backyard she managed just fine."

"The willow tree?"

His expression was wicked. "The branches make

pretty slick switches. My brothers were on the wrong end of more than their share of them. Since I was older and much better behaved, I escaped that particular brand of discipline.''

''Humph.'' She wasn't buying it. ''You were probably just sneakier.'' But he was several years older than any of his siblings. And the death of his parents had probably meant instant adulthood for him.

Since his grandmother made an unlikely suspect, she moved on to the next name on the list. ''Marcus Rappaport, Lucy's husband, received a twenty-five-thousand-dollar settlement upon his wife's death.''

''And he donated most of that to the library. There's a plaque bearing her name in the most recent addition.'' He shook his head. ''Well, I knew it was a long shot. I think this lead was a bust.''

''Maybe.'' Although she strove for a noncommittal tone, his expression grew instantly wary.

''What are you suggesting, Tori, that my grandmother had her own son and daughter-in-law bumped off so she could share the joy of raising four young heathens?''

She refused to rise to the bait. ''I'm suggesting that enough money can make people do unforgivable things. And your godfather received a large sum of money after the accident. A policy the size of the one he had on your father would have had a pretty hefty monthly premium. Seems to me after they separated he had quite a few years to relieve himself of that expense. Why didn't he?''

''I don't know.'' And it was apparent from his expression that the uncertainty didn't sit well with him. ''But if he was out to make a bundle of money, it's doubtful he'd wait for three or four years to do so.''

He might be right. Or Cartwright might have wanted

just to deflect any suspicion from him. "Did your father and he part amicably?"

James jerked a shoulder impatiently. "I was fourteen or fifteen at the time. I barely remember hearing my parents talking about it. Dale was in California when the accident happened, though, I do recall that. He was one of the first people I called. He took a red-eye flight back and was at our place by dawn."

She didn't point out that being half a continent away made for a very solid alibi. Or that the alibi didn't mean he hadn't ordered someone else to do the dirty work for him. She straightened up the papers before her, bundling them with paper clips. "It's difficult to have suspicion cast on someone you love," she said simply. From his struck expression, she knew her words had found their target. It was a moment before he spoke again.

"You're right. And we can't allow emotion to cloud our judgment." With deliberate movements he tore the list he'd made off the legal pad and folded it, slipping it into his pocket. "I'll check around. See what I can find out about the details of Dale and my father's separation."

It was a peace offering of sorts, she supposed. He didn't relish the thought of it any better than she enjoyed him entertaining ideas about her father betraying him. His vow didn't make it any easier to swallow his distrust of her dad. But it did make her like him a bit better.

She rubbed her face and yawned hugely. "I'm beginning to believe that you run on batteries, but my energy wore out a couple hours ago. Since it looks like we're done here for now, I'm heading home to get some sleep."

A quick look of concern passed over his face. "You

can't drive back to New Orleans now. You'll fall asleep at the wheel.''

"I'll stop for a tall coffee and put Bruce Springsteen on full blast," she promised. But in truth she was dreading the drive. Right now she wanted nothing more than to fall face-first on the nearest horizontal piece of furniture and sleep for ten hours.

He stood and went to the door, pushed it open and waited for her to precede him into his outer office. She was shocked to see that it was later, or earlier, than she'd assumed. Dawn had come and gone, and the early-morning sun was shining through his office windows.

"I'll take you to my place."

She gave a startled laugh. "To the Tremaine estate? You've got to be kidding."

The expression on his face said he was dead serious. "Be reasonable. You haven't slept in twenty-four hours. You're swaying on your feet as it is."

The idea of sleeping down the hallway from James Tremaine, or even in the same building, made her blood heat and panic claw in her stomach.

"Thanks, anyway, but I don't think so. I'll pull over on the road if I get too tired and nap awhile." She would have promised to push the car back to New Orleans if that's what it would take to shake him from this idea.

"You're staying with me." His tone was final. "I'd never forgive myself if something happened—" His gaze went beyond her, toward the door, and his brows rose. "Don't you knock anymore?"

Tori turned to follow the direction of his gaze and saw a petite blonde standing in the doorway of the office, head cocked to one side, surveying them. Despite her bright head of hair and diminutive stature, Tori identified her instantly. This would be James's younger sister, Analiese.

The woman's bright-blue gaze, so like her brother's, was a dead giveaway.

"Actually, I did knock. You must not have heard me." Despite her brother's unwelcoming tone, or perhaps because of it, she strolled into the room.

"Ana, I'm in the middle of something here. I'll get back to you in a half hour."

Ignoring the command in James's tone, the woman approached Tori, stuck out her hand. "He really has exquisite manners when he cares to use them. I'm Ana Jones, James's sister. And you are?"

"Tori Corbett." Ana's handshake was quick and firm. At five-ten, Tori was never more uncomfortable than when standing next to tiny women like this. She had a brief mental image of herself as a gangling giraffe, neck awkwardly bobbing above a sleek, petite feline. It took a conscious reminder not to slouch, in an effort to shave off a few inches. She was only marginally successful.

"So." Ana's bright smile didn't hide the speculation in her eyes. "You must have gotten here early. It's barely light out."

"Ah..." Tori sent a wild glance at James, but he only folded his arms across his chest, an enigmatic expression on his face. "We...ah...had business and, um, worked late."

Ana's sweeping gaze took in her wrinkled clothes and unkempt hair. "I see." It was apparent that she did see. Too much. And was drawing her own conclusions about it.

Tori had just opened her mouth to set her straight when James reached out, brushing her cheek as he pushed a strand of hair away from her face. The gesture was indulgent, unfamiliar and shockingly intimate. "I'm afraid I mussed your hair. I'll have to make that up to you. Later." The promise in his voice, in his eyes, fogged her brain and heated her blood. Both made it damn hard to think coherently. And maybe that was his intent, because it left her speechless.

He shifted his attention to Ana, casually draping his arm around Tori's shoulders. "Out, brat. I'll talk to you later."

"Oh, you will." Looking pointedly at his arm, she smirked, turned to leave. "You definitely will."

The door was closed behind her before Tori found her voice. "What the hell was that?" With a violent shrug, she dislodged his arm, took a step back. "She's going to think that we're…that we…"

"Yes." His face was coolly amused as he listened to her stutter. "She is. Ana has always displayed too much interest in my personal life. And she has an unfortunate habit of making her opinions on it known. She's also an incurable romantic. With very little effort we can have her thinking we're sleeping together."

Although she'd been mentally heading toward that conclusion herself, hearing him utter it was like taking a fast jab to the solar plexus. Needing a little distance, she turned, put a chair between them before facing him again, her hands clutching its back. "She may be a romantic, but she doesn't look stupid. I'm hardly your type."

He rolled his sleeves down his arms and fastened the cuffs, while watching her calmly. "And what type is that?"

"I don't know." She jerked a shoulder, reached for a sliver of coherence. "Tall, glamorous and empty-headed. The kind to fill her days doing good works and her nights doing you."

His mouth twitched, once, before he firmed it.

"You're tall," he pointed out. "And from what I can tell, you do good work."

She looked at him suspiciously, but if that last was meant to be an innuendo, she couldn't tell from the bland expression on his face. "You know what I mean. There's no way she's going to buy that, and why would you want her to? What's the point?"

"Think about it. I'll admit I hadn't given it a great deal of thought until she barged in here—another unfortunate habit of hers—and found us together. But this can suit our purposes exactly." He went to a low cabinet behind his desk and opened it, revealing a minifridge. Withdrawing two bottles of water, he returned, handed her one. "We're going to need a reason for us to be together all the time. Letting people think we're seeing each other fills that need admirably."

"No," she told him succinctly. "It doesn't. It makes me look like a sap. You can just tell her—tell everybody—that I'm a…consultant, or something. We're consulting on a new project."

James sat on the arm of the chair whose back she was still clutching with white-knuckled desperation. "Since people around here are very aware of all of our projects, that explanation won't wash. My idea, on the other hand, gets you in to every event I attend with no questions asked. The Technology Expo is in three days. Simon Beal will be there, as will every other major and minor player in the business. I assumed you'd want to attend, as well, but maybe I was wrong." He twisted off the cap of his bottle, took a drink.

His words stopped her, but only for a minute. "I can get a fake press pass. That'd give me a better motive for moving around and conversing with the participants, anyway."

He nodded, as if her idea made sense. Taking another long pull from his bottle, he lowered it to inquire, ''And how will you explain that to my sister? Especially after telling her we were in here 'consulting' all night?''

Tori opened her mouth, snapped it shut. The man was never more annoying, she decided, than when he was right. ''I'll think of something.'' Because there was no chance she was going to miss the opportunity to talk to Beal and several of James's other competitors. She wanted to make her own observations; draw her own conclusions. She didn't fool herself into thinking that James had given up suspecting her dad of betraying him. Whoever was behind these notes could probably point them to the truth of the matter, and in doing so, clear her dad's name. That had become almost as important to her as making sure the anonymous sender didn't make good on his threats against James's life.

''The expo's by invitation only,'' James informed her. There was a wicked glint in his eye that warned of a man accustomed to getting his own way. ''Security's pretty tight.''

A sudden suspicion occurred to her. ''Just who puts on the expo anyway?''

''This particular one happens to be sponsored by Tremaine Technologies.''

A sense of resignation filled her, but she wasn't about to give up so easily. ''I'm going home to grab a few hours' sleep and I'll call you later, when I'm thinking more clearly.''

He went to his desk, pressed a button and leaned closer to the intercom to say, ''Tucker, grab someone and come to my office, will you please?'' Straightening, he corrected, ''I'll have someone drive you home since you refuse to stay. Sleep's a good idea. I'll pick you up at six.''

Tori had the sensation of being on a rapidly sinking ship. ''That won't be necessary.'' Surely it was sleep deprivation that wiped her mind completely clean of even one logical argument. ''I'll call you when I've come up with a plan. There's a better way to work this out. You'll see.''

A knock sounded on James's door and he nodded agreeably. ''You're right. I think this is going to work out admirably.'' And then he was guiding her out the door, handing her over to the two polite young men standing outside it and giving orders to have them drive her back to New Orleans. But as she was being led away she was fully aware that he hadn't given up. And she needed to come up with one heck of a strategy to avoid playing along with the deception he had contrived.

Because even pretending to be involved with James Tremaine was too dangerous to her state of mind to consider.

''Funny, with your background in technology, that you should be so averse to using a device as simple as a telephone.''

James grinned at Tori's caustic tone and held up the cartons he'd picked up from a nearby Chinese restaurant. ''I brought a peace offering. Are you going to refuse to let me in?''

For a moment he thought she was going to do just that. Then her gaze lingered on the cartons for long enough to ease his mind. Unlatching the screen door, she swung it open. ''Don't think you're going to get your own way by buying me Chinese, Tremaine. I have higher standards than that.''

"I wouldn't dream of it. Not when I know that all it takes to buy you is Hornets tickets, courtside. But I thought our discussion would be more fruitful on full stomachs." Walking past her, he went to her kitchen and set the cartons on the table. Opening up her cupboards and drawers until he found plates and silverware, he set the table with swift movements. He looked up then, found her standing in the doorway contemplating him. James couldn't say exactly why he found her wary expression so appealing. He pulled out a chair, indicated for her to sit.

When she'd done so, albeit slowly, he began opening cartons, deftly spooning food onto her plate. "Did you get some sleep?"

She grabbed his hand before he could make the mound on her plate any higher. "Yes. And I've been feeding myself for a few years now. I think I can manage."

Circling the table, he sat opposite her and reached for the cartons. "I'm sure that brain of yours has been clicking away all afternoon. Let's hear what you've come up with."

Picking up a fork, she began digging into the food on her plate with obvious appetite. "You'll have to put your male ego on hold for this idea, but give it a chance. I think we can introduce me as your personal bodyguard."

The food he was attempting to swallow abruptly threatened to choke him. It took several moments before he could manage. "I'm assuming you're skilled in that area."

"I am, yes. And you said your company was expanding in that field, so it seems a logical explanation."

He pretended to consider it, and to keep his mind firmly away from the more personal implications of the term. "Of course, Jones is in charge of that department, so my hiring you would be difficult to explain." A hint of amusement entered his voice. "Is it really more appealing to pretend to be employed to lay down your life for mine, rather than to date me?"

Her gaze firmly on her food, she said shortly, "Your idea has *complication* written all over it."

Although true enough, that wasn't precisely the term he'd use. Enticing came to mind. Tempting. And that, he thought, a slight frown forming, was exactly what made this sticky. "We need a pretense that would have you accompanying me to both social and family events. The week after the expo is my brother Sam's engagement party. Family and friends will be in and out of our lake home for the entire weekend." He waited a moment, before adding meaningfully, "Including Dale Cartwright."

Judging from the sudden look of interest on her face, he'd gained her attention. "It doesn't matter whether I call you my personal assistant, a consultant or a bodyguard. Once we're seen together more than once everyone is going to assume the term is a euphemism for lover."

Now it was she who seemed to have trouble with choking. He rose and helpfully thumped her back. Waving him off, she said, her voice strangled, "Are you telling me that people assume you're sleeping with any woman you appear with?"

"I'm afraid so. And before you ask, I can assure you that if my personal life bore any resemblance to the rumors about it, I'd have died of exertion years ago."

"Good to know." There was a hunted expression on her face that almost made him feel sorry for her. Would have, if he hadn't sensed that success was imminent.

''I've always found it's easiest to stay as close to the truth as possible. This way you don't have to manufacture a consulting firm that you supposedly work for, and I don't have to answer uncomfortable questions about why I would need a bodyguard.''

Her gaze was direct, as were her words. ''Allowing people to believe we're dating isn't staying close to the truth. We're not lovers.''

Not yet. The words blazed across his mind, startling him with their clarity. For the first time he wondered at the wisdom of his idea. Tori was right about one thing— a personal relationship between them was out of the question. He had grave doubts about her father's integrity and concerns about her willingness to look at all the facts, especially if they implicated the man. She wasn't a woman he'd have considered getting close to in normal circumstances. If it hadn't been for this case, their paths would never have crossed at all. She was different in just about every way from any other woman he'd ever dated.

It was just too damn bad for him that he'd always been a man to appreciate the unique.

With effort he shook off those thoughts and looked at his watch. They had a full evening ahead of them. But first he had a few things to check out. Rising, he carried his plate to the sink, set it down. ''Grab your purse. We need to leave in a few minutes.''

''Where are we going?''

''However you want to explain it, the fact remains that we're going to be appearing in public together fairly often in the next several days. You'll want to look the part.'' He gave her dark khakis and plain blouse a bland glance.

Her brows lowered. ''Whatever you're thinking, Tremaine, you can forget it. And just to be clear, there is no way you're getting me into a dress.''

He headed for the stairs, figuring he'd find her bedroom—and closet—fairly easily. ''Actually, it's the thought of getting you out of one that I find most intriguing, but I promise to keep your preferences in mind.''

Chapter 9

"You are so dead, Tremaine," Tori muttered between gritted teeth.

The volume of the threat was muffled by the three hair dryers pointed in her direction. And it didn't lack conviction, despite repetition. It was at least the third time in the past hour and a half that she'd threatened him with grave bodily harm.

Sipping at a very decent complimentary Chardonnay, James realized with a faint start of surprise that he was actually enjoying himself. Oh, there had been a few pangs of guilt when he'd noted the look of sheer terror on her face after he'd delivered her to the tender mercies of Claude—no last name needed—and his associates. He'd much preferred the mutinous expression that had followed when he and New Orleans's leading and most temperamental hairstylist had discussed the styles that would suit her best. Or the lethal looks she'd shot at the women busily doing her manicure.

''Relax. Think of it as a disguise.'' Temper, he noted, turned her eyes nearly gold.

''And so much less conspicuous than a rubber nose and multicolored wig.''

Being a cautious man, he carefully hid his grin behind his glass. The dryers shut off, and Claude wielded a styling brush with almost frightening competency. She would recognize the wisdom of the makeover once she got over her fit of pique. When one confronted the enemy, it paid to take him unaware, to don the mask that would be expected, and use it to disguise your real intent.

Certainly that was what his enemy appeared to be doing, and fairly successfully.

The truth of the thought burned, but it couldn't be denied. Whoever was behind the messages could easily be someone who knew him well. Perhaps someone he did business with. Even trusted. Whoever was threatening him was going to be destroyed. That wasn't a vow, it was a fact. It remained to be seen whether he'd be destroying friend or stranger.

''Monsieur?'' Claude whirled Tori's chair toward him and whipped off her cape with a flourish. James surveyed her critically. The new length suited her, he thought, barely topping her shoulders in a sleek style that had required deft styling and straightening. He'd ordered the color to be left alone, and commended himself on the decision now.

''Well done.''

Tori bolted from the chair and strode toward the door. ''Wait.'' He followed her, used his automatic start to turn the car on and the alarm off, then handed her the keys. ''I expect it to still be there when I get out.''

''No problem.'' She bared her teeth. ''You could save

me some trouble by lying down in front of it when you come out, though.''

Wincing, he turned to write Claude a very generous check to compensate him for staying open late. The man looked at it, then beamed, followed him to the door. ''Anytime, Mr. Tremaine. It is my pleasure to serve you. You have but to call.''

Somehow James was certain that ''pleasure'' wasn't what he was going to have in store for him on the way back to Tori's house. He went to rejoin her at the car, and found it running, with the hood up and Tori bent, quite delectably over the engine. ''It misses just a bit when it idles, do you hear that?'' Although she didn't straighten to look at him, he cocked his head obediently and listened, heard nothing but a car engine running. ''Your spark plugs don't look corroded but the points may need cleaning. I can take care of that when we get back to my place if you want.''

''That's…ah…a very generous offer,'' he said bemusedly, watching her thrust her fingers into the unidentifiable tangle of machinery without a care to the ensuing damage to her one-hundred-dollar manicure. ''But it's almost dark. Maybe we could put that off for now.''

She didn't respond right away, which gave him time to appreciate the very feminine backside defined by her position. The casual clothing she favored did a masterful job of hiding the curves of her long, lean build. Crossing his arms, he angled his head for a better view. ''Or, you could take your time, if you prefer. I'm in no hurry.''

Reluctantly Tori backed out from beneath the hood and straightened. Taking the handkerchief he held toward her, she said, ''Well, okay, but you aren't going to want to wait too long on something like this. Regular tune-ups really pay off in the long run.'' Absently she wiped her hands on the handkerchief and handed it back to him, a part of her mourning when he slammed down the hood. There was no telling when she'd get her hands on an engine like this one again.

"I'll keep that in mind." He waited to get in the car before continuing, "But if allowing you to tinker with my car is all it takes to distract you from your earlier death threats, I'll count it as an action well worth it."

"Hmph. Well." She yanked her seat belt on, snapped it securely. "High-handed seems to be your MO, but I can't say I'm surprised, all in all."

He waited several moments for a break to appear in the heavy traffic before pulling away from the curb. "People will be less apt to give your presence with me a second thought if you look the part." He allowed a meaningful pause to pass. "Whatever that part turns out to be."

She lifted a shoulder, slid down to a more comfortable position in the seat. "Your attitude doesn't surprise me."

"And that's supposed to mean…"

Tori lifted a shoulder, as if it didn't matter. She wished, more than was comfortable, that it didn't. "Let's just say, I'm familiar with your type. Appearances mean everything to guys like you. What people think. What they say about you. I was married to a guy a lot like that. I was expected to transform myself into someone that would suit his idea of a fitting wife."

"You've been married."

The way he said it wasn't a question, but still spoke of surprise. Slanting him a glance, she wondered at the cause for it. A person didn't have to be a P.I. to figure that out since she didn't share her dad's last name. "To a guy who thought he could change me into a simpering debutante in twelve easy steps.''

''And you think that's what I'm doing here.''

Pushing aside the edge of disappointment that threatened to well, she said, ''Hey, don't sweat it. You probably can't help being that way. It's the money or something, I don't know. But just for future reference, I've been through one major silk-purse-out-of-a-sow's-ear operation. Like the rest of my marriage, it was a miserable failure. You might want to consider that before you decide just what 'part' I'm to play in the next few days.''

He was quiet for a few minutes, long enough to have her regretting her unusual openness. The last thing she wanted to do was to let James Tremaine into her head.

But when he spoke again, there was genuine puzzlement in his voice. ''Why do people get married if they just want to change their spouse into someone or something else?''

She gave a startled laugh. That was, and had been, the million-dollar question for the twenty-eight excruciating months of her marriage. ''He seemed satisfied while we were in college. We had a lot in common— we were both on scholarships, and we were only children. But when we went back to Dallas, back to his family, his friends, his social group...'' She shrugged. ''The contrast was too much for him. And I couldn't be what he wanted.'' That fact had hurt far more than his infidelity. Because she'd tried. The memory of her attempts to meet with his approval could still make her squirm. She'd lost a healthy dose of her self-respect along the way. Although time had eased the pain of her shattered marriage, it hadn't dimmed the resulting self doubts. It was difficult to trust her judgement again after she'd been so wrong about the man she'd married.

James pressed the gas pedal and turned the corner just as the light was turning yellow. "Your ex sounds like an ass."

She laid her head back, smiled slightly as she watched the scenery pass by. "He is." But thoughts of him didn't wield the same sort of hurtful power they once had. He'd long since ceased to matter.

"I know people like that. They define themselves by a certain style of living, the right clothes, cars and vacation spots, as if the surface appearance is all that matters."

Without lifting her head from the soft leather headrest, she turned to face him. "As far as surface appearance goes, yours is pretty polished," she observed dryly.

His teeth flashed. "Ah, that's the thing about polish. It reflects back what the viewer expects to see. A smart man, or woman, cultivates that trait. Exploits it. It's easier to take people unaware that way."

Her eyes narrowed, half-admiringly. "That's a very devious point of view." Once he'd voiced it, she didn't find his words surprising. She'd long suspected there was far more to the man than his meticulous tailoring. But what, exactly, remained a mystery.

He gave an elegant shrug. "You can't tell me that your profession doesn't call for the same thing. Fostering contacts, gaining their trust, requires donning a certain demeanor befitting the situation, or the people involved."

She couldn't dispute it. But the difference, which she didn't bother pointing out, was that her job didn't require her to live the pretense. Didn't have her believing that was all there was. Not for the first time, she was convinced that there was far, far more to James Tremaine than met the eye.

With a start she realized he was pulling up across the street from her address. The curb directly in front of her house was blocked by a large truck, it's side emblazoned with the name of a well-known boutique. Even window shopping outside the establishment made her billfold ache.

With a long-suffering sigh, she closed her eyes, wished she could transport herself elsewhere. Anywhere else. "I am not…" she enunciated precisely, "…wearing anything sleazy."

James looked wounded. He parked, turned off the car and got out. "Would I dress you in something sleazy?"

"Yes," she said decidedly, pushing open her car door. "If it suited your purposes, you definitely would."

"Luckily for you, my purposes are better suited with you in styles of understated elegance."

Even knowing it was a lost cause didn't stop her from trying. "I've got my own style, Tremaine. I know what suits me."

"Really?" He took her elbow in his hand as they went toward the house. "You couldn't prove it with the flowered thing I found hanging in your closet. It was the only thing in there that might have been a dress, although it more closely resembled a shower curtain." At their approach the truck doors swung open and a burly man carrying a clipboard got out the driver's side.

Stopping in the middle of the street, she gazed at James menacingly. "You were in my closet?"

Exerting subtle pressure, he got her moving again. "I wanted to double-check sizes. You should be a perfect size six."

"I'm a size eight."

"Let's see, shall we?"

"We're looking for Tori Corbett." The driver's voice interrupted them. He took a pencil from behind his ear. "You her?"

Tori looked past him to where workmen were already wheeling racks and carrying boxes up the walk to her modest home. A shudder went down her spine. She detested shopping, and she absolutely loathed trying on clothes. She glanced longingly at her car, nestled snugly in the carport attached to the house. She could make it; she'd attended college on a track scholarship. Her keys were in her purse. In five minutes she could be a couple of miles away.

James stepped to her side then, effectively cutting off that means of escape. The image shattered, leaving her staring at a middle-aged man in a brown uniform, impatience stamped on his pudgy features. Gritting her teeth, she said, "Yes, I'm Tori Corbett."

Two hours later she looked at the shambles of what used to be her living room and wanted to scream. After a great deal of strategic planning and direction from James, the workers had crammed the racks and stacked the boxes so as to leave a narrow traffic pattern through the room. Of course, she couldn't get to the furniture or TV, but efforts to point out those details had been in vain.

The door closed behind the uniformed men, and she collapsed against a stack of boxes, knocking the lid of one loose to reveal very sheer, very exotic lingerie. With a look of horror, she dove to replace it, but not before James hooked his index finger in the strap of a daring lace teddy and drew it out to admire it.

"Nice."

When his glance went from it to her, as if picturing

her wearing it, Tori snatched it from him and crammed it back into the box, jamming the lid in place. "Somehow I don't see how my choices in underwear can affect our investigation one way or another."

"The investigation? No. My imagination, however…" His grin was wicked, seductive, and caused a shiver to shimmy down her spine. She damned both the cause and the reaction. "They took me seriously when I placed an order for a complete wardrobe. Can't say that I can argue with their selections so far."

She really, really wasn't in the mood for exchanging suggestive witty banter with James Tremaine. To be truthful, she'd never had much experience with it, and definitely didn't want to learn now. He'd shed his suit jacket and tie, and rolled up the sleeves of his white-on-white striped shirt. He'd pitched in and helped with the organization, and his hair wasn't as perfectly groomed as usual. There was a lock, directly over one eye, that had tumbled free and gave him a faintly disreputable look. He appeared entirely too human and outrageously sexy. Under normal circumstances she might have found the combination nearly irresistible.

As it was, all she had to do was force her gaze away and note the clutter in her home to feel her resolve stiffen. "There is no possible way for one person to wear all this in a month, much less in the next week or so. It was a waste of money. I could have just picked a couple of outfits up for whatever event we'll be attending. Now I'm just going to have to mess with sending most of this stuff back."

"Actually…"

He let the sentence dangle until she looked at him again. Propping one shoulder against the wall he went on, "Since the purchases are in my name, the returns will have to be, too. They won't accept any returns from you.''

"Of course not.''

Pretending not to notice the sarcasm in her voice, he suggested, "Why don't you wait until tomorrow to try on the rest of this?''

Horror must have shown on her face then, because he hurriedly added, "Or not. What you've tried on so far fits, so the rest probably will. But it can wait until tomorrow to be put away. Just leave the tags on. That way anything you don't use you wouldn't have to keep if you don't want to.''

She didn't point out that just storing this amount of stuff was going to take up every ounce of closet space in the entire house. "Nice try, but I don't think so. I'm going to have to spend hours going through this junk and setting aside the stuff I absolutely can't wear.'' The thought of the time it would require to do just that made her want to weep. So she bared her teeth at him and added, "Don't worry, I'll bill you for the hours.''

"I'd expect nothing less. But from what I've seen so far, there isn't anything inappropriate in the entire collection. Remember, your goal is going to be to blend in. Think of this—'' he gave an elaborate sweep of his arm "—as disguise.''

She went to one of the racks and pulled down a hanger with a very short, very low-cut cocktail dress in flaming-red sequins visible through the clear garment bag. "I'm guessing this will disguise very little, but maybe I'll have to use my imagination.''

His smile was slow and wide and devastating. "Do. I'm certainly going to.''

She shook her head, careful to hide an answering smile. The last thing the man needed was encouragement. "I've discovered a new and alarming part of your personality, Tremaine. Depravity."

His raised eyebrow didn't dispute her observation. "I'm a man. And so will be seventy percent of the attendees at the expo. Any guy who gets a look at you in a dress like that isn't going to be worrying about what you might be snooping into."

Oddly enough his words cheered her. "That's true. Maybe I'll happen on to some information that will clear this whole mess up."

"Maybe." Pushing away from the wall, he began to roll down his shirtsleeves. "In the meantime, have you heard from that friend of yours? Juicy?"

"I'll reach out and nag him tomorrow."

James went to the adjoining kitchen and retrieved the suit jacket and tie he'd hung over the back of one chair. She was too tired to even sneer at the care he'd taken with them. Shrugging into the jacket, he hung the tie around his neck and began moving toward the door. "You can call me after you contact him and let me know when we can see that reconstruction. I'll want to be there."

She followed him through the narrow pathway toward the door, a sudden thought occurring. "When was the last time you got some sleep?" Once she'd gotten home that day she'd hit the bed for a good six hours before stirring again. She was certain that he couldn't claim the same.

"I plan on getting some. I'll stay at the lake tonight."

She trailed him out onto the porch and down the front steps. The night was clear, with a half-moon surrounded by a night sky of diamond-studded velvet. But any thought of enjoyment of the evening was shattered by the sight of her next-door neighbor walking quickly from his garage to his house.

Suspicion surged. "Dammit, Junior, what have you been up to?" James stopped and turned, his gaze going to the man Tori was already closing in on.

Joe Jr., neighborhood lech, affected a surprised look. "Hey, Tor, what's up? You just get home?"

Rapidly closing the distance between them, she said between her teeth, "What were you doing in that garage?"

He hitched up his low-riding jeans with his free hand. "Hey, it's my ma's garage. Guess I have a right to be in there."

"Don't make me kick your ass again, Junior." Reaching out, she grabbed a handful of his ribbed undershirt and yanked him closer. "So help me, if I go in there and find out you've set up your telescope again, you won't be walking upright for a week."

He must have heard the promise in her voice, because he covered himself with one hand. "Calm down, Tor, that was a big misunderstanding, just like I told ya back then. I didn't even know how to work that thing. I didn't aim it at your bedroom window on purpose."

She hadn't bought it back then, and she wasn't buying it now. "Uh-huh. And the window of your garage doesn't give you a perfect view into my living room." A discovery that had had her searching for the thickest curtains she could find.

"Honest, Tor." The fury in her voice must have made him nervous. A whine crept into his tone. "I was out there trying to fix Ma's radio. See?" He waved the tool he held as if for proof. "That's all. But I couldn't fix it. Maybe you'll take a look at it later, huh?"

She gave the tool a pointed look. "Fixing a radio with

a wrench? Either you're dumber than I thought or you think I am.''

"Do you acquire some assistance?''

For a moment she'd forgotten James. But he was beside her now, a lethal undertone to his otherwise innocent words that Junior obviously recognized. He backed up several feet, babbling the whole time.

"Hey, buddy, there's no problem here. Just a little neighborly chat, you know? I gotta go in now, gotta check on my ma. She doesn't like me to leave her alone too long.'' He was backpedaling rapidly, putting as much distance as possible between him and the man at her side, who was fairly radiating menace.

She glanced at James, put a hand on his arm. It was tight with bunched muscles. She had the impression of a big jungle cat, ready to pounce. There was a feral expression in his eyes, like a hunter who had scented prey. "There's nothing going on here that I can't handle. C'mon.'' It was several long seconds before he allowed her to turn him, and fell into step with her as they crossed the yard.

"How long has that been going on?'' His voice was clipped.

Tori thought it wiser to pretend to misunderstand. "Joe Jr.? Oh, he moved in with his mom about a year after I bought the house.'' And had been a royal pain in her side ever since. "He's annoying but harmless.''

From the tone of his voice, he wasn't buying it. "A polite description of a lowlife Peeping Tom. Have you reported him to the police?''

"I took care of it myself, okay?'' He stopped, just looked at her. Finally she blew out a breath. "Look, he's a slimeball, but his mother, Pauline, is the sweetest woman I've ever met. As long as I can keep things strictly between him and me, she won't have to be upset." She had to exert more force to get him to turn, accompany her across the yard. "You, of all people, should appreciate the sentiment."

"I don't like it," he said flatly. "Sure he's a loser, but even guys like him get a little braver with some booze or their drug of choice in their system. How can you be sure..." His gaze returned to the street before them and he stopped dead in his tracks. He threw out an arm to halt her, as well. "Do you recognize that car?"

Puzzled at his abrupt change of subject, she followed his gaze to his vehicle, and the one parked in back of it, close enough for the bumpers to almost touch. "No, why?"

He grabbed her sleeve, spun her around and pushed her toward the house. "It doesn't belong to your neighbor? One of his friends maybe?"

Bewildered, she looked over her shoulder, difficult to do as she was stumbling over the lawn with his hand at the small of her back. "No, I've never..."

The night erupted into an inferno that shook the ground and singed the air around them. Heat enveloped them, brutally intense. Time fragmented, split into short stills. There was the sight of Joe Jr. standing on his porch, his jaw agape. Then the hard ground rushing up to meet her, the oxygen streaming out her lungs when a heavy weight landed on her. She had a single last image of the street, James's car and the one behind it engulfed in flames. Then something flew through the air, and her head exploded in agony. After that, there was nothing at all.

"Someone sure went to a hell of a lot of trouble to plan a bonfire in your honor." Detective Cade Tremaine looked up from his notebook, his green gaze sweeping between James and Tori. "If you have any ideas who, you'd better be letting me in on it, and quick."

Broodingly, James looked toward the scene half a block down the street, where the bomb squad had cordoned off the entire area. The fire was under control now, showing the skeletal remains of the two cars. "If I was the target, and that's a big if, there are any number of people who might have reason to want me out of the way."

"Yeah," Cade deadpanned, "but do any specific names spring to mind? I mean, outside of family?" When Tori's attention jerked to him, his mouth quirked up and he shrugged. "Hey, I'm joking. But you haven't pissed Ana off lately, have you?"

That remark pulled a smile from James. "No more than usual." He blew out a breath. "But she's going to be hard to contain once she hears about this. Unless…"

Cade was already shaking his head. "Not a chance, buddy. I'm not going to try to keep this from her. And I couldn't if I wanted to. The press is all over this already."

As if on cue, a white news helicopter flew low across the scene, a cameraman leaning out the door, filming the scene. That sight, and the chaos on the street, had James choosing his words carefully. "I'd appreciate you being as vague on the details as possible. I don't need this kind of publicity right now."

He felt the shudders working through Tori next to him, and without a thought he shrugged out of his jacket to hang it over her shoulders. That was the first time he noticed that it was completely missing one sleeve. Anchoring it in place with his arm around her waist, he ignored his brother's interested stare and went on. "I'm delivering on a big contract tomorrow. I hope to be awarded the bid on another very soon. This sort of publicity I can do without.''

Jotting down a few notes, Cade inquired, ''Is that what tonight was about? These projects of yours?''

''Hard to say. We don't even know that I was the target.'' Tori stirred beside him, but James tightened his arm warningly. ''If I were you I'd check out the guy that lives right there.'' He gestured with his free hand at Joe Jr.'s house. ''He's a dirt ball, and there's no telling what he's mixed up in.''

''I told you before, he's harmless. Joe's got nothing to do with this.'' Tori finally roused from her shell-shocked state and entered the conversation. ''Can I get into my house now? I want to get an idea of the damage.''

Cade half turned, and motioned to a uniformed cop standing nearby. ''The homeowner would like to get into that house. Has it been cleared?''

The cop approached them and nodded. ''The windows are blown in on the street side, but no structural damage has been observed. I can take her in.''

James frowned. ''Why don't you wait a few minutes. I'll go with you.''

''Hey, I handled your idea of a fun evening, Tremaine.'' Tori's attempt at a smile wobbled at the edges, but she seemed steady enough. ''I can handle this.'' She moved away, fell into step with the uniform and headed to her house.

''So…'' Cade let the word dangle. ''She's the reason you were in the neighborhood, huh?''

Bringing his attention back to his brother, James said shortly, ''She's an…associate of mine.''

''Yeah, got that.'' Cade rocked back on his heels.

Damned if it didn't look like he was enjoying himself. "And you were in her house…associating…for how long before the bomb went off?"

"We'd only been home about two hours," he started, and then another thought had his blood running cold. Using abandoned cars full of explosives was typically a terrorist stunt, designed to take out an entire block of buildings and create the greatest damage possible. But someone had gone to a great deal of trouble to limit the destruction. The only person meant to die in the blast had most likely been him.

"Well, if it was meant for you, the guy took some risk. Most would have hooked it to the ignition or accelerator to detonate when the vehicle was turned on, or pressure applied to the gas pedal. It's chancier to hang around the vicinity waiting for the chance to blow it."

Looking back at Cade, James said, "All the vehicles used by me or by the company are protected by Safe-T, an antiterrorist alarm system. If anyone had gotten close enough to try, to wire the engine or the body of the car, I would have been alerted."

Cade tapped his pen against his pad. "So someone either made an incredibly lucky choice, or they knew about that protection." His somber stare met James's. "Who's that narrow it down to?"

"Hell, anyone who'd done their homework." He jammed his hand into his hair, frustration riding him. Any of his rivals would know, since his system, minus some perfections for his own private use, was on the market. Anyone who worked for him would know, as well.

After that thought, a brief mental image flashed across his mind. His curse had his brother's brows raising.

"What?"

"Tori had the hood up and her hands in the engine less than three hours ago." The blood in his veins seemed to ice up. If he'd brought a car that hadn't been protected and someone had tampered with it, it might have blown the moment she'd unlatched the hood.

The ice in his blood dissipated, melted by the fury that began to simmer. He'd brought the danger to her doorstep, literally. Through their association, she was at risk, too. And he wasn't quite sure how he was going to cope with that.

In succinct sentences he told Cade as much as he'd shared with Jones about the threats, purposefully staying as vague as he could. "It wouldn't hurt for you to stay on guard," he concluded. "And alert Sam, too. I don't know if the purpose is to distract me or get rid of me, but going after anyone in my family would be just as sure a distraction as something like this." They exchanged a sober look. "Be careful."

Cade's notebook shut with a snap. "Sounds like good advice for you to be taking yourself. Why the hell didn't you come to me when those notes started arriving? Do you still have them?"

Carefully he skirted the last question. "It's not the first time something like this has happened. It won't be the last. I had the notes analyzed by a lab I use, and no fingerprints were found, except for the outside of the envelopes. I didn't think you could guarantee they wouldn't leak to the press, and as I've said, that could really scuttle things for the company right now."

Cade's response to that was unprintable. "You're unbelievable, you know that? You're actually more worried about *business* than being straight with your family?"

James drew back, watched his brother more warily.

The man was obviously furious. There was a nerve twitching in his jaw that always indicated temper kept tightly leashed. "I didn't want to worry you all unnecessarily. This kind of thing…" He hesitated, finally deciding that half a truth was better than none at all. "There's danger in all of our jobs. Sam's—despite the fact we're all supposed to believe he's an international attorney—and yours. You're the one who had three bullets dug out of his chest just months ago, remember? I'm already taking precautions. I'm asking that you do, too."

Jaw still tight, Cade looked away, slapping his closed notebook in a rapid tattoo against his leg. "You have a point. But there's another you're refusing to consider here. When someone targets one Tremaine, he takes on all of us. And if you think the rest of the family is going to sit back and let you handle this alone…well, you're even denser than I thought."

The brotherly insult was mild, given some he'd endured in the past, and when Cade brushed by him, he let him go. The memory of his own stunned grief when Cade was in the operating room for hours, his life hanging in the balance, was still fresh. Recalling it, remembering the helpless rage that had filled him at the time, gave him some insight into his brother's feelings now.

Scrubbing his face with his hands, he removed them to see Tori approaching him again. He watched carefully, but there was nothing showing in her expression but resignation.

"Well, the damage doesn't look too bad, although I'm told everyone on this block will have to have structural assessments done. But glass is everywhere. I'll probably have to replace the furniture and the carpet." Irony was rife in her voice. "The clothes you bought seem to be fine. Everything was still boxed or covered."

"I'll take care of your house." He raised a hand to stem the protest he sensed on her lips. "There's little doubt that if I hadn't been here, you'd be sleeping peacefully right now. The police will be in the area for hours yet. I'll have workmen here first thing in the morning." He waited a moment before adding nonchalantly, "We'll have to get those deliveries out of there so they can work, though. I'll have the collection sent to our place on the lake. That's where I'm taking you."

The medics on the scene had pronounced them both fine, but for a few bruises and lacerations. He wasn't so sure. He was still worried that she might have a possible concussion. She'd been out a couple of minutes when a piece of debris had hit her. There was a good-size lump on her head, a dark smudge across one cheek and a rapidly spreading bruise along her jaw. Yet she showed no signs of crumpling. What she did show signs of was temper. Ridiculous, really, to be reassured by the sight.

"What makes you think I'm going to let you call the shots? And I'm not staying with you. That's out of the question."

Pulling his cell phone out of his pocket, he called for a cab. There was no way she'd be able to get her car out and maneuver around the emergency vehicles blocking the street. Not for a few more hours at least. As an aside he said, "I suppose you could always bunk in with Joe Jr. over there." She followed the direction of his glance, where Joe and his mother stood on their porch, watching the goings-on avidly. This was more excitement than their quiet neighborhood had seen in decades.

"I could go to a motel."

"You could." Having ordered the taxi, he flipped the cell phone shut and slipped it back in his pocket. "You're not going to."

Hands still clutching his jacket around her shoulders, she narrowed her gaze at him. "You know, you really irritate me, Tremaine."

The words, the tone in which they were delivered, lightened something inside him. Wrapping an arm around her, he rested his chin on her hair, for just a moment. "And you fascinate me, Corbett. I guess we're both going to have to learn to deal with it."

Dawn was still hours away when a cell number was dialed for the third time that night. This time it was answered by a familiar voice, sounding groggy. "H'lo?"

"You failed tonight. Miserably."

There was silence for a few moments, as if the man on the other end of the line was mounting his argument. "Look, it was a clean attempt. How was I to know he'd spot the car and get wise before he got close enough to—"

"It's your job to *know*. I pay you to *know*. You failed, and now Tremaine will be on his guard. The police have been alerted. It will be more difficult next time." Thoughts of there having to be a next time made fury surge. Incompetence was intolerable. And time was growing short. "Had you done your job correctly, he would have been eliminated standing within a half block of that car."

"Hey, that was your idea. You said you wanted as little collateral damage as possible. I put enough C-4 in the vehicle to blow Tremaine to hell and back if he'd gotten closer. You want me to take out an entire city block, I can do that."

Calm was never more difficult to summon. Deep cleansing breaths were hauled into lungs, attempting to push aside the haze of fury. "You can't try the same thing again, you idiot. I'll have to think of something else. Did they get near enough to see you tonight?''

''Hell, I was long gone before the cops arrived. And there's no way they can trace the vehicle or the explosives back to me. Relax. You've got nothing to worry about.''

Nothing. If only he knew. ''I'll be in touch.'' The caller abruptly ended the conversation, set the cell phone down on the desk with more care than the act called for. Shimmering waves of rage mixed with panic. It had been a mistake to trust another party to do the job correctly. Tremaine's elimination was going to require a personal touch, and, thanks to the bungling idiot that had been hired, it had just grown more complicated.

Things had come together so much more neatly twenty years ago. Using outsiders was risky.

But the calendar on the desk was a taunting reminder that time was growing precious. Another plan would have to be devised. But first the man who'd made a mess of things would have to be taken care of.

Leaving loose ends was sloppy work.

Chapter 10

Despite the comfort of the surroundings, there was always something disorienting about waking up in a strange place. Tori rolled over in the huge four-poster bed, opened her eyes and blinked several times. Then she sat bolt upright and reassessed the space around her, trying to summon memory into her exhausted brain.

The lake house. Tremaine's. The explosion.

She fell back on the bed, burying her face in a pillow. Before James Tremaine had walked into her office, she'd been spared this type of excitement. Oh sure, there was the occasional knife fight. And she'd once chased down a would-be mugger and subdued him until the police arrived, but most of her work was pretty mundane.

There was nothing mundane about her current client or the feelings he elicited in her.

Discomfited by the thought, she flopped over in bed, opened her eyes again. She would have been as concerned about any client of hers who had barely avoided getting blown up in front of her place, she assured herself. Would have felt the same fears for anyone she knew who was being stalked by someone who might very well have killed before. Who was intent on killing again.

The reassurances were rational and should have soothed her. Unfortunately, Tori wasn't one to lie to herself about anything. And she couldn't pretend, even to herself, that James Tremaine was just a client. Couldn't pretend that she didn't have deeper feelings that went far beyond the client-P.I. relationship.

Recognition of that fact was anything but calming. Throwing back the covers, she noted that the clothes she'd shed the night before were lying in a heap on the floor beside the bed. She snagged her shirt and surveyed it resignedly. There were streaks of dirt down the front, and one sleeve was hanging by threads. Her pants weren't in much better shape, sporting two ripped knees and covered with grime. It was difficult to say how much of the damage had been sustained when James had knocked her to the ground and covered her body with his and how much had come from the debris that had showered upon them.

That memory sparked another, and her fingers went to her head, probing tenderly. There was a sizable lump there, but she thought her hair should cover it well enough. The biggest problem right now was getting cleaned up and out of Tremaine's house wearing little but the rags that her clothes had become.

Reaching for her purse, she dug out her phone and rang his cell number. From the look of the sun pouring in the windows, it was nearly noon. She knew him well enough to be certain that he wasn't still in the house, enjoying some well-deserved sleep.

He answered on the second ring. "Tremaine."

"Where are you?"

"Good morning." His voice warmed several degrees, and so did her blood. "Did you just wake up? How are you feeling?"

"Taking inventory. I think I'll live and if goose eggs and rags are in style, I'll be the height of fashion."

"If I remember correctly, the clothes need to be destroyed. Your new ones should have been delivered by now. Use the house phone to check with the maid."

House phone. Maid. She definitely wasn't in Kansas anymore. "I'll do that. You never told me where you are."

"Approaching D.C. in the corporate jet. I decided to deliver the project personally." A touch of dark humor laced his tone. "Call me paranoid, but I didn't want to leave anything to chance."

"You had the jet thoroughly checked out?" She wasn't able to keep the worry from her voice. She didn't even try.

"Don't worry, it's secure. And I'm not alone, Jones is accompanying me. We'll be back by the middle of the afternoon. You may as well take it easy. There's a hot tub in your bathroom. Use it. You must be sore."

"Thanks." She tried and failed to remember the last time she'd sat naked in bed and talked to a man on the phone. Come to that, she tried to remember the last time she'd been naked with a man, period. And on the trail of that thought came a mental image of James in bed with her, his body as bare as her own, his skin against hers, limbs tangled, mouths melded...

The uncustomary thought had her throat closing. Where had *that* come from? She didn't engage in fantasies about men she barely knew. Well, okay, Russell Crowe, maybe, but that didn't count. She didn't actually *know* him, so he was safe enough to star in the occasional X-rated daydream. Far, far safer than the man on the other end of the line, who would be all too available, all too tempting and maybe, just maybe, willing, as well. Her intuition about such things could be rusty, and God knows, it had never been too keenly edged.

"...today?"

Belatedly she realized James was talking again. "What?"

"Do you have anything planned that can't wait until I get back today?"

"I'm going home." She hadn't realized just how badly she needed to until the words left her mouth. "I want to get a look at the house in the daylight, and see about repairing the windows and stuff."

"Let me know if there's anything you need." There was a burst of static, before she heard him say, "...approaching Dulles now. I'll call you later."

"Later," she echoed, but the line was already dead. It wasn't until she'd lowered the phone to stare blindly at it that she managed to shake herself out of her funk and get out of bed. It definitely had to be related to the blow on the head she'd received last night, she excused herself. Because she'd never mooned over a man in her life. And she wasn't about to start with one as totally unsuitable as James Tremaine.

Resolution filling her, she reached for the house phone, pressed the red button. "This is Tori Corbett, in—" she had no idea what room she was in "—the guest room? James ordered some deliveries..."

"Oh, yes, Ms. Corbett, they've arrived. Would you like them delivered to your room?"

No, definitely not. She didn't think she could face that again. "Would you mind going through them and bringing me the most casual outfit you can find?'' It shouldn't be so hard talking to a maid, she decided, if she just pretended she was speaking to a clerk in a clothing store.

Come to think of it, that was one of the reasons she never went shopping. ''Jeans, if you can find a pair.''

''Yes, Ms. Corbett.''

Hanging up the phone, she headed to the bathroom, becoming aware of a chorus of aches and pains from various parts of her body. She gritted her teeth and started thinking seriously of that hot tub James had mentioned. She may as well take advantage of it, before she called a cab and headed home. She had no intention of coming back here tonight, regardless of what James had to say about it.

Money worked magic, she mused a couple hours later, standing in front of her home. Workmen streamed in and out of the place. The windows had all been replaced, and the carpet ripped out. She wondered wryly whether James had intended to allow her to pick out new carpeting and furniture or if that would have been decided for her, too.

But when she saw one man wearing a home security logo on his uniform passing her to go back to his truck, she snagged him and asked what he was doing there.

''Orders from Mr. Tremaine, ma'am.'' The worker, a tousled blonde just shy of thirty, gave her figure an approving glance before going on. ''Putting in a state-of-the-art alarm system, and installing new dead bolts. The work will be finished by the end of the day, as promised.''

Clenching her jaw tightly, she nodded curtly and marched away. High-handed didn't even begin to describe James Tremaine. He'd never know just how lucky he was to be a thousand miles away right now.

There was nothing she could do here, besides trip over the men he'd hired, so she went next door and knocked on Pauline's door. Joe Jr. opened the door, peeked out and then made as if to shut it again.

"Wait a minute." Tori pressed the heel of her palm against the door. "Where's your mom?"

"Ma ain't here. I put her on a bus to stay with her sister in Shreveport until I get things fixed up."

Given Junior's work ethic, Tori thought, the work could take years. "Have you called the insurance company?" Worry filled her at the financial hardship this might mean for the elderly woman. "Are they sending out an adjuster?"

"I dunno. That guy is taking care of it. At least that's what he said." Her expression must have been as blank as she felt because he added sullenly, "That guy you were with last night? Came by here this morning and said how he'd be sending workers over here once they're done with your place. But then he started making threats and stuff. That is one mean dude." A familiar whine entered his voice. "I don't know what you've been telling him, but he's got some wrong ideas about me. Dead wrong. He might dress all uptown but he's got a vicious streak a mile wide." The door closed a bit more. "And I'm not supposed to be within ten yards of you, he said, or else he's coming back. I don't need that kind of trouble."

James had threatened Joe Jr.? Over her? It was possible to feel an undeniable warmth at his concern, she decided, while still wanting to throttle him.

"Wait." It may have been the authoritative tone to her voice, but Joe stopped in the act of closing the door the rest of the way. ''I wanted to ask you some questions about last night.''

''I don't know nothing.'' His voice was sulky, but he pulled the door open a bit more. ''I told that to the cops. But if you asked me, that guy that was with you pissed someone off, big-time. And I can see how that would happen, because like I was saying, he's...''

''...a mean dude. I remember.'' She stared at the younger man, long enough to have him shifting from one bare foot to the other. ''What were you doing in the garage last night, Joe?'' she asked slowly, a thought beginning to form in her mind.

''Nothing.'' The word was vehement. ''It's just like I told you last night, I was working on the car and I...''

''You told me last night you were fixing your mom's radio.'' She spun on her heel, jogged down the steps and toward the garage.

''No, wait!'' Joe Jr. raced after her, stumbling over the hems of his low-riding jeans and nearly falling on his face. ''The thing is, what you won't understand is...''

She pushed open the door of the garage, unsurprised to see the telescope on its tripod once again. She looked from it to the slimeball standing in the doorway. ''I'm really, really going to hurt you this time, Joe.''

''Don't tell that friend of yours, he'll kill me,'' he babbled. ''C'mon, I'm beggin' ya. It's not like I could see anything, anyway. You got curtains on all the windows. Thick ones, too.''

It took effort not to kick him in the teeth. ''Why should I do you any favors?''

''Who'd take care of my ma if I wasn't around? Huh? You gotta think of that.''

Pauline had seemed to do very well for herself until

her bum of a son had shown up, but Tori left the thought unuttered. "How long were you at the telescope?"

"I wasn't, I swear!" He hitched up the back of his pants and tried a sickly smile. "Really I was just trying to fix it and…"

"How long, Joe?"

"Oh, hmm, well just since you got home with the guy. And that truck came and I was just wondering what they were carrying in."

"And you didn't leave the garage until we left the house so you must have seen the guy who left the car there." Having painted him neatly in a corner, she pounced. "What did you see, Joe? Who did you see?"

He was swinging his head wildly from side to side. "I didn't see nothing, I swear. That big-ass truck was in the way about the whole time and I never saw the car until the truck pulled away."

"And its driver?" she pressed. She was on to something and she knew it. She could tell by the way he began to sweat.

"I don't know. I never saw anyone get out of the car."

"But you saw someone, didn't you, Joe? Something kept you in here until we left the house, and since you couldn't see in my windows you had to be looking at something."

The fight seemed to stream out of him them, and his shoulders slumped. At the moment he looked rather pathetic. "I was just checking out the sports car, the one that belonged to the dude, you know? And I saw a guy, but I don't know who he was. He was just walking away, real fast like, when the truck pulled away."

"Describe him." Excitement began to pulse inside

her. Maybe, just maybe, this would be the break they were looking for.

"A little guy. Shorter than me, about one-fifty. Bald, but not old. Had on jeans and a dark shirt." He shrugged. "That's all I noticed. I was looking at the car, you know?"

"And did you tell the detective this?" She already knew the answer to that question, even before seeing the hunted look on Joe Jr.'s face.

"I can't do that. I'd have to explain how I seen him, you know? And then they'd start getting bad ideas about me, like that friend of yours."

"You're going to call the NOPD," she ordered, "and ask for Detective Cade Tremaine. Then you're going to tell him everything you just told me. Yes," she retorted, when he began to shake his head again, "you are. I don't care how you explain it. Tell him you're a junior astronomer, if you want to. But you are going to talk to the detective right away. And if you don't, the dude," she mimicked him, "is going to come back. And he's not going to be happy with you."

He wasn't eager, but he obviously feared James more than the police. After gaining his agreement to make the call and to look at some photos she promised to drop off later, she got into her car and drove to the office. It wouldn't hurt to have him examine any pictures she could find of Cartwright and the CEOs of the other companies competing with Tremaine Technologies for this next contract. And she'd call Cade herself to suggest he have Junior take a look at the mug shots they had on file. Maybe something would pop that way.

And after she did all that, she had another stop to make. The sun was shining brightly, so she found her sunglasses and slid them on. This seemed to be her day for sleazeballs. Because she had every intention of paying another visit to Kiki Corday.

If Joe Jr. looked like an oily, wannabe Lothario, Kiki Corday reminded her of a man who'd long since traded away pride, and hadn't missed the quality overmuch. His gut hung over his waistband, and the button-down shirt he was wearing was grease-stained. The few strands of hair that he still had were combed over his pink scalp and sprinkled heavily with dandruff. There was white powder all over his hands and dribbled down his chin. She'd obviously interrupted his brunch of Irish coffee and beignets.

The house he lived in seemed to have given up hope years ago. Even in this questionable neighborhood, his seemed to slump a bit more on its foundation. The siding seemed older. The roof sagged. She'd heard rumors that the man actually had a heck of a stash put aside. Tori thought it might be true. He sure didn't spend anything on himself or his surroundings. The only top-of-the-line products he was interested in were cameras and photographic equipment.

Kiki pushed open the door minus a screen and greeted her with a grunt. "Yeah? You need more pictures? 'Cuz I got to thinking, I shoulda charged ya more. Those were high quality shots, every one of them."

"Actually, I came to see if you were interested in a job." She hadn't run this by James, but after the decisions he'd been making for her recently, she dared him to disagree with this one. "Have you heard about the Technology Expo starting tomorrow?"

He licked the powdered sugar from his fingers. "Yeah, so? You need a press pass to get in. I already checked." His expression went sly. "Not that I can't get my hands on one, you understand, but there's not likely to be anything of interest going on there, anyway.''

Meaning, he didn't think he'd be able to sell any of the photos to a news rag. ''Maybe it'd be more interesting to you if I can arrange for your admission, and pay you to take pictures.''

That piqued his interest. He held open the door. ''C'mon in.'' She did, gingerly. She'd been inside before, and each time the place seemed to get dingier. She could see the clutter in his kitchen from here. He'd been eating on a tray in front of the TV, she saw now. Filing cabinets lined one wall. She already knew there were more in the spare bedroom that served as his office. He never threw away a picture. That room would also be the only part of his house that he kept in halfway respectable shape.

''Here are some shots of people who'll be there, that I'm especially interested in.'' She handed him a manila envelope with duplicates of the pictures she'd shown to Joe Jr., who hadn't seemed to recognize any of them. ''I want you to mingle, seem to take pictures of everything, but the actions of these men are of particular interest. I want a shot of whoever they talk to.'' She couldn't be certain if Cartwright would be at the expo, but she'd included his photo just to be safe.

He grunted again, shook the pictures out and studied them. ''How much?''

She quoted a price that had his eyes going beadier than normal. She knew it was too much when he smiled, revealing stained crooked teeth. ''Sweetheart, for cash like that, I'd take pictures of myself getting up close and personal with a donkey.''

Tori didn't have to feign the shudder that ran down her spine. ''Consider this an advance against that, as

well. I'll arrange to have a pass delivered for you, and
get you cleared at the door.'' She edged toward the exit,
anxious to be gone. After dealing with Joe Jr. and Kiki
in the same day, she felt the need for another shower.

Once safely on the porch, however, another thought
occurred. Speaking through the windowless door, she
said, ''Oh, and Kiki? Search your closet for something
that might have been in style in the last decade, all right?
And laundered in the last year or so.''

''You've been busy.''

The words seemed innocuous, but Tori was getting to
know James well enough to know when he was dis-
pleased. She also knew him well enough not to care.

When she'd called Juicy earlier and prodded him
about the project, he'd promised to have it done that
evening. She'd relayed the information to James when
he'd called, and they were on their way there now after
he'd insisted on picking her up at her house, in a limo
complete with driver, no less. She spent the trip filling
him in on her day while trying to ignore her surroundings.

''I'll make you a deal. You don't rag at me for making
decisions without you, and I won't even start on what I
found at my place this morning.''

He opened his mouth, then, with a quick glance at
her, seemed to reconsider. ''Well,'' he finally said,
''when you put it so charmingly... Was there something
wrong with the arrangements I made? From the quick
look I had, it appeared as though the workmanship was
topnotch.''

For a man who'd risen to the position he had, he could
be singularly dense. ''It is. And though I would have
preferred to be consulted before installing a new alarm

and dead bolts, they seem top of the line, as well. Trouble is, I'm used to taking care of myself. And I don't like people making decisions for me without consulting me first.''

"I'm sorry."

The apology had her swinging her head around, gaping at him. There was a slight frown on his face, and his gorgeous profile was serious. "It's a habit of mine, and one that regularly ticks my family off. I'm used to making judgments in my business and don't always remember the need to consult others in—'' he hesitated. ''—my personal life.''

Tori very nearly squirmed in the plush leather seat. He'd managed to make her feel churlish. If she thought that had been his intent, she would have made a sarcastic retort, but he looked so genuinely puzzled, so nearly *abashed,* that something inside her softened. ''Oh, well…no harm done, I guess.''

There was a part of her deep inside that actually gave a derisive hoot at that. The man had hijacked her hair, showered her with clothes she wouldn't normally be caught dead wearing and then commandeered her house, and no harm was done? That voice, along with a measure of spine, forced her to add, ''But it has to stop. You can't go around arranging things to suit yourself and expect people to forgive you. Most of us feel pretty capable of running our own lives.''

''So I'm told. Frequently.'' From the curve of his lips, she figured he was thinking of his family again. Maybe his sister. Ana didn't seem the type to take an older brother's interference quietly.

''In any case, I contacted your brother to double-check that Joe Jr. actually called and gave him the information he told me about. He had, and they were pairing the description with the details from the bomber's MO to see if something shows up in the database.''

''I'm annoyed as hell with you for approaching your sleazy neighbor on your own.'' He sent her a quick admiring glance. ''But very impressed with your detective work. How did you know he had information that he hadn't given the cops last night?''

''It never really occurred to me until I spoke to him again today. But the more I thought about him in that garage, the more certain I was that he had to have seen something.'' She made a rueful face. ''Something other than what he was hoping for, obviously.''

''At the risk of being accused of being pushy, again, I'd like to point out that having you live next to a pervert doesn't do much for my peace of mind.''

There was an odd jitter in her pulse, and she took care not to look at him. A woman could read all sorts of things into words like that. Like thinking that he cared, on a deeper level. That he'd forgotten the distrust between them—his belief that her father had betrayed him…and his fear that she would do the same.

All of a sudden a vast distance seemed to yawn between them that couldn't be bridged. Despite all that had happened in the last twenty-four hours, nothing had really changed. She was still intent on proving her father's innocence as she solved this case.

And she was just as intent on making sure James stayed alive while she did it.

''Did Joe happen to mention our conversation this morning?''

She sent him a droll look. ''Yes, he did babble incoherently about the 'mean dude' who was going to do unspeakable things to him if he got within ten yards of me.''

There was a definite note of satisfaction in his voice. "Good. Then he's smarter than he looks. I did wonder." He leaned forward and fiddled with the back controls of the CD player until some mournful jazz filled the interior. "I don't like him living next door to you." The simple words were anything but, when delivered in that tone. With that intense light in his eye. It fired an answering warmth in her system, suffusing her with heat.

And because she could hear the genuine concern in his voice, she kept her words even. "It's not like I haven't taken precautions. Unless he's got an X-ray lens on that scope of his, he isn't going to see anything at my house. Peeping Toms rarely escalate into more violent crimes." And she knew this precisely because she'd researched it. She gave him a slight smile. "However, if your brother was to be tipped off and the telescope got seized and not returned, I wouldn't be upset."

James nodded grimly. "Consider it done." At the risk of offending her sensibilities yet again, he was planning on telling his brother far more than that. If the NOPD could put a little pressure on Joe Jr., he just might be convinced to move to a climate better suited to his health. Because James certainly couldn't guarantee the man's continued well-being as long as he was within speaking distance of Tori.

"So." In an obvious effort to lighten the mood, she looked around the limo. "Some ride. Bet you hate not being at the wheel, though, huh?"

He shouldn't have been surprised at the accuracy of her observation. "More than you can imagine." The words, the feeling behind it, were heartfelt. "But having a driver gives me another pair of eyes." The limo also had the added safeguard of armored doors and bullet-proof glass, but he knew better than to put too much stock in that. There were myriad ways to kill someone. It was impossible to protect against all of them.

The driver and car was a concession to the concerns of his family. Cade hadn't been the only one who'd given him hell last night, or, rather, early this morning. Ana had ripped into him, as well, and he didn't totally blame either of them. He owed it to his family's peace of mind to take precautions. And he owed it to them to stay alive to solve the mystery of their parents' deaths, once and for all. To bring the person responsible to justice.

The car glided to a halt, and James looked up to see a familiar, flickering neon sign. Anticipation mixed with trepidation was snaking through his chest, squeezing. The trouble with finding answers, he thought, was dealing with the emotions that came along with them.

In the next moment a slim soft hand slipped into one of his and gripped hard. Startled, he looked down at the woman beside him, saw the understanding in her warm hazel gaze. She didn't speak; she didn't need to. For better or worse, he wasn't by himself in this. It was a disconcerting feeling for a man who was used to dealing with whatever life threw him at him decisively and alone. But not an unpleasant one.

For just a moment he squeezed, returning the pressure. And when they got out of the car and walked up to the tavern door, they did so hand in hand.

"Sorry this took so long. I got another job for a defense attorney." Juicy looked exactly as he had the last time they'd seen him. In fact, James was certain even the patrons outside in the bar were the same. It was as if the place had been caught in a time warp since they'd

last been there. "There's this guy up on vehicular man-
slaughter, see, and his lawyer wants to show…"

"We're glad you could fit this into your schedule,"
Tori put in, with a sidelong glance at James. Unable to
remain still, he roamed the small area, studying the
prints hanging on the bulletin board. One set obviously
belonged to the new case the man was working on. But
the set next to the computer were from the file they'd
left with him. He didn't recognize the three photos hanging above it.

The vise in his chest eased, infinitesimally, as impatience edged out other, darker, emotions. "What are
these?" He gestured to the three.

Juicy ambled over, pointed to each in turn. "Those
aren't from your accident scene, I just got them as ex-
amples to refer to when I explained something. Most
people see skid marks on a road and think they're all
the same. But they're actually very different. Here," he
pointed to the first photo, "is a picture of an acceleration
skid. Laying rubber, we used to call it in my day. This
next one," he moved his finger to the second photo,
"well, that's what laymen think of when they hear the
term *skid mark*. It's left by a tire that's locked, not rotating, while the car continues moving forward. That's
what you see on the road when the driver slams on the
brakes for whatever reason. And this—" he moved to
the third and final picture "—is a yaw mark, left by a
vehicle when a wheel is rotating and sliding sideways."

James peered intently at the last picture. "So if my
father took the curve too fast, lost control on it, this is
the mark we'd expect to see on the road."

Juicy was bobbing his head enthusiastically, a teacher
pleased with a particularly bright student. "Exactly.
Problem is, that's not the kind of mark shown in the

accident photos.'' He pulled several from the envelope and tacked them up beside the ones already hanging on the wall.

"What?'' Tori crowded closer to them, peering at the photos. "You mean the investigating officer misidentified them? How is that possible? Accident investigation has been included in police science for decades.''

"Since the fifties, for sure,'' Juicy said cheerfully. He bent his thin frame into the seat before the computer and punched up a program. "Problem is, it's still the most common police investigative error. Sometimes what we think we see is warped by what we expect to see, ya know? The officer probably figured since there was nothing in the road, those marks were left by a car going too fast on the curve. But the rear end would break loose, see, and swing to the side if in that were the case.''

He tapped the screen, where a close-up of one of the photos appeared, with the tire marks evident. "Person screws up the kind of skid mark, it's going to affect the projection of how fast the vehicle was traveling, too.''

James felt as though each of his organs was encased in ice. Frigid waves radiated throughout his body, numbing his system. His mind, though, remained dangerously clear. "So you can be certain that these marks are braking skids.''

Juicy nodded. "The accident driver was trying to avoid hitting something.''

"The left front fender was smashed.''

Juicy nodded at James's flat statement. "Whatever was on the road, the driver didn't completely miss it. I performed some photogrammetric calculations to determine just where the object was. If you hadn't brought me those other pictures, I'd have figured maybe an oncoming car veered into the lane. But look at this.'' His fingers danced over the keyboard, and yet another scene appeared. This one was obviously a 3-D simulation.

The man stabbed a finger at a spot on the screen. "Now, a second car, if there was one, would have needed to be at this angle here in order for your driver to start braking where he did. But there are no corresponding skid marks to indicate another car was involved. Which means the driver hit something else."

He quickly typed a command and a close-up of the road appeared on the screen. "See that gouge there?" He pointed to the asphalt. "The road crew had just blacktopped that section a week earlier."

James bent lower and stared at the dirty gouge visible on the road's surface. "Something a lot heavier than a car rested right there."

With another quick press of the keys, he had a picure of the boulder, with the fresh scar marring its surface, sitting in the precise spot the gouge had been. "Long story short, I did some calibrations from past photos. If that boulder was sitting right there, it could have caused the damage to the left front fender, and the braking skids would match up exactly."

"It was gone when the police got there, so whoever moved it must have been waiting," Tori put in softly. "He would have had to act quickly to move it back."

"Yeah." James couldn't look away from the photo of the boulder. "Which means there was a witness to the accident after all. The killer himself."

James was grateful for the silence in the car. His mind was a chaotic jumble of anger, despair and a wild, unchecked grief. It was almost like reliving that night all over again. The shocked disbelief. The curious numb-

ness that propelled one to go through the necessary mo-
tions. The overpowering sorrow.

And layered over it all, a shattering sense of failure.

He laid his head against the back of the seat, exhaustion punching through him. For twenty years he'd lived
with a delusion. One far more comfortable, if he was
honest, than the truth he was faced with now. For twenty
years a murderer had gone free. Free to enjoy what life
had to offer. Free to plan James's own destruction when
the timeline was right.

The razored fury would come later, slashing all other
emotions until it pushed to the surface, all cutting edges
and white-hot heat. But for now there was only a deep,
abiding sense of sadness, and an almost unbearable sense
of guilt.

He knew, deep in the darkest corner of his mind, that
it was an emotion he would never dislodge.

"You couldn't have changed anything, you know."

Tori's voice, any voice, was unwelcome. Her words
particularly so. But she was unrelenting, speaking in the
dark confines of the car like a persistent echo in the
shadows. "No matter what you'd done. Who you consulted. If you'd found the killer back then, the only thing
that would be different now is you wouldn't be targeted
yourself by the same person. But the result back then
would have been the same."

He shoved aside the logic of her words. Of course it
would have been different. Someone would have paid.
There would have been a sense of justice, revenge. And
that at least would have counted for something. He and
his brothers and sister wouldn't have lived a lie for two
decades. Wouldn't have accepted a shattering act of vi-
olence for truth.

"Your actions after the accident wouldn't have

changed the results. You couldn't bring them back, James, regardless of the outcome. So don't sit there beating yourself up now because of it. It's pointless, and distracts you from the real issue facing you.''

Her words were annoying, only partially because they might be correct. He opened his eyes, turned his head to look at her. She was shrouded in shadows, but he could make out the reflection of lights in her eyes, the shape of her mouth. ''Do you know what's more irritating than a woman who's right?'' He could barely make out the shake of her head. ''Nothing.''

Her low laugh filled the car, and something shifted inside him. He went quiet for a time, too many thoughts and emotions crashing inside him to identify any one. Finally he spoke again. ''Knowing that, understanding it, doesn't make it better.''

''No.'' Her voice was soft.

There was understanding in the single word; in the touch of her hand when she reached over to take his. He laced his fingers with hers, amazed to find a measure of peace in the simple touch.

The intercom beeped. ''Where to, sir?''

He looked at Tori, an unfamiliar need battling with a lifetime of solitary competence. ''Come home with me tonight?''

She was still for a moment, before her fingers curled more tightly in his. ''Absolutely.''

Chapter 11

The ride home was accomplished mostly in silence, wrapping them in a shroud of intimacy. James had opened up the overhead panel so the stars glittered above like diamonds sprinkled across an inky sea. And then he'd wrapped his arm around her, pulled her close. She spent the remainder of the ride with his heartbeat sounding in her ear and emotion filling her heart.

It was easy to resist a man who seemed invincible; a well-trained warrior who needed no one and nothing. It was a far different matter, she was finding, to turn away from one who was reaching out. Especially when she knew how rare that was for him.

Still, she would have tried. Could have succeeded if her own heart didn't ache for the emotion she knew was twisting through his. If she couldn't imagine the way he was blaming himself. Wrongly. And if she didn't care, all too much, that he was hurting.

There was no heat in his touch as it smoothed over

her shoulder and down her arm, back again. It was more of a promise, a gilded kiss of sensation that whispered of things to come. The certainty of it calmed anticipation until it was just a quiver in her belly. For now, this quiet embrace was enough.

She undid a button on his shirt and slid her hand inside, resting it quietly upon his chest. The warmth of his body transferred to her fingertips, danced along those sensitive nerve endings.

When he tipped her chin up with one finger, she expected his kiss to be light, languorous, like his touch. And for the first few moments it was just that. His lips brushed hers, gossamer soft, as if relearning their shape. She gave a little sigh and sank into it, hazily wishing to capture this moment in time; to freeze-frame it for replay later, when reason returned and doubts resurfaced.

But then he caught her bottom lip in his teeth, applying just enough pressure to have the muscles in her stomach clenching. The angle of the kiss changed, and the world abruptly shifted. Her lips parted and she met his tongue with his in one long, heated stroke.

The stars above were more seductive than candlelight. The mournful tune of lost love more sensual than harp song. But she didn't fool herself into thinking that atmosphere played a part in the sensation crashing through her system. Her response was due to the man beside her.

With one smooth move he tugged her onto his lap, settled her there with her head against his shoulder. She had a moment to marvel at the fit before his mouth went to her throat and a shudder of pleasure worked down her spine. She'd known he'd be good at this, but hadn't counted on her own reaction to his touch. His teeth scraping the cord on her neck sent off electrical currents that flickered to life beneath her skin. And when her eyelids fluttered shut, she firmly closed the door on the last bastion of reason. Whatever happened, she'd deal with. What came next, she'd handle. Now was a burning pulsing need that wouldn't be quieted. Whatever the outcome, she wasn't going to deny this, or him.

What had begun as a languid slide into pleasure quickly became more. The moment James felt her shiver in his arms, a silent savage hunger leaped to life. Desire, too long suppressed, took him unawares, made a mockery of control.

It wasn't supposed to be like this. He had the dim thought even as he pressed his mouth to the pulse beating wildly at the base of her throat. Sex, in all its varied faces, was meant to be a natural, pleasurable release. He didn't treat it casually, because intimacy made the act fuller somehow. More complete. He didn't know this woman in any of the usual ways. Hadn't spent quiet times sailing or at the theater; hadn't done the usual courtship dance over expensive meals and fine wines.

And yet she understood him, and he her, in a way he never could have foreseen. Circumstances had thrown them together and stripped them of their usual guard. With defenses lowered, vulnerabilities peeked through. And every moment with her had him more intrigued.

He caught the cord of her neck in his teeth and drew a gasp from her. The sound called to something primitive buried deep inside him. Caution reared, distant but insistent. There was danger here. Feeling too much too fast wasn't his normal way.

But the unexpected could be damn inviting. The foreign an almost overwhelming temptation.

She twisted against him, and he pulled her closer, inhaling the scent found below her ear, at her temple. Her skin was silky there, baby soft. And he was suddenly eager to explore the rest of her, to discover all the textures of her body. Find out what made her sigh and moan and gasp.

Need rose in him, edgy and fierce. He tugged the blouse from her waistband and slipped his hand inside, finding sleek skin molded over fascinating curves. He covered her breast with his palm, felt the warmth of her radiating through the lace. Her heart was hammering against his hand, and he knew its pace matched his own.

He took her mouth again and felt her hand slide to his hair, fisting there. Her flavor was heady, and it was difficult to get his fill. Especially when her tongue was flicking the roof of his mouth, sliding along his teeth, darting daringly against his own. He was certain in that instant that whatever the outcome of the night, he wouldn't regret this. Or her.

Tori didn't know how long it was before she became aware that the car had stopped. James barely lifted his mouth from hers to murmur against her lips. "I want to take you somewhere. Show you something."

His low voice was raspy with desire. The same emotion was reflected in his hooded eyes. He caught her hand when she smoothed it over his hard jaw; pressed a kiss in its center. Closing her fingers, she trapped the warmth that lingered there. "Show me," she said.

He helped her from the car and then laced their fingers. Tugging her along with him, they started off across the drive at a leisurely pace. But when the limo moved away toward the garage, James shot her a grin of pure wicked sin. "This will be easier barefoot."

A delighted smile crossed her lips at the playful challenge. It was unexpected. And, like many other experiences tonight, showed a side to him she wouldn't have guessed at. Once he'd shrugged out of his jacket and tie, and they'd both shed their shoes and socks, he grabbed her hand again and they ran flat-out across the dew-kissed grass.

The yard was long, lush and rolled softly toward the shore of the lake. They dodged the shadowy gardens and ornate walks and raced across the lawn.

Tori reached her stride easily, lungs expanding with air that seemed unbelievably fresh, amazingly sweet. And when a glance at James showed that he was matching her stride for stride, an innate competitive streak kicked in.

She could hear his low husky laugh behind her as she pulled ahead, could imagine his long legs stretching to keep pace. And felt a flash of pure enjoyment as sensation layered over sensation. The damp grass beneath her feet and the studded velvet sky overhead.

And most provocative was the presence of the man beside her. A man who, until now, she never would have pictured doing anything so carefree.

A small building loomed on their left, several yards away. His arm snaked around her waist, spun her to meet him, and then they were both tumbling to the grass, rolling across it. By the time they came to a stop she was dizzy and laughing helplessly, pushing at his chest. "Get off me, you fool."

James propped himself up on his elbows and grinned down at her. "Is that any way to show your appreciation of my seduction technique?"

"You've finally convinced me that your reputation in that area has been overstated."

"I told you." His easy agreement was in contrast to the kisses he strewed along her jawline, leaving fire in their wake. "It's always a mistake for people to believe their own press."

Her hands linked around his neck even as a sneaky sliver of doubt stabbed her. "I've made my share of mistakes. I don't want to regret this. I don't want you to."

James paused. Her words, the shadow of uncertainty in them, unleashed a bolt of tenderness that was as unfamiliar as it was undeniable. "No. No regrets." To convince her, his kiss was slow, rife with promise. Her flavor was still sweetly unique. It still fired his hormones to instant readiness. But beneath the desire was an understanding that this wasn't going to be easily dismissed, or easily forgotten. And any regrets he experienced would be most likely to come at their parting.

The moonlight dappled the lawn, painting it with threads of silver. He wanted, quite desperately, to see her skin streaked with its pearly glow. To taste the areas bathed in light and explore those left in shadow.

To drive them both mad, he unbuttoned her blouse slowly, starting at the bottom, distracting each of them from his actions by pressing light, nibbling kisses to her lips. Two buttons open. The warm, smooth stretch of skin beneath his palm. He didn't look, but his imagination supplied him with an image that was temptation personified. Pressing her lips open with his, he found her tongue, sucked lightly.

Two more buttons undone. He heard the slight hitch of her breath when the night air met her bared skin. He kept his eyes closed and his touch restrained. Light brushes, fingertips on satin. Anticipation thrummed through him. Muscles grew tight with tension. And her mouth opened more eagerly for his, her hands clutching at his shoulders.

When the last two buttons were released, he gave a slight tug and the fabric parted. And only then did he raise his head, open his eyes and send up a fervent prayer.

Her long lean form was a delight to the eyes, a treat to the senses. Spreading his hand over her rib cage, he kneaded lightly, watching the shadows meld into glistening ivory and back again. The lace covering her breasts was rough in comparison to her skin. He wanted to see her wearing nothing but moonglow. He unsnapped her bra and tossed both it and her blouse aside.

Her breasts were high firm mounds that begged for a man's hands, for his mouth. He took a nipple between his lips and sucked, filling his palm with her other breast. He was aware of her hands in his hair, pulling him closer, but even more aware of the taste of her, unspeakably erotic; the exquisite softness of her curves; the bite of need in her nails digging into his shoulders.

Tori fumbled with the buttons on his shirt, lacking his finesse or restraint. She wanted to feel their skin pressed together; chest to chest; hips to hips. When she had the garment unfastened, her hands streaked inside, in a hurry to chart every inch of flesh she'd bared.

He had the long, spare build of a runner, lightly padded with muscle. She wasn't surprised to find strength lurking beneath the polish, but she was tempted by it. Incredibly so. Hands greedy, she slid them over his torso. There were surprising hollows beneath angles, sleek skin stretched over bone and sinew. The ribbon of hair trailing below his navel was silky where she traced it, the muscles quivering beneath her touch a stark testament to a need that mirrored her own.

She dragged her eyes open, tried to focus. He was leaning half-over her, part of him in light, the other in shadow. He still cupped her breast, the thumb rubbing over her nipple, drawing it to a tauter point. Odd, with the distrust that lay unspoken between them, that at this time, in this place, she trusted him as no other. Hunger painted his face nearly savage, but it wasn't fear that quickened inside her at the sight.

Leaning forward, she ran the tip of her tongue over his collarbone, tested it lightly with her teeth. Then lost her breath when, with one quick move, he had her in his arms and was rising, like a statue of a Roman god come to life.

She stretched, muscles tight with anticipation, and hooked an arm around his neck to anchor herself. The other was free to roam across his hair-roughened chest, finding the flat nipple hiding there and flicking it teasingly.

He nipped her throat for her efforts, then laved the spot with his tongue. With a sense of disorientation, she realized he'd brought them to the building she'd seen earlier.

"Look out there. See that view?"

Obeying his low, raspy voice, she turned her gaze on the lake and caught her breath. The half-moon hung low in the sky, painting the ripples in the water with a pearly stripe of ivory. The sky was an endless glittering spread of midnight, deep and unpenetrable.

"I've been all over the world, and nothing can match this spot for beauty." His eyes looked dark in the night, fathomless. "I'll never look at it again without remembering you here. Remembering this moment."

Her heart did a slow roll in her chest. An aching thread of tenderness, far more dangerous than passion, filled her. Words failed her, but words weren't needed.

His mouth found hers, gentleness quickly turning to something sharper. More urgent.

Once inside the screened gazebo, James reluctantly set her on her feet. His mouth traced the curve of her shoulder as he swept his hand over the surprisingly delicate line of her spine, found the intriguing hollow at its base. Her slacks impeded his exploration, and patience proved elusive. He managed the zipper but wasn't as careful with the scrap of silk beneath. There was a sound of shredding fabric, before he filled his hands with her silky bottom.

There was more, far more than he'd imagined to stroke, to knead, to explore. The curve of her waist, the underside of her breast, the sleek line of thigh, the slick softness of her femininity. He tolerated, for as long as he was able, her hands at his waist, unfastening his pants. But when she inched the zipper of his trousers down one excruciating inch at a time, he was certain he was being punished for forgotten sins. Breath hissing between his teeth, he stepped away, stripped off the remainder of his clothes and drew her close again, marvelously close.

Bending his head, he took her nipple between his lips and filled his mouth with her. Her broken cries torched the fever of his desire. Stoked it higher. He could feel the hunger rise in him and strove to check it. Not yet. There were too many discoveries he'd yet to make. And far too much of the night remained to rush through this now.

And then those intentions fragmented when she found him, wrapping knowing fingers around pulsing heat and stroking him to madness. His eyes went blind. His lungs strained for oxygen. And the sharp and vicious edge of need grew keener.

His hands became increasingly urgent, just shy of desperate. He caressed her thighs, found her damp cleft and pressed rhythmically. When she softened against him he cupped her femininity and slid a finger inside her damp center.

The cry that escaped her scraped over nerve endings already taut and straining. She was exquisitely soft, tight and warm. Even days ago he would have sworn that lovemaking could hold no surprises for him. And yet here he was, sensation raining over him, a storm in his system. And the indisputable cause of that was the woman going wild in his arms.

Her response shredded the veneer of civility he was usually careful to maintain. It called forth an untamed element that he'd always been aware of, had always hidden. It drew from him a determination to take all she had to give and then push her higher. Further. Until the image of what had passed between them was etched forever in her memory, as it would be in his.

He felt the precise moment when she stiffened against him, surprise and pleasure drawing her up into a tight fist of need. One more stroke, one deep touch would send her crashing over the edge, leaving her gasping and limp.

He withdrew his fingers, muffled the low whimper she made with his lips. When she went over the first time, it would be with him buried deep inside her, with every inch of their bodies touching, straining toward release. And it would have to be soon. Sweat slicked his forehead, and he couldn't see through the haze of his own desire.

Moving more from memory than sight, he tumbled them both to the futon. Ragged breaths mingled. Greed took over, on both their parts. Damp skin pressed against damp skin. Hands raced over tense muscles. Mouths met while teeth clashed and tongues battled.

Control shredded.

He had a moment of clarity, as the hunger sliced through him with a single savage stroke. Blindly he reached for his pants, dug out the foil-wrapped package in the pocket. And then what was left of his tattered control was tested, as Tori took the condom from him and sheathed him with it, fingers staying to caress.

His brain misted, reason receded. Moving her hands away, he slid over her body, positioned himself between her thighs. His intent was to go slow. He entered her by excruciating inches, his throat clogging at the tight perfection of her, his muscles quivering with restraint. And then intent was shattered when her hips rose wildly, forcing him deeper, faster.

He needed to see her face. He dragged his eyelids open, fought for focus. Her eyes were open, dazed and huge, fixed on his. And in that moment he was certain that what they shared was a first of sorts for both of them.

She clutched him closer, the tiny sting of her nails on his back whipping his hunger to fever pitch. His hips lunged against hers, each frantic movement edging them closer to a brilliant culmination. He felt her body buck beneath his, swallowed the helpless cry on her lips. He tried to fight against his own climax, but she was liquid fire around him, her inner muscles clenching and releasing, milking his own response. With his gaze still locked on her face, her name on his lips, he felt the sensations slam into him. He surged against her one last time before following her headlong into pleasure.

Time and distance were qualities necessary to steady the pulse and resettle sanity. Tori hadn't seen James all day, which, she considered, was for the best. Perspective, she decided, was something she very much needed to restore.

The night they'd spent together defied description. Melting tenderness, primitive hunger and, laced through it all, a burning desire that had been quenched, over and over, only to quicken again. She had expected the lovemaking to be hot and, given her response to him, satisfying. She hadn't known that it could be meltingly touching at the same time. That it would wipe out every previous experience she'd ever had and stamp her indelibly with his touch.

A frisson of worry shot through her at the thought, and her spine straightened. Obviously lack of sleep had affected her brain, as well. She wasn't *stamped*. She didn't do *stamped*. Okay, it had been good between them, she told herself, struggling to pour herself into the dress he'd had the maid bring to her room. Great even. He'd needed someone last night, and she'd happened to be handy and available.

Maybe a little too available—where was the zipper in this thing? Contorting herself into an impossible position, she yanked at one of the myriad straps that crossed what she fervently hoped was the back and inched the dress up a fraction. But she wasn't going to waste time second-guessing herself. They'd both said last night they weren't going to do regrets. And despite how this thing ended, and it would end soon she was certain, she couldn't be sorry for something that had been…almost magical.

Once she finally got the garment on, she strode to the mirror, gaped in horror. Where was the rest of the material? In vain, she tugged at the hem in an attempt to lengthen it a few inches. And the back—she half turned to peek and gave a groan—was completely bare, save for the criss-crossing of stretchy straps that didn't seem to be much more than decoration. Certainly they meant she'd have to lose the bra.

She scowled at her reflection, considered her options. She could track down the maid and ask her to select something else. But she had no idea where to find the woman, and she was running short of time as it was. She was very much afraid that anything else in the collection would be as bad as or worse than this one.

Finally giving up that idea, she shifted so she wouldn't be faced with her reflection and dragged a brush through her hair. She started to strap on her watch, then noticed that the functional style would hardly go with the dress. Muttering beneath her breath, she laid it back on the dresser and snatched up the shoes that went with the dress. Resignation filled her when she noted the heels. They added a good three inches to her already over-average height. In the bright-red dress, which she had a sneaky suspicion James had selected on purpose, she now looked like a flaming Amazon.

A knock sounded as she attempted to jam her cell phone into the tiny matching purse. Starting for the door, she didn't get two steps before she darn near twisted her ankle. Cursing the uncustomary heels, she hobbled the rest of the way and threw the door open, glowering at the man standing there holding a flat case in his hand.

''Why don't you just take a gun and shoot me? It'd be less painful.''

Brows raised, James strolled in, his gaze traveling over her form and lingering on the shoes. ''Is it the dress or the heels? Both, by the way, are very becoming. I knew they'd suit you.''

She shut the door behind him, with a little more force than necessary. ''The dress is about four inches too short to wear in public, and the heels should qualify as lethal weapons. I'm not sure I could chase down a suspect in them, but if I happened to trip one I could always use a shoe to beat him to death.''

Tori saw the smile quivering on his lips and the admirable effort he took to firm it. Neither endeared him to her. ''Easy to be amused when you're not the one attending this thing half-naked wearing stilts.''

''I don't suppose it will improve your mood to add some glitter to the mix. You're not the type to go gooey-eyed over jewels.'' He flipped open the jeweler's box to reveal a gold necklace dripping rubies and diamonds. Taking it out, he said, ''Turn around and I'll fasten it for you.''

She didn't move. Couldn't. She was very much afraid her mouth was agape, as well. ''Is that real?''

''A hundred grand worth of 'real.''' Since she still hadn't moved, he stepped behind her and fitted the necklace beneath her hair. Latching the clasp he turned her in his arms, studying her critically. ''Perfect.''

''Are you crazy?'' Each jewel seemed to burn like a brand. ''I can't wear this.'' She slapped a hand over it, as if to keep it in place. ''What if I lose it?''

''Then the insurance company used by Hansen, Hansen and Smith are going to be very upset with the store manager. I've borrowed this for the night. I'll messenger it back in the morning.''

That made her feel only a modicum better. ''So all I have to do is manage not to lose it for a few hours. Great.'' Another thought occurred, and she frowned. ''They actually lend this stuff out? Are they crazy?''

''I'm a very good customer.'' He cocked his head,

appreciation obvious in his expression. "And at the risk of having you use one of those heels on me, I have to say you're a gorgeous advertisement for their jewels. And you're breathtaking in that dress."

"I look like a stork," she said shortly. "All legs." She couldn't begin to count all the times in her life that she'd wished to saw about four inches off them.

He moved behind her again, shifted her so that the mirror reflected both of them. In the heels, she was only a couple of inches shorter than he was. "You look like every man's fantasy," he murmured in her ear. "We're a pretty primitive lot, darling. When we see endless legs like yours we tend to think only of how they'd feel wrapped around our waist."

His words robbed her of speech. The stinging kiss he placed on the side of her neck stole her breath. Raising his head again, his eyes met hers in the mirror, an unmistakable sheen of desire in them. "And having had that exquisite experience recently, I'm going to have the devil's own time tonight keeping my mind on business."

Because her throat seemed clogged, she cleared it. "Well, I wish I'd known that before I invested in all those self-defense courses I took. Next time I get in a jam, I'll just flash some leg."

He reached past her, picked up the red-sequined purse. The sight of the frivolous accessory dangling from his arm relaxed her in a way nothing else could have. He nudged her toward the door. "And if you get in a jam tonight, remember I've got your back." As if to accentuate his words, his hand slid to her butt and squeezed.

A well-placed elbow dislodged his hand and brought a satisfying wince to his face. "Don't you think we're a bit overdressed for a…what exactly is a Technology Expo, anyway?" He was dressed in a dark suit that looked every bit as formal as a tux. They headed down the staircase and out the door, where the driver had the limo running.

"The expo actually starts tomorrow and runs for three days. Tonight is a more formal cocktail gathering for the participants and press." Reaching into his breast pocket, he withdrew an ID for her, slipped it inside her purse and handed the purse to her.

The sight of it reminded her of something. "Did you remember to have an ID sent over to Corday?"

"I did. I also..." His cell phone rang then, and he answered it, even as he helped her into the car. It was a struggle to swing her legs inside while maintaining her modesty. Catching the look of sheer male appreciation in his expression at the sight, she lost no time reaching over to slam the door.

Once he was inside, she listened unabashedly to his side of the conversation. It wasn't difficult to discern that he was talking to Cade. She waited impatiently until they were down the drive and on the road before he ended the conversation.

"NOPD got a lead on the bomber," he said without preamble. "Nothing popped in the database, but the detectives worked some snitches. With Joe's description and the MO, one name kept surfacing. Dennis Francis."

Hope leaped to her throat. "Did they catch up with him?" He nodded, face grim. "But not before someone else caught up with him first. He's dead. Shot three times in the front seat of his car, close range."

As quickly as hope had surged, disappointment replaced it. "But we can look into his history. See if he might have been acquainted with your father..."

James was already shaking his head. "He was only thirty-three. He would have been too young to have anything to do with the accident. More than likely he was hired for the bombing and was killed when he failed.''

Mind working furiously, Tori said, ''Well, this still might shake loose a lead. What about his phone lines? Have they done a dump on them?''

James gave her a look that was half admiring, half amused. ''You're right on track. He didn't have a land-line, and no cell was found on him. But they did find cell phone bills when they tossed his apartment. Cade said they put a rush on the order, but it will still take a couple days.''

''Something tells me we may not have that long.'' She looked at him consideringly, knowing he wasn't going to like what she had to say next. ''I heard back on some feelers I put out a few days ago on Dale Cartwright.''

He stiffened, very slightly. Voice cool, he said, ''That wasn't necessary. I told you I'd take care of it.''

Silence stretched, the tension in it palpable. Then, with obvious reluctance, he asked, ''What did you find?''

Discreetly, Tori tried, and failed, to tug the hem of her dress farther down her thighs. ''He and your father didn't part especially amicably. Word I heard was your father forced him out. Apparently he had an alcohol problem and it cost them too many contracts.''

''And where'd you get these details?'' There was a light in his eye, a dangerous burn. She refused to quail beneath it.

''From information brokers I use from time to time. I got the same story from two of them, so I tend to think it's credible.'' And because she saw through the anger to the hurt beneath, she said, ''I'm sorry, James. I know it's not what you wanted to hear.''

He took a deep breath. ''No. But then, there's been

damn little I've wanted to hear in the last few days. But a lot that I needed to know. So.'' He seemed to draw himself in, a warrior preparing to rejoin the battle. ''He could have harbored a grudge over that, I agree. I tend to think if he had, however, he wouldn't have waited three years to get revenge.''

Tori wasn't so sure. There were plenty of people who believed that the best revenge was served cold.

''I don't want it to be Dale. I admit that.'' She knew the admission didn't come easily for him. ''It'd be easier, less personal, if it turns out to be one of the CEOs of one of the other companies.''

''Tarkington's and Beal's were the only two of the other competitive companies you cited who were even around at the time. Your parents' accident and the threats on your life are linked. So the suspect almost has to be someone from that time period.'' She thought for a moment before inquiring, ''If I were the sender, I'd have followed up the bombing with another message.''

''Another came today,'' he admitted. ''Said next time I'd be dead and to withdraw my bid from the upcoming Pentagon contract.''

The chill that broke out over her skin had nothing to do with her scanty dress. ''And when do they award the contract?''

''Next week.''

Time was running out, and the sender's desperation was sure to escalate. The concern she felt wasn't new. The stark fear was. ''So what are you going to do?''

''The only thing I can do.'' His voice was even, full of promise. ''I'm going to find this bastard and nail him to the wall. And if I find out that the same person threatening me killed my parents...'' His tone sharpened, a sword whetted on stone. ''The law will be much more merciful than I will be.''

Chapter 12

It resembled theater opening night rather than Tori's idea of a technology expo. The hotel conference rooms were overflowing with people, and more of them were wearing press passes than she'd expected. She saw Kiki in the distance, camera flashing away, and winced. He hadn't taken her fashion advice. With his loud, plaid polyester suit coat and striped pants, he looked more like a seventies used-car salesman than a photographer. But he appeared to be doing the job she'd hired him for, so she would have to be content with that.

James kept her close to his side, introduced her to a dizzying array of people, but none were the ones she most wanted to meet. If Beal, Cartwright or Tarkington were somewhere in the crowd she was busily scanning, she'd yet to see them.

"Tori." She pasted a smile on her face and turned to greet the woman James was greeting. She looked vaguely familiar.

"You remember Celia, don't you? My assistant?"

The name didn't ring a bell, but the job description did. The woman who vetted all of James's visitors at the company. "Of course. Nice to see you again." Rather than the colorless suits she'd seen the woman wearing at work, tonight she was dressed in a tasteful navy dress and pearls. Tori felt positively bare beside her.

"Miss Corbett." There was a puzzled note in the woman's voice, as she looked from Tori to James. "I didn't expect to see you here."

"Well, actually, I'm Mr. Tremaine's..."

"Companion." James slipped an arm around Tori's waist, ignoring the way she stiffened. "She was kind enough to accompany me here tonight. Looks like we've got a good crowd."

"Yes, I knew you'd be pleased." Celia turned to scan the mob. "I arrived with Marcus a little bit ago. I believe he's searching for you."

"I'll look him up. Why don't you see if Tucker and Jones need any help? And if Corley and Soulieu have the Micro Secure set up and ready for the demonstration."

Celia took a pad from her purse and began scribbling his orders, the picture of competence. "I'll do that. Do you have your cell with you?" At James's nod, she promised, "I'll let you know what I find out."

Once the woman had departed, Tori slipped away from his arm. "Can we at least go with 'associate' rather than companion? You make me sound like the faithful family dog."

He snagged two flutes of champagne from a passing waiter's tray and handed her one. "'Associate' works for me. Of course, when I introduced you that way to my brother the other night he immediately assumed we were 'associating.' The word dripped innuendo."

Throat suddenly dry, Tori sipped. It was rather hypocritical, she supposed, to object to having people thinking they were sleeping together, now that they were, in fact, doing just that. Wisely, she kept the rest of her protests to herself. So far she'd managed to avoid any discussion about last night, and she would like to keep it that way. They'd moved from the gazebo sometime before dawn to her bedroom. And when she'd awakened, he was gone. The only signs he'd been there at all was the indentation on the pillow next to her, and her clothes, neatly folded on a chair.

She took a bigger drink. Yes, any discussion regarding their relationship, real or pretended, was something she'd rather evade.

''What's on the agenda tonight?''

James checked his watch. ''Happy hour will continue for another forty-five minutes, and then the participating companies will begin the exhibition. Each will highlight one of the products they'll be showcasing for the next few days.'' His voice was laced with certainty. ''Of course, we feel that Tremaine Technologies will garner the lion's share of attention with our product.''

''All modesty aside, I'm compelled to agree.''

Tori immediately identified the tiny blonde in the black cocktail dress who'd joined them. Ana ignored her brother for the moment and said, ''Tori, isn't it? How are you? Cade said the bomb went off in front of your house.'' She swept her figure with her gaze. ''I'm glad to see that you don't look any the worse for wear.''

''I've got a bump on the head and makeup took care of the worst bruises.'' Tori shrugged. ''We were lucky.''

Ana sent a meaningful glance to her brother. ''His luck is about to run out. He's been avoiding me all day, but I want to know what kind of precautions he's been taking. This psycho who almost killed the two of you isn't going to stop. Did he tell you the family wanted him to delay the expo?''

Tori shook her head. She wasn't surprised, however, that James had refused. He wasn't the type to back down in the face of danger.

"We've got security all over this area," James informed them quietly. "And I'm using a driver and an armored car.''

Ana smiled, but the worry was still evident in her expression. "I know exactly how much you hate that, too. When I'm tempted to brain you for being bull-headed, thinking of that fact cheers me right up.''

Looking slightly hunted, James said, "I thought you'd be getting in position to see how the Micro Secure performs.''

"I already know how it will perform," she replied sweetly. "Magnificently. Tell me you're wearing Kevlar tonight.''

He looked down at his suit. "No, Armani.''

"Don't be cute, James. This would be a perfect spot for someone to take a shot at you." At the real concern threading Ana's voice, Tori looked around uneasily, wondering if she was right. Certainly the mob of people would make discovering a sniper more difficult.

"You can talk over the security details with your husband. He arranged them. We tightened up the registration ID process, and the metal detectors make smuggling in a weapon unlikely." He reached out, gave her a hug. "I know you're worried, but you shouldn't be. This is probably the safest place I can be.''

Ana didn't look satisfied, but she hugged him back, hard. To Tori she said confidingly, "He tends to think he's indestructible, which has the rest of us a bit worried.

Add to that his irritating quality of thinking he knows best, and he can be a bit of a trial.''

''I'm familiar with the trait,'' Tori said meaningfully. ''Maybe we could double-team him.''

Ana laughed delightedly. ''I like her, James. She's not a fawner.'' To Tori she said, ''Most of his women drip all over him. It's absolutely nauseating.''

Tori was beginning to enjoy herself. Certainly she was enjoying the pained expression on James's face. ''I'm standing right here,'' he reminded them. ''And I thought you wanted to quiz your husband on the security details.'' He turned his sister firmly around. ''He's over there by the windows. When you're finished with him go make sure Corley and Soulieu are ready to start.''

''Okay.'' She began moving away. ''I can take a hint.''

''Not well,'' he muttered. Grasping Tori's elbow, he began leading her away. ''Don't believe anything she says.''

''I don't know.'' She pretended to consider. ''Seems to me she had you dead to rights.''

His cell phone rang again then and while he answered it she did another scan of the crowd. It had grown considerably in the past few minutes. Taking advantage of his distraction, she tugged on his sleeve. ''I'm going to mingle.'' His answer, if he made one, was lost as she moved away.

James had just finished his phone conversation with Celia when he felt a clap on the shoulder. ''Hell of a shindig you got going on here, son. Can't say I'm surprised.''

The familiar voice elicited twin feelings of happiness and dismay. Turning around, he exchanged a handshake with Dale Cartwright and wished he'd had more time to prepare for this meeting.

"I didn't expect you until the engagement party later this week."

Dale beamed at him. "Got to thinking a few extra days in town wouldn't hurt a bit. Give me a chance to catch your expo and a little extra time to flirt with Ana. She here tonight?" He sent a searching gaze across the room. "Might steal her away from that new husband of hers to catch up. Shirley sent along pictures of the grand-kids, and Ana always gets a kick out of those."

The man never seemed to change. Big, bluff, hearty, with hair that had been gray for as long as James could remember. Shirley, his wife of forty years, matched him in looks and in personality. The two had been a mainstay in his life since he'd been able to walk. Try as he might, he couldn't imagine the man capable of anything as ne-farious as the plot they'd uncovered.

He imagined Tori felt the same way about her own father.

"Ana's here." His next words, as distasteful as they were, had to be spoken. "I'm glad you came tonight, though. I've been wanting to talk to you."

"Well, shoot, son, why didn't you say so? Let's head out to a balcony." James set his empty glass down on a nearby tray and didn't pick up another. For as long as he remembered, Dale had been a nondrinker.

Once outside, he had difficulty summoning the nec-essary words. So he listened as Dale rambled about his wife, their travels and their grandchildren. It was several minutes before the man wound down, saying, "Well, listen to me go on. You had something you needed to talk to me about, and I haven't stopped rattling on for a minute. What'd you need? Business advice?"

James responded to Dale's hearty laugh with a faint smile. "I need you to help me understand some history. Specifically how you and my father parted ways after years of partnership."

Dale's laughter abruptly halted. Eyes narrowed, he said, "That's old news, and better left alone. Why would you be asking about that after all these years?"

"Indulge me."

The man studied him a moment, a serious expression settled over his face. Finally he gave a slow nod. "All right. We wanted different things for the company, your father and me. We each had our own ideas for how to make it grow. Heck, you can imagine how that would be if you had a partner. You're a fella who thinks he knows how things should be done. Take a couple strong-willed guys like your dad and me, and we didn't always agree, I can tell you that."

James looked away. It was hard to have this conversation with a man he respected. One he loved. Harder yet to deal with the uncertainty of what had transpired all those years ago. "You had an alcohol problem, I heard. It affected your work. Affected the business."

Dale took a step back, leaned heavily on the balcony railing. "Yep. I sure did." He waited for James's gaze to meet his again. "It's not something I'm proud of, but it's something I deal with every day of my life. I'm an alcoholic, son. Been on the wagon more than eighteen years, but it doesn't change what I am. They say everyone of us has to hit rock bottom before we admit we have a problem. Well, your dad shoving me out of the business was the beginning of my bottom. It took me three years to forgive him. Another three to get sober."

"But you did forgive him," James probed. He

wanted, badly, to believe him. He wanted it to be the truth.

Now it was Dale who looked away. "I loved that man like a brother. Loved you kids like my own. That didn't change, but I'd be lying if I said I wasn't angry with him at the time. I had my problems, God knows, I'm not denying it. But shoot, son, we were all young upstarts back then, wild in our own way. With me it was drinking. Marcus liked to gamble more than he should have, and Celia…well, your father nearly fired her when we found out she'd been consorting with one of our rivals."

James felt like the recipient of one too many right jabs. "I never heard that about Marcus. And Celia…who was she involved with?"

"Simon Beal." The man shook his head sadly. "Whoa, that was a long time ago. He took advantage of her, of course. Wooed her and then tried to use her position to get information on the company. Once she found out what he'd been up to, she came right to your father and me and told us the whole story. Took us a couple days to wrestle with it, but eventually we decided to keep her on. Don't think she ever got over it," he mused. "She never did get married, did she?"

"No." James swallowed. "She never did."

The man seemed to shake himself from his reverie. "Well, like I said, it's ancient history. Old hurts, old scars. But you know what they say, time heals all wounds. And I gotta say, most of them are better left covered." Clapping him on the shoulder again, he moved away, back into the crowded conference room.

Broodingly James considered the street below without really seeing it. Old wounds, he knew intimately, didn't ever really heal. Sometimes they could still throb viciously two decades later.

He didn't catch up with Tori until people had begun drifting out of the area. Then he spotted her standing across the room wearing an expression that could only be described as dangerous. The sight lightened something inside him. There was something about the contrast she presented, he supposed. In the feminine dress and foolish purse, she'd appear at home on a fashion runway. But the look on her face spelled trouble for whoever had been foolish enough to raise her ire. He started toward her, half expecting her to take off one of her heels and start swinging at the poor sap.

He saw her shift, a deliberate movement designed to dislodge a hand from her rear. Then the crowd parted around them, and James identified the man at her side.

Allen Tarkington.

There was a single savage leap inside him, something primal. It took a moment to tuck away that flame of visceral possessiveness before he started toward them again. It wasn't an emotion that Tori would welcome. He didn't welcome it himself. Since he didn't get possessive over women, not ever, he chalked up the emotion to the dislike he had for Tarkington.

He'd never been able to link the man to the fire at his corporate headquarters nine years ago, but that didn't mean he didn't still suspect him as the arsonist. There was little the man wouldn't do to get ahead in their field. His tactics hadn't won him many friends in the business and his personality even less.

"Allen." His voice pleasant, he stopped next to Tori, nodding at the man. "Caught your presentation on that new password decryptor. Interesting."

Tarkington straightened his jacket. "We're thinking it'll start a buzz. Who knows? Might even give us a leg up on that contract next week. That'd be ironic, wouldn't it? If the exposure from your expo sent some attention my way from the Pentagon bigwigs?"

James thought of the arson once more, and smiled. "Funny, I've always thought exposure would do you good, too. Will you excuse us?" Tori moved away with him, leaving Tarkington to stare after them.

"I didn't catch your company's presentation," she said. "How'd it go?"

"The Micro Secure performed well. Sometimes there are glitches in the preliminary programs, but Ana did a great job working them out. I have high hopes for it."

They strolled back toward the entrance. The rooms were quickly emptying of people. "I had occasion to talk to several of your competitors," she murmured.

"Form any conclusions?" He raised a hand to acknowledge Tucker, Corley and Soulieu, who were heading for the door.

"Well, Tarkington's a grab-ass who'll chase anything in a dress. The man's lucky I didn't drive my heel through his jugular."

The mental picture brought a smile. "There are more people than you know who'd pay good money to see that."

"I also had a few minutes to speak to Beal." She stopped them, turned to look at him, concern apparent in her gaze. "He's the one that scares me, James. He's cold all the way through. And he'd take any advantage, use anyone, to get a jump on you. He must have known I was with you, because within thirty seconds of my getting near him he was pumping me for information. He was smooth. He disguised it as small talk, but the minute I convinced him I had nothing to do with Tremaine Technologies, his interest in me dried up fast.''

"He's an opportunist." A fact that, according to Dale, Celia had learned the hard way. "But that doesn't necessarily mean he's our man."

Tori looked around. "How much longer do you have to stay at this thing?"

Checking his watch, he said, "Maybe a half hour. Since we sponsored the expo we're assisting the hotel staff with security for the setups. Why?"

She slipped her arm in his and began walking again. "Let's make it fast. I'm betting Kiki went right home and started developing those photos. He can be very industrious when there's cash on the line."

Interest piqued, he glanced at her. "You're planning a trip over there at this hour?"

"I think I can safely guarantee that where money is involved, Kiki's visiting hours can be very flexible."

But when they pulled up in front of the man's home an hour later, James wasn't so sure. There wasn't a light on in the house Tori directed him to, although the man's car was in the drive.

"It's barely midnight," she said impatiently when he pointed that out to her. "I know him. The first thing he would have done is come home and load the pictures on to his computer. Where money is involved, Kiki is meticulous."

He'd have to take her word for it. The slovenly man he'd briefly seen at the expo certainly hadn't seemed meticulous about much else.

"If he's awake, he'll still be at the computer. It won't hurt to check."

Giving a shrug, he followed her up the cracked front

walk to climb the steps. "That's weird," she muttered. The front door was open, as it had been the day she'd come to hire him. The screen was still missing from the storm door.

"Kiki," she called, banging on the door. "It's Tori. I've got your money." Her greeting failed to get a response.

"Maybe if we call," James suggested.

"The heck with it. He's one guy you don't have to stand on ceremony with." She pulled open the storm door, stepped inside. "And he's never been unhappy to see anyone with money in hand."

Warily James glanced around before following her inside. This wasn't exactly the kind of neighborhood that inspired faith in humanity. But there was no one in sight. Not a sound could be heard, other than Tori still calling out the man's name. Her voice echoed in the too-silent house. "Exactly where is this office of his?"

"Right back here." She continued through the house, pushing open the office door. "Talk about engrossed in your work, Kiki, you really take the—" She stopped so abruptly that James nearly ran into her. A moment later he saw the cause for her reaction.

It was instinct rather than comprehension that had him reacting. He pushed her behind him and searched for the light switch, flipping it on for a clearer look, but that first glance had been enough.

Kiki Corday lay crumpled on the cracked linoleum floor. And from the amount of blood pooling around him, there was little doubt that he was dead.

"Ohmygod." James heard Tori's low moan, turned to see her staring horrified at the figure on the floor. "Is he…"

"Yes." From this angle he could see the man's sightless eyes aimed at the ceiling. "Use your cell to call my brother." He recited the number as he gingerly stepped over the body and went to the computer. Taking off his tie, he wrapped it around his hand before touching the mouse, bringing the screen to life.

"It looks like he was loading the pictures, all right," he said grimly. The compact flash reader was hooked to the USB port, but there was no sign of the memory card itself. The CD carousel was standing open and empty. Muttering a vicious curse, James used his covered hand to type in commands, but it was quickly clear that the images had been erased. A quick check proved that the recycle bin had been emptied, as well. "Damn."

"He's on his way." There was a slight shake to Tori's voice. He looked at her sharply, noted that she was keeping her eyes firmly away from the body on the floor. "He said not to touch anything." Despite the words, she moved closer. "Everything's gone?"

"Looks like it." Frustration rose, keen as a blade. "It could be retrieved. The only way to really get rid of them is to format the hard drive, and he sure didn't have time to do that. If I could have a half hour and an undelete program…"

"Somehow I doubt your brother will hold off on the crime-scene investigation until you get that done. They have a tech department for that, though, right? So eventually we'll get a look at them once they're recovered."

"Eventually being the operative word." He rose, frowned down at her. "You said he was meticulous."

"He is…was." Her voice stumbled over the past tense of the word. "He wouldn't have made just one CD, he'd have made several. He'd give me one and then keep the rest in case he could sell them to someone else later. I suppose the killer took them all.'' She stopped, looked toward the door. ''Unless...''

''Unless what?''

When she didn't answer, just nearly ran from the room, he followed her. Flipping on a light in the living room, she went unerringly to a filing cabinet, reached for a drawer.

''Here.'' He handed her his tie, and she wrapped it around her hand before pulling the drawer open. Looking over her shoulder, he observed, ''He'd have filed it under Tremaine wouldn't he?''

''Nope. I hired him, you didn't.'' She stopped when she found a file folder marked ''Corbett.'' Taking a deep breath, she pressed it open.

And revealed two disks inside, marked with tonight's event and date.

''Thank God,'' she breathed. ''This should speed things up for the police.''

A siren sounded in the distance. James blew out a breath. ''We should wait for Cade outside.'' At his suggestion, she straightened shut the drawer. He slipped an arm around her shoulders, and they walked out together.

Cade Tremaine held his flashlight in one gloved hand and shone it at the figure on the floor for a few seconds. Then he looked up at his brother. ''Okay, here's the deal. This isn't my territory, but if this guy's murder is connected to the bombing, that will give us jurisdiction. And judging by your presence here, I'm guessing there's a pretty strong link.''

''He was hired to take pictures at the expo,'' Tori said. ''James tightened security, but we thought there was still a chance someone attending might have had something to do with the bombing. So he was taking photos to give us an idea of who talked to whom, maybe pick out some faces that shouldn't have been there." She stopped, swallowed hard. "It was my idea to hire him."

James heard the guilt beneath the words. He was familiar with the feeling. "Don't. He took the job because we were paying him handsomely." Tightening the arm he had around her waist, he looked at his brother. "He dumped the images, but a good tech should be able to recover at least some of them. If you need a good undelete program, we manufacture the best. And there's a disk filed under Tori's name in the file cabinet in the living room. Hopefully it's a copy of what he loaded tonight."

Cade rose and took out his cell phone. "I'm calling this in. Do you remember what you touched before you phoned me?"

Tori drew in a shaky breath. "The front door. The light switch in here. The doorjamb and knob to this room. For everything else James wrapped his hand. We didn't touch the disks."

From his narrowed gaze, it was obvious that Cade was less than impressed with his brother's forethought. "Made yourselves at home, didn't you?" He pressed a button on his cell, held it to his ear. "It'd probably be best if you two waited outside. I don't want you contaminating the scene." Tori turned, seemingly anxious to reach fresh air. As James followed her, his brother's voice trailed after them. "Oh, and stick around for a while. You're going to need to give a statement."

Disaster had been narrowly averted. A deep breath was taken. And then another. It was easy now to remember how distasteful it was to involve oneself personally.

There was no thrill in taking a life. Just relief that a crisis had been averted.

The CD was snapped in two, and then each half broken again. The pieces could be disposed of easily, as could the CF card. It wasn't so much what the man had photographed that could have caused complications; it was what he may have heard in doing so. There could be no real regret in ridding the world of yet another bottom-feeding paparazzo, snooping and prying into matters that didn't concern him.

One had to create one's own opportunities. Tremaine couldn't be awarded that new Pentagon contract. His death would be the most certain method to ensure that. But he'd be on his guard now, more difficult to take by surprise.

The woman, however, was a different story. Corbett, that was her name. Tremaine seemed taken with her. And as single-minded as the man could be, it was unlikely that he could complete any new project if she suffered an unfortunate accident.

Lips were pursed and the idea given consideration. There was usually more than one way to reach an objective. Whether Tremaine died or the woman, if the end result was the same, the choice really made very little difference.

Chapter 13

"I don't want to go back to the lake," Tori objected, after James gave the order to the driver. They'd just left Cade and it was nearly three in the morning. "I just want to go home." Sneaky fingers of regret tugged at her conscience. Kiki would still be alive if she hadn't hired him. That fact was indisputable.

"I can take you home," he said agreeably. Then his hand went to his suit jacket, withdrew a flat object. "But I thought you'd want to see these."

She stared at him, aghast. "Tell me you didn't steal evidence from the crime scene."

"*Steal* is such a negative word. Since I have every intention of returning it, I prefer the word *borrow*."

"When did you get that? We were together the whole time." Tori was beginning to believe that the man had more than a hint of the criminal in him.

"Not every minute, obviously."

Her initial shock had been replaced by temper. "I

doubt very much whether your brother is going to share your fine distinction between stealing evidence and borrowing it. You just may end up in a jail cell before the killer does.''

''Let me worry about my brother. The killer went to some pretty shocking lengths to get those pictures. Given the investigation we've done so far, if there's a clue to the killer's identity in those photos, you and I are far more likely to pick up on it than the police will. And much more quickly.''

The fact that he was right didn't excuse his actions. Interest stirred, but she wasn't about to admit it aloud. ''I hope,'' she said huffily, folding her arms across her chest, ''that you still feel that way when you're introduced to your toothless bunk mate named Bubba.''

''Darling.'' Amusement threaded his voice. ''Your concern overwhelms me. And here I was counting on you to bake me a cake with a saw inside.''

''You'd better pin your hopes on a good lawyer. I'm not much for baking.'' But despite her sarcasm, hope was unfurling inside her. Hope that the images would finally elicit a clue that would bring the killer to justice.

And hope that they could do so before another attempt was made on James's life.

Since she couldn't tolerate the thought of him looking at the disk without her, her objections subsided. Besides a few more pointed remarks about his light-fingered ways, the trip to the lake was made in silence. He was grateful he didn't have to argue with her about going home.

He wanted, more than was comfortable, to keep her near him. To keep her safe. And the logic of that particular emotion eluded him. He was accused, on a regular basis, of being fiercely protective of his family. This was the first time he'd felt the same emotion for a woman.

It was the situation, he told himself, discomfited. He was a man accustomed to taking responsibility for others. But it wasn't solely a sense of responsibility that made him remember, far too often, what she felt like in his arms. It wasn't responsibility that made him anxious to have her there again.

When they reached the house he led her to the den where he kept a secure computer. He put the CD in the drive, clicked on its icon when it appeared on the screen. She seemed to be holding her breath until the first image opened and showed a scene that had unmistakably been taken that night.

"Meticulous to the end," she murmured. As one, they leaned closer to the screen while he clicked first on one image, then the next. "If you get me copies of the registration photo IDs, I can cross-reference the people in the images to identify them," Tori suggested.

"We'll work on it together so we can eliminate the people I know by sight. The preliminary count was close to five hundred."

He clicked through the images fairly quickly. Even with his powerful computer, it took several seconds for each to open. After a few minutes Tori leaned closer to get a look at an image he'd just opened. It had been taken from a distance, and depicted Dale and him on the balcony. "I didn't know Cartwright was going to be there tonight."

"Neither did I." Nor had he considered the emotional impact of the conversation they would have. Briefly, he filled her in on the information the man had imparted.

"Sounds like there were hard feelings, at least at the

beginning,'' she said. ''And plenty going on with several of the employees at the company at the time.''

He clicked out of that image and opened another. ''Ancient history, that's what he called it.'' There was, he supposed, skeletons buried in every decade. It was damn impossible to tell which ones, if any, were relevant.

Several pictures later she said, ''This one's interesting.'' It showed Tarkington and Beal in a corner of the conference room, in what appeared to be deep discussion.

''Not necessarily nefarious,'' he commented. ''I spoke to both of them tonight myself.'' A few minutes later, though, he paused on a different one, a frown forming on his face. There was an image of Marcus and Tucker talking just inside the entrance of the building. From the expression on their faces they appeared to be arguing.

''I know him.'' Tori pointed at Tucker. ''He's one of the young men you had drive me home that day. Who's he with?''

''His father, Marcus Rappaport, my vice president of production.''

Obviously recognizing the name, Tori peered more closely at the shot. James took a moment to study it, as well. Marcus doted on his son; James had rarely heard a cross word spoken between them. The man could, however, be something of a perfectionist. He made a mental note to ask if there had been any complications in the expo setup that would have had Marcus more stressed than usual.

Tori took control of the mouse and was clicking more rapidly through the images. Apparently, he hadn't been moving fast enough to suit her. Pausing on one, she observed, ''Here's your assistant.'' Celia was shown clearly, but her companion was only half-visible. James gave it a cursory glance but Tori was peering at it more closely. "That almost looks like…" She tilted her head. "It is. See that tie? What's showing, anyway. I recognize the suit, too." She looked up at him, expression sober. "She's talking to Beal." Sitting back in her seat, she drew a deep breath. "Think they're discussing ancient history?"

By the time they'd been completely through the images twice, exhaustion was taking its toll on both of them. At least, Tori assumed that James felt it, as well. For the first time since she'd met him, there were signs of weariness on his face. "When was the last time you got some sleep?" she asked abruptly. If she'd rested as little as he must have in the past few days, she'd be walking into walls by now.

He sat back, stretched. "A full night? It's been a while. And something tells me it will be a while longer."

She looked out the window, where the pearly dawn was beginning to lighten the sky. "Then let's wrap this up for now. Tomorrow will be soon enough to figure out our next step." She was half-surprised when he complied, ejecting the CD and locking it in the desk drawer. She was even more shocked when he rose, caught her hand and pulled her up to bury his face in her hair, holding her tightly to him.

"I know you feel guilty about Corday," he murmured, rubbing her spine soothingly. "But I have it on good authority that blaming yourself doesn't change anything. Leave the guilt to the person responsible. Your hiring him didn't get him killed—the person who shot him did."

A long breath shuddered out of her. Despite his words,

despite hearing her own advice parroted back to her, she knew it would be a long time before she would forget the inadvertent part she'd played in the man's death. "Do you know what's more annoying than a man who's right?"

His low chuckle was response enough. He loosened his embrace, leaving his arm around her waist. "Let's go to bed. I think I could sleep, eventually, with you in my arms."

The invitation summoned a smoky wisp of need. She could feel her pulse beating, strong and slow. After tonight she was even less sure than ever that this thing between them was right. But she was also less prepared than before to turn away from it. Life, as the past few hours had shown, was a fragile thing. And surely at its end, it would be the chances not seized that would elicit the greatest regrets, rather than the risks taken.

And so she allowed him to lead her up the stairs. Walked with him hand in hand into her bedroom and, at his urging, into the bath. While he turned on the jets, she stepped out of her heels, and her feet sobbed in gratitude. He straightened and shrugged out of his jacket. But when her hands went to her dress, he stopped her. "Let me."

Slowly she swayed toward him. Hooking an arm around her waist, her brought her closer. "I've been wondering all night what keeps that darn thing up." His hands ran down her back, over her bottom and back up again. "No zipper? How'd you get it on?"

Her limbs were taking on the consistency of melted wax. "Ingenuity…" She paused, and nipped at his chin, "and dexterity."

"Well…" His fingers stroked her back, where it was bared by the straps. "Never let it be said that I lack

ingenuity.'' With a quick twist of his hand, he had two
straps separated from the material. The bodice sagged,
revealing the tops of her breasts. Another tug, and the
rest snapped free. The dress slid to her hips.

"Most would consider that a terrible waste of
money," she informed him.

"Honey, for this view, there's no price I wouldn't
pay." He was looking entirely too pleased with himself,
so she took her time working the dress over her hips,
down her thighs, one excruciatingly slow inch at a time,
until at last it was puddled around her feet, leaving her
clad only in a scrap of silk panties. The look on his face
more than made up for the fact that she was practically
naked, while he was fully clothed.

When he would have reached for her, she stepped out
of reach. "One of us is overdressed." Hooking her
thumbs in the sides of her panties, she whisked them
down her legs. "And I don't think it's me. *Honey.*''

His low groan drew a smile to her lips, and she
stepped into the water, sank low in it. He dug in his
pocket, withdrew a foil-wrapped package and set it on
the edge of the tub. Then it was her turn to watch as he
stripped off his clothes, with considerably less finesse
than she'd exhibited. His body was, she decided dream-
ily, rather magnificent. She would have liked a chance
to study it, a visual journey to map each plane and sinew.
But in the next moment he was joining her, drawing her
to kneel with him in the center of the tub. The bubbling
water lapped at their chests while their lips met with
scorching intensity.

The world careened, receded. There was only the taste
of him, the unchecked urgency of his mouth, his teeth,
his tongue. The hint of wildness in his kiss should have
alarmed her. Instead it excited, igniting heat and desire

that had only seemed to simmer until bursting forth again, summoned by his touch.

He had quick, clever hands, and had already committed to memory which places made her go weak and boneless. She slicked her hands over his torso, enjoying the feel of sleek wet masculine skin beneath her fingers. Her touch faltered when he took the lobe of her ear between his teeth, and her body jerked helplessly against his. It didn't seem quite fair the way her body betrayed her so easily, passion fogging intent.

His mouth was as heated as the water, and avid as it followed the line of her throat, skimmed over her shoulders. Wanting, needing to give the same pleasure, she leaned forward, used the tip of her tongue to scoop up the tiny rivulets of water that ran down his chest. Her hands glided down his back, settled on his hard masculine buns and kneaded.

Her breath hissed out and her head lolled as he bent his head, and took a nipple between his lips. With each tiny tug of his mouth, the ache in the pit of her belly intensified. It didn't seem possible that the passion between them could burn this hot, return this quickly. She was helpless to deny a response; helpless to temper it. Recognition of that fact made her doubly determined to elicit the same from him.

She found the hard length of him, slid her fingers up and down in a slippery dance that had his jaw clenching, his muscles tensing.

His arm banded across her back while the pressure of his mouth grew more hungry. The evidence of his desire only stoked her own, sending the blood sizzling under her skin. Sensation slapped against sensation. Wet flesh twisted against wet flesh, the friction a delight, a torment.

He reached blindly for the condom, swore viciously as he struggled with it. Then, hands beneath her hips, he pressed her against the smooth back of the tub, the water splashing precariously high, as he urged her legs around his waist. The position left her open to him, vulnerable. With a movement that hinted at desperation, he seated himself deep inside her.

His possession was sudden, complete, and drove the breath from her lungs. She tried to regain a measure of control, but he was driving into her now, each thrust deeper than the other, and thoughts of restraint went spinning away. They were as close as they could be, and yet still not close enough. Her hands streaked over his skin, trying to draw him nearer. Her teeth scraped ungently on his shoulder as one of his hands reached between their bodies, fondled her, applying pressure that drove her higher, wilder.

And when the dual assault had her back arching, the climax ripping through her, she was distantly aware that it had taken him, too. They tumbled together headlong into the rush of pleasure.

It had a been a singularly satisfying experience for Tori to wake up in James's arms that morning. Even more so when she'd managed to sneak from the bed and leave him sleeping. He'd put up a fierce battle, but sheer fatigue eventually overcame even the strongest will. She'd left him a note detailing her plans for the day and slipped from the room, fervently hoping he would sleep another few hours before his internal clock would wake him up.

She'd summoned a cab to take her home, and once there she determined that the workmen must be finished with her house. There wasn't a soul in sight. Of course, the front room was stripped bare of carpet, sofa and chairs, but once this was over, the first thing she'd do would be to get them replaced.

Once this was over. The phrase replayed in her head all the way to her office, making it difficult to concentrate on the work she needed to accomplish there. She had a bad feeling about this, a niggling blade of foreboding that warned of future catastrophe. It was worry for James, she told herself. But if she was honest, there was worry there for herself, as well.

A wiser woman, one with a faster learning curve, wouldn't have fallen for a man like James Tremaine. The admission was there, unvarnished and terrifying. She was in love with the wrong man. Again. The recollection of her failed marriage no longer stung, but the memory remained of how glaringly out of place she'd been in her ex's world.

The one bright spot in the whole mess was that James wasn't aware of her feelings. When it ended, she'd be able to slip from his life as easily as she had his bed, with a modicum of pride intact. She was certain that pride was going to be less than satisfying, compared to what she was leaving behind.

But first she had to keep James Tremaine alive. And the only way to do that was to hunt down the killer and see that he paid. For everything.

To that end she worked feverishly all afternoon. She'd directed one of her information brokers to dig up more information on Celia. James hadn't seemed overly concerned, but the digital picture they'd seen last night of her with Beal, after hearing of their past relationship, made Tori wary. She spent several hours combing any databases she could access for more details on Beal and Tarkington. The most interesting tidbit she'd gleaned was that thirty years ago, for a brief time before he'd started his own company, Beal had worked for the other man.

Tori was still leaning back in her chair, chewing on that piece of information when her phone rang. A quick glance at the caller ID showed that it was the real estate agent for her father's house.

His news brought mingled emotions. He'd found a buyer, but they wanted to move quickly. And he wouldn't end the conversation until he'd gotten her promise to empty the house within the next week.

Giving a resigned sigh, she shut down her computer. If the information broker came through with anything today, he'd contact her cell, she consoled herself as she locked the office and headed to her car. It was about time to take a little personal time for a task she'd been avoiding for too long.

Heart growing abruptly heavy in her chest, she headed out the door.

James never slept until noon. And he rarely put in only six hours at the office before heading back home again. Albeit six very productive hours.

It hadn't hurt that several employees had been busy at the expo, and he had been relatively undisturbed while he was in his office.

The sight of a familiar car in the drive gave him pause. But it was the scene that awaited him when he opened the door into his den that made him immediately wary. Cade, Sam and Ana were gathered there, and from the tension in the room, their conversation hadn't been pleasant.

Cautiously, like an animal testing the air, he stepped inside. "Sam. I didn't know you were back."

His younger brother came up to him, and the two slapped backs, a gesture of genuine affection. But the stoic expressions on his siblings' faces were starting to worry him. Looking from one to the other, he observed, "What's wrong? I know Jones is at the expo." He frowned, looking from Cade to Sam. "Are Juliette and Shae all right?"

"They're both fine," Sam said, dropping his long frame into an easy chair by the desk. "It's you we're worried about."

The tension in his chest eased, just a fraction. "Don't be. It won't be long before this guy is caught. Then we'll all rest easier." Easier, when he'd unmasked his parents' murderer. When the person responsible for all their suffering was dead or behind bars.

"I'll tell you what would have me resting easier," Cade said evenly, strolling across the room toward him. "If you gave anyone in your family credit for having a brain. If you treated us with an ounce of the respect we give to you."

A quick glance from one sibling to the other told him that they were all in agreement. It was time to tread carefully. "Why don't you tell me what has all of you upset. We can talk about it."

Cade stopped before him, rocking back on his heels, his jade eyes snapping with temper. "I suppose we could talk. Or I could just haul out some cuffs and throw your ass in jail for tampering with evidence."

James took a deep breath, released it. "Ah."

"Ah," Cade mimicked. "I thought it was odd that Tori referred to the disks as plural, while you made it sound as if there was only one. Our tech squad was able to recover part of the images today. They also determined that three copies had been made. Now if I can trust you enough—'' his voice dripped sarcasm ''—to believe what you said about the killer taking one, that still leaves us one short.''

Through James's wariness filtered real admiration. ''That's some pretty fast police work, son. We may make a techie out of you yet.''

Cade's fists balled. Years of experience had James certain he was aching to take a swing at him.

Sam must have thought so, too, because he said warningly, ''Let's tone it down, shall we?''

Cade's smile was lethal. ''Shoot, if that tech work impresses you, you'll really like the investigating I did into your relationship with Tori Corbett.''

James's amusement immediately faded, to be replaced by a simmering anger. ''What the hell are you talking about?''

''You came to me, remember? A few weeks back you came to headquarters and asked me to look into finding one Rob Landry.'' He let the words settle. ''You never did tell me why you were looking for a P.I., and hell, I never asked. Until it became clear to all of us that you were up to your neck in trouble that you wouldn't admit.''

Suddenly weary, James rubbed the back of his neck. He walked away from his brother, moved to the desk and leaned his hips against it.

''I should have known it was too good to be true,'' Ana muttered, her eyes flashing at him. ''I just knew you couldn't have suddenly gotten the sense to start dating a real woman, instead of one of those empty-headed bimbos you usually favor. I just don't know how you got her to go along with letting you pass her off as your girlfriend.''

"It wasn't easy," he said feelingly, remembering how Tori had balked at the prospect.

"It didn't take long for Cade to start wondering why you were looking for Landry," Sam put in. "But if it hadn't been for Ana, I doubt we'd ever have known."

James went still. The silence in the room stretched. "Known…what?"

"That you hired him twenty years ago to investigate our parents' accident."

The floor seemed to shift beneath his feet. Then it righted itself, and he sent a killing look at his baby sister. "You were in my files?" The defiant angle of her chin was his answer.

"Hell, why should *your* files be safe from her," Sam asked feelingly. "Serves you right. You taught her everything she knows. She didn't discover anything that you shouldn't have told us yourself."

"Such as…"

"We figure there's a relationship between the threats you've been getting and the investigation Tori's dad ran for you two decades ago," Cade said flatly. "But we're through with the guesswork. It's time for you to level with us. For once in your life, have a little trust in your family."

Genuinely bewildered, James looked from one of them to the next, saw the agreement on their faces. "I was just trying to clear this up without letting it hurt you all. If I had turned out to be wrong, there'd be no reason you'd ever have had to know about it." God knew, there had been many times he'd wished he could be free of the doubts. The worry. The guilt.

"You'll always be the oldest, but we've been adults for a long time, James." Sam's voice was sober, his gaze direct. "It's about time you realized it. If you have reason to believe that accident was something else, you should have told us at the beginning. But barring that, you'll tell us now.''

In an unspoken gesture of unity, the three had drifted to stand facing him together, a united front. And it was hard, much harder than he'd imagined, to start at the beginning. To watch their shock and despair when he starkly told them what he'd suspected twenty years earlier. The entire story about the threats. And about what Tori and he had discovered so far.

When he was finished, there wasn't a sound in the room, but the emotion was thick. And the sight of the tears in his sister's eyes made him regret he'd been forced into divulging the information at all.

It was second nature to push away from the desk, to pull her resisting form into his arms and to soothe. He'd been trying, to the best of his ability, to take care of her all of his life. He couldn't stop now if he tried.

"Don't," she sniffed, the word muffled against his shirt. "I have a right to grieve, James. We all do. You can't spare us that, and you shouldn't have tried. We won't let you again."

There was a murmur of accord from her brothers.

"As of right now," Sam said, resolve evident in his voice, "we're all in this together."

Cade nodded, and Ana stepped away, wiped her eyes. "The first thing for you to do is catch us up on the ground you've covered so far. We may think of an angle that you haven't. With all of us working on it, we're bound to come up with something."

Cade's cell rang then, and he stepped to the other side of the room to answer it.

"You need to be prepared for the fact that this might

be motivated purely by business," James said. "And it might involve someone we trust."

"My money's on Tarkington," Ana said darkly. "A man that smarmy is capable of anything."

Cade rejoined them, gaze trained on James. "Francis's cell phone dump came back. We've got six calls to his phone within twenty-four hours. Three have been identified as coming from his girlfriend. Two came from different phone booths and the last came from this number." He handed him a slip of paper with a number scrawled on it. "Recognize it?"

James glanced down and froze. There was a moment of incomprehension, of utter denial. Swallowing hard, he nodded. "Yeah. I recognize it." It took a moment for the tight band in his chest to ease, for his lungs to work properly again. Thinking rapidly, he turned, headed for the computer.

"What are you doing?"

He didn't look up at Ana's question. "Checking out something that should have occurred to me a long time ago."

Tori looked around the attic of her dad's house with a sense of quiet satisfaction. She'd made some headway up here, at least. Everything was organized in neat sections to be thrown away, put in storage or sold. She'd arranged for a Dumpster to be delivered tomorrow, to get started on the project. Once she sorted through the downstairs, she would place an order for a small moving trailer and rent a storage unit.

But for now she was content to sit awhile, in the light afforded by the single overhead bulb and steep herself in memories of him once again.

Raised without a mother, she supposed it was normal

that she'd be close to her dad all her life. Normal to want to keep his memory untarnished. She reached out, dragged the ragged sweater off the top of one of the boxes, and sat on the floor cross-legged, holding it on her lap. Of all of the things he'd left her, she thought the ones she would value most were this tattered garment and the box of love letters he'd kept, from all those years ago, when her mother lay dying. With these things she could keep them both close, while getting to know a mother she barely remembered.

She reached out, drew a letter from the box, opened it. Her eyes swam at the obvious love poured out on the page. Her father hadn't been an especially sentimental man. To read the raw emotion in the words had her throat going full.

One letter led to another. Soon she had a pile around her feet, and she was bent over the papers in her hand to make out the words in the dim light. She decided to organize them chronologically. Then when she had the time, she could read them in order and...

Her gaze scanned the letter in her hand, froze, then swept back up again, to read her mother's writing more carefully.

"You have to learn to forgive yourself. You were faced with an awful choice, and I understand why you had to do it."

Tori dropped the paper as if scalded. There was a roiling in her stomach, an internal realization that arrived ahead of true comprehension. Then, frantically, she rose to her knees, started pulling handfuls of letters out, discarding all but the ones with dates close to the one she'd just read. One of them would hold an explanation. It had to.

And the next one did. But it wasn't the explanation she'd been hoping for.

My dearest Lisa,

Not a night goes by that I don't reach for the phone, wanting to call that boy back and tell him the truth about his parents...

There was a roaring in her ears. Her stomach lurched, and she thought for a moment she'd be ill. Her hands were operating independently of her mind. The letters were raining like brittle confetti as she dug frantically through them, skimming, tossing them aside to pull out another, phrase after damning phrase leaping off the page to sear her eyes.

I had to protect you and Tori...

It was too late to help those people, but I could save my own little family...

God forgive me. I'll never forgive myself.

She dropped the last letter and this time she didn't reach for another. Rising awkwardly, she backed away from the box, pressing both fists against her mouth to stifle the cry that she could feel trembling on her lips. She closed her eyes, wanting to shut out the damning evidence, but she could still see the words, could hear her dad's voice sounding in her head.

Integrity, above all else.

...tell him the truth about his parents...

Integrity, above all else.

God forgive me...

Unconsciously she wrapped her arms around her middle and began to rock, her mind frantically supplying, then eliminating, possible explanations for what she'd read. One would come, she assured herself. When her mind cleared and her thought settled, an alternate answer would present itself.

But deep inside she knew the heartrending truth, and the pain of it threatened to shred her soul.

Her father had betrayed James and his family twenty years ago. Because of it, a killer had gone free.

Chapter 14

"You've checked her house?" James asked tersely.

Cade nodded. "It's empty. I've got officers stationed there, though, and an APB out. It's just a matter of time."

Pacing the length of the room, James took out his cell phone, tried Tori's cell again. There was still no answer. He tried her house next, with the same result. He had no more luck with her office number.

Making a decision, he headed for the door.

"Whoa." Sam leaped from the chair he was sitting in, he and Cade closing in on James. "Where do you think you're going?"

"I can't reach Tori. I'm going to find her."

His brothers exchanged a glance. "There's no way we're letting you out that door, especially now. Have you forgotten there's someone out there who'd like to see you dead?"

"Then prepare to offer some police protection,"

James said, shoving between them and through the den door. "Because I'm going, and there's not a damn thing either of you can do to stop me."

The two men looked at each other, shrugged. "Oh, hell." Cade grabbed his shoulder holster. "Wait for us."

Feeling raw and battered, Tori drove back to her home in a fog. Her cell phone had rung for the third time. The caller ID identified James's number. She didn't answer it. Couldn't. She couldn't summon the words for him. Wouldn't have been able to utter them if they occurred.

There would come a time, probably much sooner than she would prefer, when she'd have to face him. And when she told him the truth, she'd watch the distrust bloom in his expression again, and know this time it was deserved.

Her body shook, a great racking shudder. But God help her, she wasn't ready now. She felt as if she'd been cast adrift. Everything she'd always believed was a lie. What she'd been certain of only days ago had turned to quicksand, shifting beneath her feet. How could she explain to him what she couldn't comprehend herself?

By the time she had pulled into her carport, her temples were throbbing, a vicious headache jackhammering in her brain. She was distantly aware that Pauline's house was dark. Maybe James had frightened Joe Jr. enough that he'd joined his mother in Shreveport.

James. Just the thought of him made the pounding in her head intensify. Hands shaky, vision blurry, she let herself into the house, locked it and, without switching on the lights, made her way upstairs. Sleep, if it would come, would offer a blessed relief both from the headache and the situation that had caused it.

She stopped in the bathroom long enough to find the bottle of pain relievers and shake three out. Swallowed them dry. She stumbled to her bedroom. She was halfway to the bed before instinct filtered through the pain, and she realized she wasn't alone.

Before she could turn around, the figure stepped out of the shadows and brought something crashing down on her head. There was a bright burst of pain before unconsciousness rushed up and sucked her under.

"Her car's here." Relief surged through James until he noticed another vehicle parked in front of the house.

Cade saw it and identified it at the same time. "So is Tucker."

James was out of the car and running before it came to a complete stop. "Cover the back," he shouted at his brothers. He leaped to the porch, tried the door. It was locked.

Without wasting the breath for a curse, he jumped to the ground, started around the side of the house, as his brothers headed around it in the opposite direction. He hadn't gotten more than a few steps before he saw the figure running in his direction.

Obeying instinct, he sped up, tackled the intruder, rolling over and over until he subdued him with a single blow to the jaw. "Mr. Tremaine, wait." Tucker shielded himself from another blow. "You have to listen to me."

"Where's Tori?" he demanded. Nasty fingers of panic were licking up his spine. There was a feeling of urging in his gut that he couldn't shake.

"I...I don't know," the young man stammered.

Sam ran up to them, stopped to pick up some containers the boy had dropped. Unscrewing the caps, he sniffed first one, then the other. "Gasoline."

James got to his feet, yanking the boy up with him. Grabbing him by the collar he growled between clenched teeth, "Is she in the house?"

But the kid was wild-eyed with fear now and babbling. "I don't know, maybe, he must have thought so. The gasoline isn't mine, though, it isn't! I found it in the back. I thought if I got rid of it, he couldn't, he wouldn't…"

"Who?" James gave him a vicious shake.

"My dad!" Tucker seemed to crumple then, started to weep. "I think my dad's going to try to kill her."

"Look!" Sam yelled.

James followed the direction of Sam's pointed finger, saw the smoke curling from the upstairs windows.

"Call 911!"

James shoved the boy toward Sam and raced to the back of the house. With one quick look he identified the window that had been broken out. Without a second thought he heaved himself up and over the sill into the kitchen. The downstairs was already filled with smoke, burning his eyes. He identified Cade, several feet away from him, gun drawn and finger to his lips.

Easing his way toward him, he heard his brother whisper soundlessly, "He's still in the house."

James nodded and took his handkerchief from his pocket, quickly tying it around his face. He pointed to the gun, then to himself and then toward the upstairs. Cade gestured for him to go ahead, and he dashed for the stairs, knowing his brother would cover him. The smoke was rolling down the steps. Dropping to his knees, he stayed as low as he could, crawling rapidly. He had to get to Tori on time. He wouldn't even consider another possibility.

There was no smell of accelerants in the house. James

wondered if Marcus had been saving it to torch the out-side. But the flames were spreading rapidly upstairs. In another few minutes there'd be no path to take to the bedroom.

Crouching down, James pressed himself as flat as he could against the undamaged wall, and inched toward her room. The heat was intense. Straining his ears, he could hear fitful coughing. His hopes soaring, he broke free, skirted the flames near his foot and ran into her room.

He nearly tripped over Tori. Dropping to one knee, he scooped her up and turned, preparing to exit the way he'd come. But once he'd got back to the door he saw that would be impossible. The stairway was engulfed in flames. There would be no escape that way.

Keeping her face pressed to his chest, he made his way back to her bedroom. Both of them broke out in a spasm of coughing, and for the first time, Tori's eyelids fluttered open. He laid her on the floor beside the bed, whipped the handkerchief from his face and tied it around hers. Then he tugged the sheets off the bed, rolled them into coils and tied them together. Tori tried to help, but her movements were feeble. Her voice, when she spoke, was more so. "Someone...was waiting...hit me..."

"I know, baby." He paused a moment to drop a quick kiss on her forehead, sending up a silent prayer of thanks that he'd found her alive. There would be time later to deal with the sick fear he'd felt before he'd discovered her.

And plenty of time to indulge in his primal need to make Marcus pay. For everything.

Shoving the bed as close as he could to the window, he secured one end of the makeshift ladder to the leg of the bed frame and then looked over at her. "Can you climb on my back and hold on?"

She nodded determinedly, but he wasn't so sure. She looked barely conscious. When he bent down for her, though, her grip was stronger than he expected. With a deep breath, he opened the window, picked up one end of the sheet ladder and threw his leg over the sill.

Every time another fit of coughing shook her, James was fearful it would loosen her grip. But she managed, somehow, to hang on. They were still several feet from the ground when he shouted, "We'll have to jump the rest of the way. Ready?"

Without waiting for an answer, he let go. Although it was probably less than six feet, the ground seemed to rush up unmercifully hard. He twisted his body, landing with Tori half on top of him, the impact driving the breath from him.

It was a moment before he could draw in air. Another before he heard the distant wail of sirens. "Are you all right?" He turned to Tori, pulling down the handkerchief to search her features frantically.

"I think so."

Helping her up, they both limped to the curb, where a small crowd had gathered. He looked around for Sam. He was standing watch over a huddled Tucker near the cars.

"Where's Cade?"

The question had Sam turning toward him. "He hasn't come out yet." The two men exchanged a grim look before they both charged toward the back of the house.

The smoke was thicker inside now. The fire had made its way downstairs. There was no sign of Cade in the kitchen where James had left him. Inching carefully into the interior of the house, they both spotted their brother's crumpled figure in the middle of the living room. There was a man standing over him, holding Cade's gun.

"Drop it, Marcus."

Marcus Rappaport let loose a wild laugh, the sound as foreign as his appearance. Usually meticulously groomed, his clothes were in disarray, and there was a bruise blooming on his cheek. He looked like a crazed stranger. "Damn you, Tremaine, it should have been easier than this. I never wanted to hurt the rest of the family." He seemed to be weeping and laughing at the same time, a sign of hysteria, or worse.

With a meaningful look at Sam, the two men split up, Sam heading toward Cade and James toward Marcus.

"Tucker's outside, Marcus," James said conversationally. "He's been injured. You should go to him."

The man jerked, seemed strangely uncertain. "Tucker's hurt?"

"Badly," James lied. "The ambulance was called for him."

"He didn't understand," the man mumbled, his gun hand shaking. "No one will understand." The ceiling overhead was showing signs of stress. Casting a look at it, James figured it was the spot where the fire had been started. They wouldn't have much more time.

"Tucker told me he understood, Marcus." It was hard to keep the pretense going. More cracks appeared in the ceiling directly above Cade. "All you have to do is go out and talk to him."

The man glanced dazedly toward the window and that was the chance James was waiting for. Leaping for him, he knocked him to the floor, grappling for the gun. Sam took the opportunity to dive for Cade, and drag him to safety.

Marcus screamed and nearly broke away. James

caught his gun hand and slammed it against the wall. Again and again. Until it dropped from the man's nerveless fingers. Balling his fist, James punched the other man in the jaw, jerking his head back, sending him staggering farther into the room. There was a giant *crack,* and James jumped backward as the ceiling fell in raining pieces of fiery two-by-sixes into the room. One struck the man across the shoulders and pinned him to the floor.

"Get the hell out of the house!" Sam's voice was in his ear, his grip on his arms, but it was a moment before James could obey. A moment before he could see from the odd angle of Marcus's neck that he realized the man he'd known all his life was beyond saving.

"You come to my hospital, you follow my orders, James." Shae O'Reilly pushed into the hospital room with a scowl on her face to match his own. "I told you that I was keeping you overnight for observation and that's final. In your own room."

"You can observe me in here." James had no intention of leaving Tori's bedside. He didn't worry about annoying his future sister-in-law. She had her hands full right now with Cade. The concussion he'd suffered had given all of them a few bad moments. "Besides," he pointed out, "your fiancé isn't in his room, either." He reached over, took Tori's hand in his good one.

Tori gave him a disgruntled look. It hadn't escaped her attention that of all the so-called patients in this room, she was the only one being kept in bed.

And being kept there.

"He will be." Shae turned her stern glance on her future husband and stalked toward him threateningly. "If he knows what's good for him."

"I know exactly what's good for me," Cade said. "A

night in my own bed with my favorite doctor applying a little TLC.''

''Give it up,'' Sam advised Cade. ''Even Juliette and I know enough not to cross Shae when she's in doctor mode.''

''That would be more insightful if we didn't all know what a horrid patient you make yourself,'' Juliette, his fiancée, remarked. ''I'm beginning to believe there isn't one Tremaine man who has the sense to take care of himself.''

Ana nodded, while Jones wisely remained silent.

Shae pointed to each of the patients in turn. ''Concussion,'' she snapped, gesturing to Cade. ''Broken wrist,'' she indicated James. ''And smoke inhalation,'' she ended with Tori. ''We don't keep people in hospitals because we like their company. You're all exhausted and need rest.''

Recognizing that her temper was dangerously close to the boiling point, James looked at Cade. Before Shae bullied them back to their rooms, he needed some answers. ''What was Tucker able to tell you?''

''He was the one sending the notes.'' Cade's voice and his facial expression were somber. Tucker had been more like a cousin than a family friend. ''You know what a brain he's got for encryption/decryption. He got the brilliant idea to take on his dad's files this summer. He saw it as a challenge, I'm sure. He cracked the security on Marcus's computer and discovered far more than he'd bargained for. Marcus had everything detailed in one of his files.''

''Rappaport arranged for the accident that killed his own wife?'' Tori sounded horrified. ''So it wasn't really your parents he was trying to kill?''

''You and I were on the right track when we hacked

into those databases for the insurance companies,''
James told her. "I just didn't look far enough. Didn't
even consider it seriously until Cade learned that one of
the calls to the bomber's cell phone had come from Tremaine Technologies.'' He shook his head. "I don't
know. I had a flash of that image of Marcus and Tucker
arguing, and decided to give the database another go.
Lucy Rappaport wasn't from Louisiana originally. She
was from Mississippi. Her elderly ailing parents had
fully paid for a million-dollar policy on her when she
was a teenager. Since they were dead, that money went
to Marcus upon her death.''

"First, though, he'd tried to get money by arranging
my kidnapping,'' Ana put in. "When that was foiled
before the ransom was paid, he came up with another
idea.''

Tori shook her head uncomprehendingly. "But why?
Just for the money? Was he really that cold?''

"Dale hit on it when I talked to him yesterday.''
James sent a thumb skating over her knuckles and focused on the relief of having her safe. "Marcus had
gambling problems, and apparently still does. At least
that's what the Nevada Gaming Commission says. He'd
been banned from Nevada nearly ten years ago. Apparently he began going to Europe after that.'' Certainly
he'd have had plenty of opportunity. Tremaine Technologies competed for projects all over the world.

"Well, going after you wasn't about the money,'' Tori
said to James shrewdly. "Unless a third party was in the
mix.''

He grinned. She really did have the most fascinating
mind. "You're quick. We don't have it nailed down yet,
but we think Beal was willing to pay him a fortune to

make sure I wasn't awarded the next Pentagon contract. Of course, we can't prove it yet.''

"That's only a matter of time," Cade put in. "We'll pore over his phone records, trace financial transactions... I doubt it's the first time he's teamed up with Beal. Hell, for all we know, they could have planned our parents' accident together. Whatever connection they had, though, we'll trace it.''

"Two people, at least, would be alive today if Tucker had just come forward with what he'd discovered," Tori said softly.

James squeezed her fingers lightly. He knew she was still haunted by Corday's homicide. "Tucker thought he could scare me into backing off the contract, which, to his mind at least, would keep me safe until he could figure out what to do about his father. He should have gone to the police. But regardless of what you discover about your parent, it's hard to turn your back on them. No matter what they've done.''

Tori turned her face away, the words like sharp little arrows, nicking her heart. All the trauma of the last several hours paled in comparison to the discovery she'd made about her father.

"Okay, everybody out," ordered Shae. "Tori needs to rest. And most of you have your own rooms to go to.''

One by one the family filed out, amid much goodnatured bickering over whose room they were going to take up residence in next. When James closed the door behind the last of them, Tori drew in a deep breath, struggled to find the words. "You were right about my dad.'' They came in a rush, amidst a jumble of pain. "I found some letters he and my mother wrote to each other before she died. I think... I'm almost certain, they refer to you and your parents' accident.''

"I know." Her gaze flew to his, incredulous. "It was in the files Tucker found."

The pain seized her heart again, gripped hard. "I don't know how to reconcile the man I knew with the one who betrayed you." Her eyes burned. She had no tears to shed, but her heart still wept. "I can't imagine what might have been different, if he'd told you the truth about the tracking device."

James lifted her chin with his finger, turned it toward him. "Honey, Marcus was following that investigation every step of the way. He managed the accident pretty much as we figured, and he knew about the P.I. I'd hired. He'd planted the tracking device in Lucy's purse, figuring he'd receive it back as her personal effects. But when it wasn't there, he knew immediately your dad must have discovered it. That fire that destroyed his offices twenty years ago? Marcus set it. And then he threatened yours and your mother's lives. Your father did what he thought he had to in order to protect the two of you."

You were faced with an awful choice... The line from the letter came back to her, and she released a shaky breath. "I don't know what to think. I'd like to think there was a better way."

"Maybe there was." His bright-blue gaze was intense. "But it doesn't affect us, either way, Tori. Some of the answers we found were painful as hell, but at least we have answers. It's time to move on."

The words seemed curiously significant. She tried to slide her fingers from his grasp, only to have them gripped tighter. "You're right. About moving on, I mean. Neither of us expected this...what happened between us. We can't let it change anything."

He reached out to smooth a strand of hair back from

her face. "Sometimes the unexpected can be the most satisfying. There's more here, Tori, than either of us looked for. I can't walk away from it. I don't think you can, either."

There was a wild leaping in her chest, but she quelled it sternly. Experience had etched a bitter brand, and she couldn't forget its burn. "I've tried living in your world before. I didn't fit there. We can't change who we are, even if we wanted to."

Her efforts at logic were rewarded with a bruising kiss. When he lifted his head, he muttered, "The hell with that. We'll make our own world, where we both fit. And changing isn't an option. Are you going to keep hiding behind excuses, or are you finally going to admit that you love me?" He seemed to enjoy the way her mouth dropped open at the words. Taking the opportunity, he pressed a soft, nibbling kiss to it. "That you can't live without me."

Her arms linked around his neck of their own accord. There was a glint in his eye, a smoky heat. But it was the softness in his expression that shattered defenses she had once thought stouter. Stronger. "I do. Love you, I mean. And the thought of living without you makes me miserable."

"You'll never have to worry about that." He brushed his lips over her brow, her eye, her jaw. "I started falling for you the moment I saw you with your head stuck in the ceiling tile. I have every intention of living with you, loving you, for the next sixty years or so."

She smiled, her heart full. Sixty years was a lifetime. And that sounded about right to her.

* * * * *

LUNA

On wings of fire she rises...

Born without caste or position in Arukan, a country that prizes both, Kevla Bai-sha's life is about to change. Her feverish dreams reveal looming threats to her homeland and visions of the dragons that once watched over her people—and held the promise of truth. Now, Kevla, together with the rebel prince of the ruling household, must sacrifice everything and defy all law and tradition, to embark on a daring quest to save the world.

On sale June 29.
Visit your local bookseller.

Sparked by passion, fueled by danger.

COMING NEXT MONTH

SIMCNM0704